VOLUME One

FLORIDA WRITERS ASSOCIATION

From Our Family to Yours

the Peppertree Press
Sarasota, Florida

Photo of Suzette Martinez Standring
by Janet McCourt of Massachusetts

Graphic design by Rebecca Barbier

For information regarding permission,
call 941-922-2662 or contact us at our website:
www.peppertreepublishing.com or write to:
the Peppertree Press, LLC.
Attention: Publisher
1269 First Street, Suite 7
Sarasota, Florida 34236

ISBN: 978-1-936051-21-2

Library of Congress Number: 2009936446

Printed in the U.S.A.

Printed September 2009

Acknowledgments

FWA's Collection #1 - From Our Family to Yours began with a spark shared among three friends, all Florida Writers Association members. It grew until it flamed our writers' creative juices and excited everyone. As the project's coordinator, I truly appreciate the input, support, and camaraderie of Greg Seeley and Lynn Ellen Robinson, who nurtured my initial idea and helped give it life. Thank you, Greg and Lynn Ellyn.

Well over two hundred entries poured in from FWA members everywhere. They were posted without author name to a specifically designed website accessible only by our seven judges. Huge thanks to Shara Smock, FWA's already busy secretary, for taking on the additional volunteer responsibility of receiving and posting these entries. Shara Smock also collected our finalists' photos.

The websites produced for viewing the stories and entering judges' votes were created and maintained by Karen Lieb, President of Florida Writers Foundation. Karen's also FWA's official photographer, and further helped by formatting the pictures for publication.

Seven judges, who will remain anonymous, read the entries. FWA is deeply indebted to them, and thanks each for their time, dedication, and willingness to volunteer for this worthwhile project.

Each finalist's entry was edited. Each of our three editors worked on twenty stories. Sincere thanks to Kaye Coppersmith of Wordsworth Editing, and Senior Editor for FWA's Editing Assistance Service, Lynn Ellyn Robinson, and Shara Pendragon Smock.

It is with heartfelt gratitude that FWA acknowledges Suzette Standring's contribution to this publication. She had perhaps the hardest job of all . . . picking only ten to be her favorites out of over sixty truly wonderful stories.

Finally, our sincere thanks to Julie Ann Howell of Peppertree Press from FWA's Board of Directors for graciously donating all publishing costs for this project. Her patience and expertise throughout the formatting of the manuscript was invaluable.

—*Chrissy Jackson,*
FWA vice president,
Coordinator, FWA Collections

TABLE OF CONTENTS

Introduction

Family forms the base camp for life's journey. Whether we are helped or hindered on the way often traces back to powerful memories and oh, our interior landscape is lush with scenery.

It is a writer's craft to transport the reader into such imagery to share the irony, pain, comic madness or luminous moments upon which our individual foundations are built. Every work contained within is a triumph of storytelling.

How have we defined "family?" An author unknown to me once wrote, "What we love deeply becomes a part of us." And the kind of love that can imprint for life comes from a personal sense of family, whether they are relatives, lovers, friends, pets or the serendipitous connections in nature. Family is about belonging.

From Our Family to Yours is the maiden launch of a short story compilation by the Florida Writers Association to showcase the talent of its writer members. It was my almost impossible task to select only ten from a "short list" of sixty-one finalists!

It saddened me to omit so many exceptional submissions. Any judge will admit that ultimately, all final choices are subjective. Yet the principles of universal resonance apply. Here the final ten vaulted into the realm of extraordinary for possessing a unique voice and writing that compelled with presence, clarity and sometimes, surprise. Long after the page was turned, the story lingered. And that which the writer loved deeply became a part of me.

Suzette Martinez Standring
2009

The Fathers Who Stayed

Mr. Martinez never cheered from any softball stands and the month of June is an irritating reminder. That's when greeting cards always portray affectionate and fun-loving dads. No Father's Day card ever featured emotionally distant dads, ones who wanted a different life, who yearned for travel and adventure but who stayed, anyway. My father was one of those.

In the Kodak moments of my mind, he's muttering something about "peace and quiet" as he slams the bedroom door. If noise invaded his sanctuary, a slipper whizzed into the living room followed by a yell, "Shut up, you kids!"

As youngsters, we thought Dad was a grouch, but we were grateful for his presence anyway. Since we lived in a lower end neighborhood, I felt safer with my dad at home. The little boys across the street had a padlock on their front door, but I rarely saw their mom and never once spotted the dad.

As I grew older, I figured out that most of the kids living around me didn't have dads. But I thought that having a father who hardly ever talked was about the same as not having one at all.

It took decades to piece together the puzzle of my father's past. When I was ten years old, he delivered the biggest batch of details. He was only 16 years old when he moved from the Philippines to California. He had no money and no friends, though he soon met other Filipinos and someone taught him how to cook. His first job was as a "houseboy" to a family and later on he cooked in hotel kitchens.

The next batch came when I was about 17 and a budding feminist. It irked me to discover that Dad had returned to the Philippines to marry my mother, Josephine. At the time of the arranged marriage he was forty-seven and she was thirty-one. After my dad had divorced a fiery Nicaraguan he thought it best to find a "good Filipino girl" the second time around. Of course, he didn't tell me that part. My mother did and when I asked him about it, my dad waved me off, saying it was "ancient history."

Usually, though, Dad's personal history leaked out in dribs and drabs over the decades. I knew that he was a U.S. Navy veteran and a naturalized citizen, but I was surprised to learn my father's original name was not Steve. It was Esteban. As was common during that time, dad worked and mom stayed at home. In his off hours he planted fruit trees and other plants behind our house. Pretty soon, our property was a flowering oasis, especially compared to the neglected backyards that surrounded us. He built a beautiful rock pond graced with a statue of "Our Lady of Fatima," which my shiny-eyed mother reverently referred to as "The Grotto," but we never saw any miracle of fatherly affection. My dad's efforts were solitary, except when he made us, like little convicts, pile up rocks for the pond.

Dad never played with us, never said he loved me or that I was pretty. He was a man who left early in the morning and shut us out when he returned home at precisely the same hour every evening.

When I was a teenager, my dad did pay a bit more attention to me, but by then I didn't want him to. All of a sudden there was a whole lot of yelling going on. As a teenaged feminist, I viewed Dad as the enemy. I wanted to come and go as I pleased and it seemed to me that his dominance was symptomatic of an unfair patriarchal society.

"Control freak," I'd whisper, when he stormed off after laying down yet another law.

Meanwhile, I pitied my mother, whose relationship with my dad appeared neither communicative nor romantic. Once I screwed up the courage to ask her what she loved about him.

"He works like a horse," she said as she folded laundry for five.

"That's it?" I asked, in 16-year-old disbelief.

$\sim$

Today, after three decades as a hard-working mother I am more wise and seasoned. Now I appreciate why my father rose every morning at four o'clock, wheezy and asthmatic, to work long hours in a hotel kitchen. His collection of prescriptions stood at attention like small soldiers on his nightstand. Dad suffered from virtually every respiratory scourge in the book. But he never missed a day of work in his life.

Finally, I understood that my dad's emotional distance was typical of his World War II generation - men who lived an attitude of "just dig in and do it and stop talking about it so much." All my young life I had wanted conversation and compliments, so I didn't appreciate my dad's daily gift of predictable security.

I had to become a parent, with all its frustrating sacrifices, before I could begin to fathom how deeply his energy was invested in keeping us together. Many men choose to abandon their kids rather than endure the relentless grind of keeping them clothed, fed, housed and schooled. I know that divorced women and their children plummet into a lower income bracket with all its attendant deprivations and stressors.

Today I wonder what would have become of us if my father's desire for a different life had prevailed. Back then, such notions did not occur to me. I was jealous of other girls whose dads doted on them openly.

Now, as a grandmother, I see how my granddaughters bloom under the sunshine of my son-in-law's attentions. Joe is much more affectionate and talkative with his girls than my dad was. Even so, I see now that my father's presence at home created stability and routine, which underscored my own sense of childhood safety.

Sometimes I wondered if my dad wanted something different from our family life. His answer was a big surprise.

"I know a lot of people think I'm just some guy living in this neighborhood in a crummy house. But they don't know that when I was young, I traveled everywhere and saw places they've never been. Nobody can take away my memories," he said.

Then, patting my hand, he said, "I want you to do better than I did." Then he went back to watching "The Mike Douglas Show" as though nothing had happened.

I was in my late twenties. Finding about his secret yearnings was like a mule's kick to my head. My own dad had adventures in exotic places! His memories had sustained him. Who could know that wanderlust beat in his heart every day when he hoisted heavy kettles and pots in a hotel kitchen so that he could the pay the mortgage on our "crummy" house?

I had always craved his personal attention, but he chose to channel the energy he had into a much bigger picture.

My dad gave up his dreams so his three kids would have a running chance at our own. Being with us tipped the scales in our favor.

Here's to the fathers who stayed and stayed.

Suzette Martinez Standring

SUZETTE MARTINEZ STANDRING is a syndicated columnist with GateHouse News Service and an award-winning author. Her book, *The Art of Column Writing: Insider Secrets from Art Buchwald, Dave Barry, Arianna Huffington, Pete Hamill and other Great Columnists*, took First Place for Educational Book in FWA's 2008 Royal Palm Literary Awards. It won Honorable Mention in the Writing Book category of ForeWord Magazine's 2008 Book of the Year Awards. She is a past president of the National Society of Newspaper Columnists. Visit www.readsuzette.com

Cover photo by Janet McCourt of Massachusetts.

SUZETTE STANDRING'S TOP TEN PICKS

FEATURING COLUMNIST

SUZETTE
MARTINEZ
STANDRING'S

TOP TEN PICKS FROM

FWA'S
COLLECTION

Variations on Mr. Cornflake

In the spring of 1983, my sister turned me into a fairy.

She claimed to know the spell for turning an ordinary tomboy with dirt under her nails and stained hand-me downs into a beautiful fairy, complete with gossamer wings and delicate little feet. I sat in the bathtub, hardly noticing the water going cold and the bubbles popping into oblivion, mesmerized as I watched her work. She carefully measured a capful of strawberry shampoo into a pink plastic cup. She squeezed in a few drops from her waterlogged Barbie doll's hair, added a dollop of our mother's Aquanet mousse, spit into the cup, and swirled the mixture. Her brow furrowed in concentration.

She lifted the potion over my head and poured. I closed my eyes and imagined the transformation that was likely taking place before her. My hair was probably turning from mousy and straight to curly and blonde, perhaps even topped with a tiny, glittering crown. My skinned knees were healing and my freckles were giving way to smooth, creamy skin. I felt her rubbing the potion into my hair and heard her muttering a few nonsense words—the magic spell.

Then she said, "Ta-dah!"

I hopped from the tub and hurried to the sink, my hair dripping and slick with congealed soap, my flesh a mass of goosebumps. The mirror reflected the same girl I'd been before: the tomboy with brown hair and crooked teeth, short and pudgy. No tiara, no wings.

"Nothing happened," I said.

"I can tell you're a fairy," she said. "You're probably just too dumb to see it."

My brilliant sister wrote and illustrated volumes of stories: Mr. Cheerio, A Horse Named Bob, plays starring our Cabbage Patch Kids and My Little Ponies, which we would later act out. I made a few attempts at my own manuscripts, but Mr. Cornflake just didn't have the same charisma, the same flair, as Mr. Cheerio.

I found one of her books while snooping though her dresser: Stupid Bekah. I was the main character. It chronicled the antics of an annoying, dimwitted little sister who constantly said the wrong thing, missed punchlines, took things without asking, irritated everyone and ruined everything in her path. The illustrations of me were even less flattering than the descriptions. I ripped it up and threw it out the window of the bedroom we shared.

"What happened to the book I wrote?" she asked me later.

"What book?" I asked, wide-eyed.

"You know what book, Bekah. Where is it?"

"I don't know."

She stood across the room, hands on her hips, glaring at me from behind her glasses.

"Liar," she said. "You really are stupid, Bekah."

I was crushed.

When she started middle school, things went from bad to brutal. Anything I said was up for ridicule. Nothing I wore was right. Nevertheless, I was still determined to impress her.

"What do you think?" I asked, modeling a meticulously color-coordinated outfit—turquoise and pink—right down to the socks and shoelaces.

"It's okay," she told me, "if you're starting an ugly club."

I'd seek her advice when experiencing dramas typical of any fifth grade girl.

"I think my friend is mad at me," I'd say, on the verge of tears.

"You probably deserve it," she'd reply.

Then we were in high school. First, she dyed her hair, then she shaved it. She wore combat boots with fishnet stockings and safety pins on her flannel shirts. I was never brave enough to venture beyond the realm of torn jeans and dark lipstick, which I always wiped off before going home. She smoked pot and dropped acid. I felt trés rebellious drinking Peach Schnapps and NyQuil. She once threw an entire ice cream sundae at a girl who made fun of her jacket. Meanwhile, I talked about people behind their backs and smiled to their faces. She was the real thing. I was just an imposter, a Mr. Cornflake.

Somehow that didn't matter anymore.

We became confidants, co-conspirators. She taught me how to smoke a cigarette. We sat together on her dresser and blew sloppy smoke rings out her window, coughing and giggling. She taught me how to sneak out of the house. We practiced shimmying down the huge evergreen that stood in front of her second floor window. Soon we were nimble as cats, able to make it from window to ground in twenty seconds flat. During family gatherings we swiped alcohol and smuggled it off into empty bedrooms, daring each other to drink it. Our throats ached from laughing hysterically as we stumbled and slurred. During these moments, inside the hysterical laughter, the commiserating about crappy relationships, disloyal friends and strict but absent parents, we were equals. We were best friends.

We went to college on opposite coasts. I still envied her life and spent my time playing catch-up. The places she traveled, the things she dared to try, even the seedy apartments and shady friends— everything was about her was so alive.

I was blind-sided when I found out she'd tried to kill herself. She told me about it when I visited her at art school one spring. We sat on the roof of her apartment, sharing a bottle of wine and smoking cigarettes.

"So don't get mad," she began, "but I tried to commit suicide last year."

"What?" I stared at her. "When?"

"Right before Christmas." She flicked her cigarette. Ashes fluttered onto the tar paper below.

"But…why?"

She shrugged. "I wasn't happy. Stressed out. Work, school, breaking it off with what's-his-name." She was calm, like she was telling me she'd tried a new recipe that didn't quite work out.

I, on the other hand, was livid.

"You were thinking about killing yourself and you didn't even call me?"

"What were you gonna do? You live, like, a thousand miles away."

"Still, you could have at least talked to me about it."

She laughed and held up her wrist, where I saw the fragile red lines running across it.

"What's there to say? I didn't go through with it."

"How could you even think about killing yourself!?" I was raging. It blew my mind that the person whose life I had always admired could decide she was disposable.

"I wasn't really thinking about anything, I guess," she said. "I was depressed and drinking. I saw a knife and I went for it."

"Jesus Christ!" I took a swig of wine, my lips making a hollow thup on the bottle.

"I didn't want to bother you," she said. "You're so busy with school and stuff. Plus you're so far away."

"I think you feeling suicidal would have taken precedence over anything else I had going on."

I felt betrayed. She hadn't trusted me to handle her at her worst, her most vulnerable. I'd always believed we were as close as two people could possibly be. Then, when she should have been running to me first, she'd shut me out.

"Really, why didn't you call me?" I asked, crushing out my cigarette.

She shrugged again, a ghostly arm of smoke escaping her lips. "I didn't think you could relate. You've always had it so together and your life is so easy. You wouldn't have understood."

"You think I had it together?" I laughed out loud. "All I've ever done is try to copy you. Don't you know that?"

She just looked at me.

"Hello? Mr. Cornflake? Remember?"

"Oh, yeah...."

"I've always tried to be like you. Everything in my life has pretty much been a variation on Mr. Cornflake."

"Great," she said, laughing. "Well, congratulations. You're better at my life than I am."

"But don't you think that's kind of pathetic? Not ever doing anything original?"

"It's not pathetic," she said. "You didn't copy everything-just the parts you liked. You'd be a complete moron to copy my mistakes. That's where you made your own life."

"I guess."

We sat there, looking out over rooftops, air-conditioning units and satellite dishes, high above the medley of car horns and laughter and barking dogs.

"I always kinda liked Mr. Cornflake," she said after a minute. "He wasn't a jerk like Mr. Cheerio was."

"Yeah, he was kind of a jerk."

"I mean, he had his reasons…he had a hole in the middle of his body. That's gotta be tough."

"Yeah, but he was interesting," I said. "Mr. Cornflake was flat and lame. Who wants to hang out with a loser like that?"

She blew another smoke ring, looked at me and smiled.

"I do," she said.

Rebekah Hunter Scott

REBEKAH SCOTT is a writer who is taking a break from sanity to raise her two young children. She is a member of Rogue's Gallery Writers, and her work has appeared in *The Flagler Review, The Storyteller Magazine* and *The Creekline Newspaper.* You can also find her work at motherhoodiseasy.blogspot.com

Storm Gathering

Drought's been going on fer months now, years by my reckon. The land's dry and crispy. Cactus growing everywhere. One spark a fire sets acres of forest to raging blazes. Taint like it used to be, that's fer sure.

I grew up here in Flor'da. I can 'member every afternoon, 'bout two o'clock, the skies'd turn blacker'n dusk, winds ripping through trees, whooshing and scooping up anything laying round. Leaves and trash'd be a-dancing, flying in the sky higher'n Daddy's head, higher'n most buildings. Sand'd blow in yor eyes if you weren't careful.

We all knew when a storm was comin'. Squalls give only a couple minutes warnin', and you had to hurry. Clothes'd be grabbed off clotheslines quicker'n you could think, 'fore the rain come to soak 'em. Toys and trashcans out in a yard'd be picked up and placed proper, cuz the winds'd have 'em scattered all over the neighborhood in seconds. Might take days to find all yor b'longings, cuz you never knew where the wind'd drop things off.

Fast as we could, we rolled up the car windas. Many times giant raindrops'd be heaving at us 'fore we could get 'em closed. House windas'd be slammed in a frantic. Anything not shut and away be drenched in a instant. If you weren't home to grab everything, you'd come back to a sopped-through mess.

I love a good storm. Most tourists never seen a rainstorm like we have here in Flor'da.

Gales still scream across Flor'da land, but not on the daily basis like they used to. Now 'days, we got drought.

When I take my outdoor shower come morning, honeybees fly round me to git a drink of water from a stray stream of water. Every morning they buzz round, collecting drops on their feet to carry back to the hive. They must be awful thirsty in there.

I make sure to keep the birdbath full so birds and squirrels got a place to drink and wash. One day I saw a lizard clinging inside the bath, his web fingers fixed to the edge and his pointy nose dipped down to get a drink. The littlest red tongue striking out and lapping the water. I'd never seen a lizard drink 'fore.

Purple, pink, red, and white azaleas fill the parch-dry air with sweet fragrance, but the flowers hang wilted. They look pitiful. Drought's been going on so long, many a lake's dried up and many a wildflower's dis'peared, and now fire burns a big stretch of land near here. Smoke chokes my throat and stings my eyes, and the fire's moving closer. Something's gotta be done.

Folk run hither and thither, full awares of the drought but not doing anything 'bout it.

What can anybody do?

Other night, I went out to take an evening shower. As I reached to turn the water on, I caught sight of a teenage-size tree frog sitting on the pipe near the cold-water spout. My hand jumped, and my heart got racing. His face lit up with a big frog smile, and he sang out, Rrreee rrreee, rrreee rrreee! announcing to his family the coming water.

After getting over the scare Mr. Frog gave me, I turned on the water. He didn't budge. He watn't the least bit afraid of me. Jus' sat there waiting. I named him Alphie.

I hadn't noticed, but direct a-hind him on the wall perched his baby sister. In a smaller voice she shrilled, Waaa waaa! Waaa waaa! and waited fer splashes. I called her Sheebu.

A big daddy frog sparked my attention, and next to him sat little twin girls, Rexie and Dexie.

Mamma frog came hopping in from under a branch.

I couldn't believe it. A whole family of frogs. Mamma, Daddy,

Alphie, Rexie, Dexie, and Sheebu. They croaked their tunes of joy under the spray leaking outta the old pipe, getting wet all over and beaming big frog grins.

Alphie suspended hisself under the faucet, catching dribbles a water on his face till he looked full slimey.

Tree frogs don't drink. They get their water through their skin, absorbing it into theirselves.

The frog family basked in the cool water, but they knew this water wasn't always there and not everybody had a way to it. Many a their friends suffered in the dried up lakes, some even dying or dead by now. And they knew something had to be done.

After I finished showering, I turned the water off and went inside the cabin and stood by the door listening to the frogs singing.

When I was little, Mamma and Daddy taught me to listen to the frogs. They tol' me, "They sing fer rain to come, and they sing after rain, like praying."

My frog family croaked and ribbited. I could almost hear 'em saying, "We thank Thee fer the water! Whee'whee, whee'whee!"

The harmony stopped. I heard some breeze and leaves shuffling.

A new song started. Pleading sounds croaking in the night. Laaack laaack! Laaack laaack! Low-pitched, vibrating cries ringing to the sky. They sang all night and next day, the frogs asking, "Please, we need rain!" Rrrreeek rrrreeek! "Please, we're withering and need water!" Rrrib't rrrib't!

They sang nonstop, Creeeek creeeek! They were good frog songs.

Guess what happened next? This is a true story.

The very next day, come mid-afternoon, the sweltering blue sky turned gray, almost black. Full-up clouds come low warning rain.

Wind blew the trees, making tall pines dance wild and oaks and palms to dropping branches on the ground. The blowing yanked leaves and trash up, and dust blew high as telephone lines. A storm gathering.

In the background, I heard the frog family singing fer the rains, Creeeek creeeek! Creeeek creeeek!

Bolts a lightning cracked the sky, and thunders shook the cabin. A storm born.

Big drops splashed the parch-dry earth. The sounds on the tin roof got louder and louder, coming heavier and heavier and going sideways against my windas.

It rained all day and night, lightning snapping the air. Over and over the clouds dumped their water and built up again to send more drenching rains.

It poured and poured near a week. Trees and flowers blossoming like spring, pools forming in low places, puddles in the high ones.

Gardens and bugs and birds and animals and people all smiled with gladness fer the rains. Sunday, folks went to church to say thanks fer answering their prayers.

But I knew it was my frog family that asked Him hardest.

~

Epilogue: I went to visit my sister and stayed with her six weeks in Miami. I saw hardly any rain there. When I came home, everything was green and had grown, the grass near above my knees. My neighbor came by.

"We had lotsa rain while you were gone," he tol' me. "Hundreds a frogs are ribbiting in the lake."

I heard 'em them that night, singing their melody. I went to sleep to them singing, thanking God fer the rain, and I sweared I heard my frog family sing the loudest.

DEBORAH LYN THOMPSON

DEBORAH THOMPSON, a native Floridian, is a vibrant storyteller and explorer of cultures, philosophies and nature, whose life experiences include living in Argentina, Alaska, India and Africa. Her unique adventures are recorded in dozens of beautifully illustrated journals. Deborah currently resides in a lake-side cabin in Keystone Heights, Florida.

Her Place in the Sun

I's writing this the best I knows how, for I wants the whole world to know how I got my freedom but loss my precious Safara, my one and onliest child.

I lost her the first time to my massa, Mr. Samuel Russell. It was 1860 and Massa Russell's wife and onliest child got kilt in a carriage accident in Durham. That's jus down the road a couple miles from his plantation. Old Jacob, the slave coach driver, he let them horses get spooked and, well, what's past is past.

Massa Russell moped round after that. He was never a hard man to work for. Strict, but not hard. After the death of his eleven-year-old daughter Caroline, though, he started seeing us slaves different. I particularly seen him looking at my Safara. Then one day he come to my cabin.

"Annie," he says in a voice as calm as the evening breeze, "I want Safara to live in the house with me."

Well, you can imagine what I was thinking, him having loss his wife and all. We ain't never knowed him to go after one of us slave women, but when you's dealing with white folk, there's no telling.

"She gonna be a house slave?" I asked.

"She's jus gonna live in my house," he said. "And she cain't be round you and the slaves no more."

"She's jus thirteen," I tells him, "but you's the massa, and I got no say."

He leads my little Safara out the door but turns round and says, "One day you will, Annie."

It musta been three months 'fore I see'd my Safara again. I see'd her from a distance and only for a few seconds. She wore one of them fancy hoop skirts. It was then and there I knowed the massa done lost his mind, dressing my Safara up like his own Carrie. The man had found a way to end his grieving over the loss of his daughter by taking mines. The onliest thing that kept me from screeching after him was thinking at least her life was better than mines, better than any negro slave.

The war started, but things went along 'bout the same the next few years, the slaves slaving. Massa did a fine job keeping Safara out of sight of everyone. I kept 'specting there to be a child, but none came. I remembers thinking how maybe Safara was spared that. Maybe God made her barren so's not to suffer indignities.

The war got to winding down, and it looked like we was gonna be freed. Massa did a fine job of keeping Safara out of sight of everyone. Then late in the fall of 1864, Massa Russell really done lost his mind. He throwed a big harvest ball and invited all the neighbors. Many come, too, cause it took their minds off the retribution them Yankees said the southerns was gonna have to pay.

Massa Russell dress me up like a house slave and had me working serving food to the white folks. I thought that a might peculiar until I see'd what happened that night, the night I lost my Safara the second time.

When I first laid eyes on her that evening, everyone was gathered in the ballroom. Musicians was playing, and slaves was serving the white folk fancy foods on trays. I had jus offered a tray to the Mayor of Durham when the massa's voice rang out.

"Ladies and gentleman," he says, "I'd like to introduce a very young lady...Miss Safara Freedman."

In walks my child through the door, and I nearly dumped my tray in the Mayor's lap. She was wearing one of them white girl's fancy hoop gowns, and a silver lace bonnet lay flat on her head.

Every eye in the place turned to her, and not a mouth said a sound. Yet Massa Russell acted like it was the most naturalest thing in the world, a dolled-up slave at a fancy white folks ball.

Right away some of the guests was so insulted they left, but many of the men gathered round the massa asking for an explanation. He stood firm and repeated some things he read in a book by some English white man. Charles Darwin, he called him and insisted that Safara and all the slaves was people same as white folks.

For them that stayed, Safara played the piano and sounded like an angel in Heaven. She sang, too, and recited poetry, and even read from the Holy Bible. It was a passage where Moses was told how to treat slaves. That's when I learnt we was supposed to be set free after slaving for seven years. The white folks never told us 'bout that part of the Bible.

There was a big argument 'tween massa and some of the more excited white men, and then all the guests stormed out. 'Fore I could get a chance to talk to Safara, the massa sent all us slaves back to our cabins. And that's where I stayed. Even after fire lit up the night in the wee hours of the morning. I was too afraid to look out my door, so I jus lay there 'specting at any moment for white men to come breaking in and do bad things to me and the other slaves. But nothing happened to us.

In the morning, I scurried outside and see'd the plantation house burnt to the ground. We rushed up there looking for the massa and Safara, but alls we found was a piece of paper stuck to a burnt porch post. None of us could read 'cept me and Joppa, the livery stable slave. He told us the best he could figure was that massa had saved hisself and Safara and taken her up north. And us slaves was free.

We was free all right. Free as long as we stayed on the plantation. Cause if we dared leave, we'd be shot or hanged as runaways if we was caught wandering the roads.

That was the last I ever heared or see'd of my Safara. But I heared one time that there was a charming young black woman who played piano and sang for President Johnson. Rumor had it she'd gotten herself married to a white man. My heart picked up after that, cause I knowed if that was her, she was better off in her life than me or any slave. And it was comfort knowing she did not endure the lesser chains of freedom we had to endure after we was freed by the war.

Her father, a negro man killed for making too many 'scapes, named her well, cause Safara means her place in that African man's language. And even though the rest of us lived in the shadow of freedom, Safara found her place in the sun.

EUGENE ORLANDO

EUGENE ORLANDO published his RPLA first place short story *My Mother's Daughter* with the *Diana Kay Publishing* magazine, now available on SeaCrestebooks.com for download. For more, visit me at www.DanaPalladino.com or on my young adult site, www.DakotaBalmore.com.

Sweet Summer Rain

Unrelenting heat and burnt grass defined that summer, whirling ceiling fans the things we saw last before we closed our eyes at night.

My brother Evan and I learned the meaning of words like swelter, drought, and heat index. The sidewalks in town were too hot for even calloused feet, and the blacktop roads sucked at tires. Even the brown dog down the road stayed under the porch all day, coming out only to gulp from his water dish.

Seems like everyone got angry that summer for no good reason. Kids hardly ever switched before got lots of them. My neighborhood gang got into such a ruckus over a game of dodge ball, our folks made us stay in our own yards, meaningless taunts flung over fences the only outlet for our frustrations.

As the dry, scorching days wore on, things at our house went bad. Daddy didn't come home until well after dark at night, smelling of beer and cigarette smoke. Momma met him at the door, blazing as the midday sun. Angry words poured from her lips like molten lava. One time our neighbor next door, gray-bearded, wrinkle-skinned Mr. Farraday, stomped out on his porch, yelling. "Stop your caterwauling, woman. I'm old and need my sleep." Momma was so embarrassed.

Some nights, Momma's going at Daddy made him turn and leave again, sometimes staying gone all night.

Whenever Daddy took off, Momma went to sit in the cellar, crying and nipping from the sherry bottle hidden behind the onion sacks. We weren't supposed to know it was there, but Evan found it one day and took a swallow. He said it dang near burned his gut from the inside out. I was too timid to try and scolded him for doing it.

Our folks fought so often that summer, we thought they might kill each other. When the bitter words flew, I'd sneak into Evan's room. We'd talk about what would happen if our folks were gone. We figured we'd either be sent to live with ancient Grandma Ritchie or smelly Uncle Fred who farted all the time. Each had both good and bad points. We discussed them at length, lying in the dark on Evan's bed, trying not to sweat through his sheets.

Grandma was a good cook, her house in the country next to a dairy farm. We were fascinated by the workings of cows and where milk came from. But Grandma was strict. She kept a ready-cut supply of switches at the back door.

Uncle Fred, on the other hand, lived in town, his place by the railroad tracks where trains roared by day and night. Unlike Grandma, who lived alone, Uncle Fred was married. "That woman," Momma called her. She told us we didn't have to call her Aunt Dahlia because, "She's Uncle Fred's second wife and not really kin to us." I'm not sure why Momma didn't like Aunt Dahlia, but they seemed to end up sniping at each other whenever the families got together.

Uncle Fred's house wasn't as clean as Grandma's, but it had three floors and an attic that went the length of the house. That attic was filled with some pretty cool stuff. But then there was Aunt Dahlia to deal with. We loathed her. She didn't like kids and us in particular, giving us nasty digs about our intelligence, "or lack thereof," she said. She couldn't cook, didn't know how to play card games like War and Go Fish. She said we should be seen and not heard. Still, she and Uncle Fred did live right by that train track.

We never did make up our minds which place we'd rather be sent, but it made for distraction while Momma and Daddy yelled at each other into the night.

At the end of July, when the red line in the thermometer rose to beat all records, Momma packed a bag in the middle of the night and left us. The note on the Frigidaire said something about "needing to find myself." We never knew she was lost.

Now it was Daddy's turn to sit alone and cry. He did it at the kitchen table, beer in one hand, cigarette in the other. Tears dropped from his face and mingled with the sweat on his chest, all of it sliding to his belt.

"If it would just rain and cool things off," he'd mutter. "It's this heat. It's this damn heat."

He tried to do his best by us, staying home from work, helping make our beds, gathering up the laundry to take to his sister Gretta. For lunch and supper, he put jelly, peanut butter, and a loaf of bread in the middle of the table and told us to help ourselves. He set out paper cups and filled them with green Kool-Aid that was warm and sticky sweet. He cried so easily, we knew not to complain.

On the third Friday after Momma left, Daddy's boss called. We could hear him yelling at Daddy through the phone on the hall table, heard him say, "You better be back on Monday or else." Daddy mumbled something and slammed the phone down hard enough to make the house jump.

Monday, Grandma Ritchie started coming for the day. Though she fussed at us constantly for being messy and rude, at least she made good meals. Like herb-baked chicken or macaroni and cheese with little cubes of ham. She even made Rice Crispy treats, which we got to have before bed if we finished all the vegetables on our plate at supper and hadn't been too annoying.

Just when we thought we couldn't endure another day of the blistering heat or another night of Daddy's crying about Momma, it rained. Not one of those quick thunder and lightning rains but a gentle rain that lasted all day. It came in the morning, dimming the world to a shimmering pearl gray, the first drops sizzling on the blacktop in the front of our house.

Grandma Ritchie let us put on our bathing suits and run around the back yard, shrieking like wild Indians. The cool wet felt so good on our skins.

After lunch, we sat on the couch beneath the bay window in the living room with our coloring books and crayons. Grandma sat in the rocker humming and looking out the window at the passing cars.

Daddy came home on time that night carrying a bucket of fried chicken and whistling a Souza marching tune. We heaped our plates full and took them to the back porch so we could eat and watch the rain. As night descended, the air grew even cooler. We'd be able to sleep without sticking to the sheets.

After Daddy sent us upstairs to bed, I snuck to Evan's room to play Go Fish. Halfway into our first game, the back door creaked open and closed. Straining our ears, we heard Daddy say, "So you're home Miranda. Have you come back to stay?"

"Oh, Ralph," Momma said. "I'm so sorry. I don't know what got into me."

A few minutes later, the back door creaked again. We sat still with dread thinking Momma was leaving again, still bitter with the anger she'd carried all summer at Daddy.

Trudging head down back to my room, I heard a sound drift up from below. I stopped to listen. Music? Yes, music! Coming from the back yard. A mushy oldies tune playing on the radio.

I popped open the little round window in the upstairs hall and leaned out. I figured I'd see Daddy outside crying in the rain to the sappy love song. Two people moved out from under the porch eave, barefoot and laughing, their faces turned to the sky. Daddy waltzing Momma around the yard. She laughed and said, "The neighbors will think we're crazy if they see us."

Daddy stopped dancing. He took Momma's face in his big hands and said, "I'm the crazy one. Crazy in love with you, Miranda. You're sweeter to me than this sweet-tasting rain, and I've missed you." He kissed her. Her eyes closed, and she made a soft moan.

Instinct told me they needed to be alone and didn't need my curious eyes. Before I closed the window, I leaned out far enough to catch rain on my tongue.

Back in my room, my pillow tucked under my chin, I agreed with Daddy—summer rain sure tasted sweet.

M. E. Landress

M. E. LANDRESS wrote *Sour Grapes and One Bad Apple,* both part of the Marvella Watson series. She was editor and feature writer for *Cedar Key News* and now contributes to several local publications. See her work at: www.sourgrapes.mysite.com.

A Lifetime of Music

Phillip walked up the steps to the front porch thinking of the day's events and wearing a big grin. It had been a great game of marbles and he was getting really good! He almost beat his cousin Miller Sam!

Phillip, at nine years old, was the youngest of the boys that gathered during the long days of summer to wile away the time. Eventually he would bet on his games but he wasn't quite good enough yet. He wouldn't bet money because no kids in 1937 rural Louisianahad any. However, once he got better at playing marbles, he would bet his chores against those of the other boys. He would bide his time until he knew he was the absolute best, and then easy street! His parents wouldn't approve of the gambling or of his passing off his responsibilities, so Phillip decided as he walked into the coolness of the foyer, that they would never know.

"Oh, here he come Mr. Ojay," Marcelite waved Phillip over to stand near her as she sat on the couch. "This is my son. Come here, boy. Which one of these do you wanna play?"

Phillip walked over to see what his mother was holding. There were two pictures, one of a saxophone and one of a cornet. Puzzled, he looked back at his mother.

"This here is Mr. Ojay, the music teacher at your school," Marcelite said pointing to the man seated on the settee directly across from them.

Phillip already knew Mr. Ojay, his school's music teacher. What wasn't entirely clear was the reason he was now in their house. As if reading her son's mind Marcelite quickly explained her plans for his immediate future.

"I decided you gonna do somethin' other than play marbles with your extra time. You gonna take music lessons. Now, which one do you wanna play?"

Phillip looked at the pictures of the two instruments. The saxophone was bright and shiny. He imagined himself playing it and everyone staring at him in awe while listening to his sweet notes. Maybe he could even play it on the street corner in New Orleans for money. As if hypnotized, Phil pointed to the sax.

"How much for the saxophone?" his mother asked.

"Sixty-four dollars."

"Ohhh wheeeee! Sixty-four dollars!"

Marcelite calculated things in her mind. She could only afford to pay one dollar a week and at that rate, it would be awhile before Phillip could even begin his music lessons.

"Well, what about that other one?" she pointed to the short trumpet.

"Let me see your teeth, young man." Mr. Ojay said.

Phillip bared his teeth, resisting the urge to neigh as the teacher did his inspection.

"He has good teeth, Mrs. Guilbeau. He'll make a good trumpet player."

"I don't wanna to play that." Phil started to whine. "Mama I don't-"

"Quiet," Marcelite cut her eyes at her son. "We're not talkin' to you. You just stand there." Then turning her attention back to Mr. Ojay she asked, "How much is it?"

"Well…we have three or four at the school, so if you want, you can use one for free."

"Well, that'll do it." Marcelite stood, which was her way of signaling the end to the discussion. "Looks like my son's gonna be a trumpet player. I'll walk you out, Mr. Ojay."

Phillip sat on the sofa and listened as Mr. Ojay and his mother said their goodbyes. He waited in the living room expecting his mother to return in order to make his final plea, but instead she walked past the living room and into the back pallor. That was her music room. When she went there she did not want to be disturbed.

Phillip listened as she began to play the violin. She loved her violin, but mostly she loved music. She had hoped all seven of her children would learn to love music too. Elliot, the older brother, could really play the piano and Phillip was convinced the boy could outplay anybody in the whole world. Elliot was a great musician, but Phillip never imagined himself being as good.

He closed his eyes, knowing his fun afternoon of today would soon be a distant memory. He would have to learn to play the trumpet and, just as his mother had planned, that would leave little time to play marbles and hang around with his friends.

It was no use trying to bargain with her on this issue. A black woman playing the violin in rural Louisiana was an indication of how much music meant to her. She believed it didn't matter what the instrument was just as long as you did your best and played with all your heart. Phillip listened as his mother played the violin in the music room. She was convinced that the talent her children had came from her musical genes. He certainly hoped not, Phillip thought, opening his eyes. She was terrible.

⁓

I watch my seventy-eight year old father toting his beloved trumpet up the walkway to the house. He never went anywhere without it nowadays. Ever since my mother died he had changed. It seemed that without her, he could no longer find his purpose or direction in life. He had the freedom of a young teenager and the loneliness of an old man. His children were grown and had left one by one. Now his partner of more than fifty years had left him too. Music, his first love, is the only thing that stayed. He would always have music and for that, he thanked his mother.

For Phillip Guilbeau and his trumpet, the past held a lot of great memories. He had played and recorded with the great ones, Frank Sinatra, Count Basie, Otis Redding, Lionel Hampton and for a great deal of his career he traveled and recorded with Ray Charles. As I watched his frail frame struggle with the weight of the trumpet in its large case, I felt the emotional weight of mortality land heavily on my heart. He wouldn't be here forever. My mother's passing was a daily reminder of the stealth-like approach of death. I heard it whisper: parents die.

All of us kids heard the tales of backstage scandals, musical highlights and funny mishaps over and over again. Knowing my father, he would want to be able to tell his stories forever. They weren't just a compilation of disjointed memories; for him they were the fragile pieces of his life. I wanted to write them down, in his own words to preserve the essence of who he was for his grandchildren and their grandchildren to read. So I requested an interview and he, carrying his trumpet, came to talk.

I asked why he was described as Ray Charles' discovery in the liner notes of the Genius + Soul = Jazz album. I asked about his traveling amid racism in the Deep South with Big Joe Turner. I asked about the standing ovation streak for his solos that started a backstage pool. I asked question after question and this time I really listened. I discovered more in one attentive afternoon about Phillip Guilbeau the man, than I had in an entire lifetime of knowing him as Phillip Guilbeau the father.

I am thankful that I learned so much in my interview with my father. Searching for the person hidden behind the image of Mom or Dad is a powerful journey. Discovering their hopes and dreams, their fears and regrets, can create a deep reservoir of understanding and, when necessary, forgiveness. Thinking back, I wonder why I never saw the similarities between my dad and me. Maybe, it was because I didn't know him as well as I thought. Or maybe, I didn't know myself that well, either.

My father fell sick and passed away shortly after our first interview and I cherish the one recorded session we had. I smile now listening to his voice on the tape. No matter how often he repeated a story, he never failed to get tickled and laugh in the same spot or pause in the exact same place for dramatic effect. He loved entertaining, even as he had on that day, for an audience of one.

Because he recorded hundreds of songs with various artists, I hear his trumpet everywhere. Each time I pause, knowing that those in the movie theatre or restaurant or watching the television hear him too. They don't realize it, but they are not only listening to the work of a masterful musician, but they are also hearing the talent of a good father and a good man. He is the most famous, non-famous person I know. I learned that he chose to be non-famous, rejecting opportunities rather than sacrificing his family. He was a father that put family first. I grew up knowing what it felt like to be loved. For that, I will always thank my father.

NINA GUILBEAU

NINA GUILBEAU authored women's fiction book *Too Many Sisters* and e-book *Birth Order and Parenting*. Her articles have been published in newspapers and online parenting magazines. For more of her work, including writings on her father's career, visit www.ninaguilbeau.com

An edited 400-word version of the essay appeared in the Orlando Sentinel, June 21, 2009.

Picture of Old Zeb

My grandmother pulled a glossy snapshot from an overflowing shoebox. Black and white photos, fading tintypes and aging sepias tumbled to the floor.

"Well, would you looky here," she said, holding up the picture. "Pays to clean out the closet once in a while." Hugging the box to her ample breast, she shuffled to her rocking chair and sank down. "I remember the day I took this. Didn't even know I was taking it. Remember the story of old Zeb?" She eyed me over her wire-rimmed glasses.

I was instantly excited. "You have a picture of old Zeb?" At ten years of age I was more interested in the comic book I was reading while sprawled on the floor than a pile of old photos. But the idea of a picture of Zeb made me scramble up to see.

The photo looked terribly normal. I felt disappointed. As if the fellow had been right there, in the flesh, he appeared exactly the way Grandma always described him, a skinny, scarecrow of a man with a scraggly beard. His battered two-button jacket and wide-brimmed hat were decades old; his boots looked heavy and were probably scuffed, and he led a dark horse.

"Ever get a prickly feeling that you're being watched?" Grandma said, her aging voice unsteady. "No, 'course you wouldn't, you bein' only a little girl. But I tell you, I always felt it when he showed up. Felt the prickly disturbance in the air before I ever seen him."

While hoeing weeds in her garden, she told me, the "prickly" feeling would wash over her. She'd look up and there he would be. Leading an unsaddled black horse, he would tromp, unhurried, around the corner of our weather-beaten barn, then stop and stare at her as if he hadn't expected to see her.

I tucked my feet under me and gave her my full attention. The same story I'd heard countless times was underway and I didn't want to miss a word of it, especially now that she'd found a picture. Mother objected to Grandma's stories, but they fascinated me.

I considered my grandmother a special kind of person. She laughed at raunchy jokes but her faith was unshakable. She could cook a meal fine enough for royalty but she preferred simple meat and potatoes. She worked her small farm and her vegetable garden from daybreak to day's end and still had enough energy to read me a story, or tell one of her own. She'd attended a one-room schoolhouse through the sixth grade, but she had more intelligence than a lot of today's college graduates. And she didn't just believe in ghosts, she saw them.

"Who'd he ever expect to find in my own garden besides me, I'd like to know," she grumbled. "I lived here from the time I was a girl. When I was a young woman, Zeb would often wink as he passed by and when I got married, I moved away from the old homestead. After my parents were gone, yer grandpa and me moved in here and took it over. Then here come old Zeb, acting surprised like he never seen me b'fore. The old coot."

According to my grandmother, old Zeb had paid several visits over the years and always looked the same.

"My daddy told me about him. He used to see Zeb once in a while. Momma too if she was in the right place."

The "right place" according to Grandma was at the corner of the garden facing the barn.

"He'd come around the west side of the barn," she said, pointing, "and walk straight off into the east." She pointed in one direction and then the other. "The story goes that there was a man in these parts who lived all alone in a house down by the creek, behind the barn there. Zebediah Something-or-Other. Folks forgot his last name. One night the house caught fire and spread, burning everything to the ground with him and all he had—the house, a small barn and a horse. Tragic, that's what my daddy said. Happened in my daddy's day, back in the 1880s or so, 'bout when I was born. It was some time after the fire that folks round about started seeing the old man wandering the hills leadin' his horse. Other folks seen'im different places but I only ever seen'im from that corner of the garden, and he'd be comin' toward me. He'd stop and look at me kinda startled, like he took a wrong turn or somethin'. Then he'd nod polite like and walk on by, toward the east."

"You mean he just disappeared, Grandma?" I always asked. It seemed expected.

"Not like 'poof,' of course, just sorta walk 'away,' you know?"

I didn't know, but in my childish imagination I could see the old man and his horse vanishing into thin air.

"Why did he make these visits, Grandma?"

As if I'd never asked that question before, and maybe I hadn't, Grandma eyed me out of the bottom half of her glasses.

"Lord, child, if I had them kinda answers. You've heard it said that there's more in heaven and earth than we are given to know, ain't you? I've told you often enough. Shakespeare, I think. Well, he was right, there's some things don't have explanations."

"But weren't you ever afraid when he appeared?"

"'Fraid of old Zeb? Heavens no! Way my daddy told it, folks were kinda glad when he come to visit. They took it to mean he was lookin' out for 'em. Keepin' them safe."

Now, even as a child I knew farming held its own kind of danger. Things were always happening, horrible things, such as the tractor accident that claimed my father's life in later years. Grandma cautioned me not to blame things on a failing of old Zeb's. He knew nothing except horses and farming and fires. The general belief was—and it seemed to hold some truth—that as long as he appeared, there would never be a house fire in that small community. Grandma didn't remember when his visits stopped.

"But it was odd," she said. "After the Chambers place burned, he was never seen again." Leaning forward, she carefully took the snapshot and held it, reverently. "It's somethin', ain't it, this picture? I took it myself, you know."

"But Grandma, if he was a ghost, how did you get his picture?" Even at ten, I knew you couldn't photograph a ghost.

"Hmm, I reckon he was a ghost, at that. Him and his horse. Never thought of him that way. More like a spirit visitor. I didn't aim to take his picture, you know. Didn't even know I was doin' it. I stood right out there at the corner of the garden with my trusty old Brownie box to take a picture of the barn's hay doors. Your grandpa had just hung new ones after a thunderstorm tore the old ones off. Well, when I got the film developed, I found I had old Zeb's picture, like he was posin' for me. If you look real close, he's kinda grinnin', too. I guess you can take a picture of a ghost, if the ghost is willin.'"

CAROL A. JONES

CAROL A. JONES writes a twice-monthly column on behalf of Freedom Public Library in the South Marion Citizen newspaper; quarterly features in Freedom's Flyer, the Friends of the library's newsletter; and has completed two novels. View some of her work at www.jonesyworks.blogspot. com

She Dances on Her Toes

Emily was an imp. It took us a while to figure that out. About six months. Our first child, we went silly documenting her new life in photographs, recordings, and baby-book entries, everything proud parents could do to celebrate their new child.

We worried over her and probably spoiled her, but we were children ourselves, or at least we felt like children.

We decided to have an oil portrait of our new family. The artist gave up trying to pose us after Emily wormed out of her mother's lap for the twelfth time, so we had a photo taken, and the artist painted from that.

A week later, the artist called. "Mr. Campbell," he said, "I finished the portrait. I had some trouble with your daughter's face. It took me a while to capture her expression, but I think I figured it out, finally."

I knew exactly what he meant. We had figured it out ourselves only a few weeks earlier. "Mischievous?" I said.

"Yes, that's it. I hadn't thought of that word, but it fits. I think you have a handful there."

I chuckled. Didn't we know it. The girl loved adventure. No ant, pan, noise, smell, or person escaped her attention. God had provided all of it to entertain her and only her. Or so she seemed to think.

I never knew what to expect when coming home from work. I walked into the family room one day to an eerie quiet. Quiet was bad, I'd learned.

A faint squeak emitted from behind the sofa. Emily's feet greeted me as I peered in the space between the back of the sofa and the wall. She wasn't frightened. She seemed to be enjoying herself, though wriggling like a cat in a big shopping bag.

My wife Jennie, who'd stopped overreacting to Emily's adventures a month and two bottles of antacid ago, asked, "What did she do now?"

"Your guess is as good as mine," I said. "I'll hold her feet while you pull out the sofa."

Another day, I came home to the muffled racket of metal hitting metal. It came from a cabinet over the oven. I opened the cupboard door to see Emily holding two Revere Ware copper bottom pots, poised in mid-strike. She glared at me. How dare I interrupt? I closed the cabinet door, shook my head, and called the negligent mother, as if Jennie she could have prevented the four-year-old from climbing up there.

The message was clear. Don't turn your back on me or suffer the consequences.

Now imagine a large dog with an extremely wet mouth, licking your face one hundred times. As horrible as that sounds, our five-year-old believed it was her way of showing love.

Jennie lifted Emily onto her lap and kissed her forehead good morning.

"A hundred kisses!" Emily shouted and proceeded to plant them on Jennie's face, each one louder and wetter than the last. At the end of the onslaught, Jennie excused herself and whispered, "I'm going to take a shower."

"Please," I said, and kept my distance.

Seven should have been an exciting time in Emily's life. The wild whirligig slowed for no one, talking, dancing, running. She had the unusual habit of running on her toes. We thought little of it because it didn't slow her down. If anything, it made her run faster.

"Isn't she adorable?" Jennie said as we watched Emily in dance class, flitting across the floor on her toes. Her teacher commented to us, "She dances so lovely on her toes. Pointe will come to her naturally. A future ballerina."

To be honest, that's probably why we enrolled her in dance, as well as soccer and swimming classes. I imagined her, the ingénue, stunning the Bolshoi, or the star striker, beating all the other girls to the soccer ball. Living the glory through the child, I guess. At least I admit it.

My selfish dreams ended that day in the park. Jennie and I watched Emily running on her toes, like Mercury delivering an important communication to the gods. Her long blond hair slapped at her face as she alternated between imaginary bridges and castles, interrupted only by swing sets.

"Is that your daughter?" the woman seated next to me asked.

I smiled. "Yes, that's our Emily." I wanted to add, "The prettiest girl out here, don't you think?"

"She runs on her toes all the time," she said.

"She's always done that. It doesn't seem to hold her back. In fact, we have trouble keeping up with her."

The woman sighed. "I work in the medical field, so I've seen this before. You might want to have a neurologist see Emily." She touched my arm. "Walking on toes is usually an indication of a muscular disorder."

I couldn't respond. I reeled from the hammer blow to my chest. Emily sick? It wasn't possible

The neurologist was a pragmatic man. In some ways, I appreciated that. In other ways, I wanted to choke him as he methodically spelled out his diagnosis and his options.

"Emily is suffering a loss of muscle mass, a wasting of the muscular structure with contractures."

"Contractures?" Jennie asked.

"A permanent tightening of a muscle that affects its shape. That's why she walks on her toes, to compensate for the weak muscles. It's common to patients with muscular dystrophy."

I'd never heard my wife gasp before. The neurologist had said the words as if he were a mechanic discussing a bent tie-rod on an SUV.

Muscular dystrophy was a cliché that other children suffered to maintain telethons, not something that could afflict my daughter. Emily had Duchene Muscular Dystrophy. Extremely rare in girls and passed genetically from us to her. One defect among millions, but deadly just the same. The doctor, again dispassionately, said she could live to puberty, but it was unlikely.

There was no way for us to explain to Emily what was wrong with her. We never did. As the symptoms worsened and she adapted to her affliction, there wasn't any need to explain.

Emily fought the disease bravely, through the crutches, the wheelchairs, until eventually, her muscles no longer supported her body, and she progressed to a negative pressure ventilator, the technical name for an iron lung. It's a large plastic container that enclosed her torso to her neck and breathed for her. An oxygen mask covered her mouth and nose.

Defying the doctor's prediction, she turned thirteen. And I waited. I waited by her side. I waited all day and all night—waited for her to die. Jennie couldn't stand to watch Emily suffer. I couldn't blame her. It's too much to ask of any parent. I'm not sure how I managed, but I did, torn between wishing she'd live and hoping she'd die.

I brushed her hair often to show her I was there and to break the monotony of the whoosh-whoosh of the beast that imprisoned her.

Then she opened her eyes. It startled me. She must have realized her end was close. I debated removing the oxygen mask, knowing if I left it off too long, it would speed her death, but it was obvious she wanted to say something. Knowing my imp, she'd probably say something clever or maybe just, "I love you." or "Thanks, Dad".

I removed the mask. Emily smiled and whispered, "A hundred kisses."

God, if only she had only said something else, anything else. My chest heaved as I gasped for air between sobs. Even as I cried, I worried about the oxygen mask and knew I needed to compose myself. I wiped my eyes with my sleeve and repositioned the mask on her.

"Okay, baby," I said and kissed her a hundred times around the mask.

Then I thought back, to the imp twirling in her dance outfit with her long blond hair slashing the air as she danced on her toes.

J. J. WHITE

JOHN J. WHITE has won numerous writing awards for his novels, short stories, and poetry. He has written for several newspapers, magazines, and websites. You can see his work at www.jjwhite.org.

I'm A Person

My dad's name is Alfred Person. The phone book lists him with only his first name's initial. Person, A.

In the mood for fun a few years ago, I called directory assistance and asked the number for A. Person in Paterson, New Jersey.

The operator said, "What is the name, please?"

"A. Person in Paterson, New Jersey."

"Look, don't be smart with me."

"I'm not, ma'am," I said. "I'm looking for A. Person in Paters—"

She hung up on me.

My dad made dinner reservations for us at a nice restaurant to celebrate my mom's birthday. He told them, "Five persons, and the name is Person." We got there but had no reservation and had to wait an hour to be seated because the hostess thought Dad's call was a prank.

When my brother left for his first year at college in another state, Dad told him to call person-to-person. A week later, my homesick brother called home.

The operator asked, "What is your name, please?"

"Philip Person."

"And who do you wish the call placed to?"

"Alfred Person."

"Let me get this straight. This is a person-to-person phone call from a Philip Person to an Alfred Person?"

"Yes."

When Dad speaks at organizational meetings, he's inevitably introduced as "Alfred Person, in person!"

My whole life I've heard, "You're a real person, huh?" "What kind of person are you?" or "Look, it's Elaine Person!" Sounds like a lame person, doesn't it?

In my teen years, one of my nicknames was Miz Personality. I liked that.

In eighth grade, a guy friend dubbed me People. I didn't care for that. When we got to high school, and he shouted down the hall, "Hey, People!" the first day there, I told him we were grown up now and not to call me that anymore.

Sometimes people don't believe their ears and think I'm Pearson, or they add an "S" to Person, which makes me plural. I am not married, so I say "Person: I'm single, and it is singular."

My dad tells people, "You're a person, and I'm a Person." In his case, he really is A. Person.

When speaking on the phone, I spell "Person" to people who want to make it what it's not. "Person," I say. "You know, the simple word you learned to spell in first grade. It's easy. Like Smith, but it's Person." My niece got married, and her last name changed from Person to Smith.

My sister Margie so disliked the Person-al assaults, she couldn't wait to get married and change her name. Despite herself, she fell in love with Charlie Reene and married him. A friend of hers asked if things were butter for her.

My parents could have made things worse for us. They could have named my brother Rich or Frank or Harry. I could have been Gay or Merry or Anita.

My brother dated Rhonda Small for a while. Had he married her, she would have been Rhonda Small Person.

In college, someone started a rumor that my last name used to be Mann, but I became a woman's libber and changed it to Person.

I'm five-four and Caucasian. Chuck Person, former NBA player, and former assistant coach for the Sacramento Kings, is six-foot-eight and two hundred twenty pounds. Wesley Person, his younger brother, is also a former NBA player. He is six-foot-six and two hundred pounds. I tell people they're my "little" brothers. "What, you don't see the resemblance?"

My name is Miss Elaine E. S. Person. Miscellaneous Person. I'm a real person.

ELAINE S. PERSON

ELAINE PERSON was an editor of the College Humor Magazine *Galumph*. Her parody of King Arthur was published in Random House's *A Century of College Humor*. As Production Coordinator for TCI Cable, she wrote TV scripts. Elaine performs poetry and stories. She created the poetry Chapbook: *Miss Elaine E. S. Person*.

Murder by Candlelight

The idea of it jolted my head off the pillow. I swung my feet and slammed them on the hardwood floor, making a thunk louder than a carriage wheel on cobblestone. I listened for my bedchamber's darkness to spring into opposition but, hearing nothing, renewed my decision—to murder the infamous three this very night.

The stillness unbroken, I reached for a match on my nightstand, struck one, and lit a candle. The odor of animal fat tallow filled my nose as I glanced round. My solitude intact, I rose in spite of the pounding in my chest, lifted the candle by its holder, and tiptoed to my bureau.

My chest muscles tightened, forcing me to pound my breast with a fist to rekindle air flow. Palpitations shook my heart, a heart I once thought incapable of performing so foul a deed but which now cried out in bloodlust.

I stared down at my left wrist in the pale light and swear a large vain throbbed inside its clammy skin. My heart prepared to commit itself to Satan's hand. Why not every other part of my being?

I opened the middle dresser drawer and dug beneath my

nightclothes, grasping a cold metal object. Yanking it from the sea of cloth, I held it up to the candle. Its icy surface seared my palm with the passion to murder.

A pistol. Yes, that's how I'll dispose of the wickedest cads to ever curse the streets of London. Boring a neat hole in each of their foreheads ought to exact all vengeance.

The infamous Wimpole brothers created an untold amount of civil unrest in our troubled times of 1842. Change hung heavy in the air, though, for tonight I took lodging in the same ill-famed inn as they with but one purpose—to dispatch their miserable lives so the people of London could be free of their prankish tortures forever.

Deciding shooting too quick an end, I reburied the pistol and withdrew in its stead an authentic Indian tomahawk from the American West. That seemed a better way to murder someone—or three someones. Splitting each of their skulls will serve quite well at revenging the agony they'd inflicted over the years. If paybacks were indeed hell, the tomahawk would deliver it.

A thought struck me. If I did them in with an Indian artifact, people would think the murders committed by Indians, and I'd not receive the well-earned credit that could make me a folk hero. No, that would never do.

Returning the tomahawk, I removed an eighteenth century Russian Cossack dagger. I thrust a quick jab into the imaginary guts of Fenimore Wimpole, the eldest and most notorious of the brothers. I next slashed the air, pretending the dagger's edge sliced open the throat of John, the middle brother. As young Shelley would undoubtedly run like the coward he is, I mimicked a throwing motion, holding the blade by its point. My mind conjured a scene wherein the weapon sank deep between the youngest rogue's shoulder blades.

Yes, the dagger would do nicely.

Toting it and the candle to my bedchamber door, I flipped up the latch, easing the door towards me to peer into the inn's main room. On the far side, the door to notoriety loomed ominous. It harbored the three treacherous brothers. Harboring them for but one night longer, because on the morrow's rise of the sky's yellow ball, England will celebrate its freedom.

My heart crashed against my chest wall. My dagger hand squeezed the weapon, the charging flood of doubt nearly persuading me to drop it, dash for my bed, and dive beneath the covers.

Did I have the courage to commit murder? I'd never committed one before. What made me think I could commit three tonight? Did my drive to revenge and justice empower me to take life? I shut it all out and shoved purpose to the fore. I crossed the main room on tiptoe and melted my back into its far wall, becoming one with it.

Coal fumes from a hearth fire long burned down weighted the air. The coals smoldered, their embers pulsating in crimson hues, the room's warmth replaced by the night's hard chill. My breath's mist floated into the dark beyond the feeble candlelight.

Reaching their door, I found it ajar and so pushed it open with caution. A tiny creak, then another, and lastly a snap, the hinge belching its resistance to my invasion. I paused, my breathing almost as loud as the clacking carriage passing the brothers' bedchamber window, its clop, clop, clopity-clop cloaking my pants. Clop, clop, clopity-clop, clop, clop, clopity-clop. Eclipsing the street lamp, the carriage shadow flickered past the window, the noise of it fading to leave the night in silence.

The smell of an extinguished paraffin lamp hit my nose, betraying the evil three's recent retirement. Perhaps they were not yet asleep. If I crept in now and they were not, they could leap up and overpower me before I could exact my revenge. I shook the possibility from my brain and eased a foot into the room.

A quick blow through my lips snuffed out my candle. I stared towards the single wide bed, a winter-cooled force inside me standing the hairs on my neck straight up. The brothers stood along the bed's side closest to me, their backs towards me, lined up as though expecting execution.

Did they somehow know I lodged here at early candlelight the day before? Was there someone hiding in the darkness waiting to foil my plan to liberate the city? My mind swooned with anxiety, and my stomach filled with nervous nausea. I might be cheated out of delivering justice to the scandalous three.

Fenimore, the brother on the far right, reached towards the nightstand and lit a candle. Though befuddled as to why he did this, I knew the moment for action had arrived. If another body waited to pounce on me, I'd have to race it to accomplish my deed.

Darting forwards and dropping my candleholder, I sprang towards the bed. To my amazement, none of the brothers looked back at me. I glanced over my shoulder but saw no reinforcement diving out of the darkness.

I plunged the dagger deep into Fenimore's back, spun him round in a wink, and buried the blade in his gut, slashing upwards, his insides spilling to the floor. He gasped and fell back on the bed as I turned to my next victim.

I expected John to retaliate and prepared to thrust. But John moved not, so I grabbed his arm and spun him round. On seeing his sick smile, I loosed a slash, tearing open his throat, spurting blood everywhere, and pushed him onto the bed. I turned to Shelley.

Instead of fleeing as expected, his hand went round my throat. I sent the dagger to his midsection, but he caught my wrist with his free hand and forced my arm up, the dagger above our heads. We fought for supremacy.

My knee slammed upwards, but Shelley pushed his buttocks back in a dodge, which gave me the leverage I needed. I shoved him onto the bed, jumped on his thighs, and sent the blade deep into his chest—once, twice, thrice. He turned his head to one side, gurgled, and passed from the Earth.

My mind screamed, London's avenged at last!

I leaped back and dropped my imaginary dagger to the floor where it evaporated wisp-like.

My three brothers rose from the dead.

"Charlotte," Fenimore said, "what fun! Shall we act out another of your famous stories tomorrow night?"

Eugene Orlando

EUGENE ORLANDO published his RPLA first place short story *My Mother's Daughter* with the *Diana Kay Publishing* magazine, now available on SeaCrestebooks.com for download. For more, visit me at www.DanaPalladino.com or on my young adult site, www.DakotaBalmore.com.

Cubs in the House

(Talk About a Blended Family)

For David and Tim Tetzlaff "family" meant an unusual menagerie of animals their father brought home to be nurtured. In the early '60s, before the Tetzlaff boys were born, their parents began Jungle Larry's Zoological Park in Naples, Florida. Columbus Zoo Director Emeritus and animal trainer Jack Hanna, one of Larry's many peers says, "When you think of Jungle Larry, you think of a man and his family who literally dedicated their lives to the exotic creatures of the earth."

The park in Naples was the realization of Larry's dream for the care and breeding of wild animals. However, it all started with his fascination with the snakes he caught as a kid in Kalamazoo, Michigan. By the time he was eleven years old, he'd collected 250 snakes. When he was eighteen, Larry leased a log cabin for his snake exhibit. He was acknowledged as the world's youngest herpetologist, much in demand by schools, colleges, and civic groups for lectures and demonstrations of snake handling and milking.

Larry left his university studies of herpetology to work for Frank Buck, the famous big game hunter of that era. During that time Larry appeared on many TV shows and he needed a public persona, so he became known as 'Jungle Larry.' Jungle Larry went on to manage the alligator farm in St. Augustine where he wrestled ten- to twelve-foot gators on a daily basis. He also worked on the Tarzan set in Silver Springs, where he was responsible for all the exotic animals and preparing them for scenes. He did the underwater stunt work with the alligators (referred to as crocodiles in the films) as the stand-in for Johnny Weissmuller's Tarzan.

Larry conducted safaris to collect baby animals as humanely as possible in order to start zoos across the United States. He trained lions and many other sorts of animals, including naturally breeding tiglons (the offspring of a tiger father and a lion mother). Jungle Larry was a conservationist years before it became a buzz word. He educated the patrons by demonstrating the animals' natural behavior.

He married Nancy ('Safari Jane') who stepped right in and worked with everything from anteaters to zebras. The couple spent their summers in Sandusky, Ohio, exhibiting animals at Cedar Point. Then they set up the fifty-two-acre Jungle Larry's Zoological Park (now Naples Zoo). When sons David and Tim came along, they were reared to love and respect animals, too. Human and animal families blended naturally. While other youngsters played after school, the Tetzlaff boys rushed home to help feed whatever newborn animals were creeping, slithering or peeping. At any given time they'd have a newborn tiger, lion, or leopard cub; a chimp, reptiles, or birds waiting for them!

These boys grew up to be big cat trainer David Tetzlaff and Naples Zoo Manager Tim. Their childhood years were spent as much in the zoo/parks as much as in the house. Their home, conversely, was the place where numerous baby animals got their start. If an animal born at the park needed to be hand fed, it spent its early months in the Tetzlaff house. Brutus and Duchess were two lion cubs that had the run of the place for a time. People joke about child-proofing to protect valuables from their toddlers. Put up the glass trinkets from the coffee table, move the silk throws, and so on. But how do you lion-proof a house? Remove the couch and chairs?

One of Tim's earliest memories is the tiglon (the tiger-lion mix) cubs having fun chewing on couch pillows and suede jackets. Several of the Tetzlaff sofas were ruined by playful cubs. The family accepted the damage as a routine part of hand-raising energetic wild animals.

Today Tim sits on a bench near one of the park's lakes and enjoys the sight of peacocks and flamingos. He reminisces about spending his childhood with litters of cubs in twos and threes.

"We raised a lot of leopard pairs, too. I remember helping care for Missy, one of David's black leopards. At the Sandusky house we had a couch that stretched out in front of the TV—one of the sectional couches you could make into any shape. The leopard liked to cruise around the house, jump over the back of the couch and land right on whoever was on the couch. After being the landing pad several times, I learned to put a pillow on top of me so she'd land on it instead of my unprotected body.

"We also had two dogs—Fritz, a miniature Schnauzer, and Gizmo, a standard poodle. When we brought a new cub home, whether a lion or tiger, the dogs were bigger and they bossed the cat around, thinking they were hot stuff. As the wild cat grew, the dogs were gradually looking eyeball to eyeball at the big cat, then looking up to him, then even farther up. By then, the dogs totally backed away as if to say, 'Okay, you're bigger than I am,' but sometimes the dog maintained that dominant role if, that is, the big cat could be bossed."

While the dogs had their regular food, the cubs got formula from a baby bottle every four to six hours, until they were old enough for a mixture of fresh ground meat, condensed milk, water and vitamins. The Tetzlaff boys got in on all the animal chores, fun or not.

Tim says, "Besides feeding the cubs, the family had to massage the cubs' rear ends to simulate a mother's licking to promote bowel movements. You don't want a cub to get constipated, because that could lead to death. When I was about thirteen years old, I remember taking young cubs to our chain link fenced backyard, bringing a wet paper towel. I'd hold up the animal's tail and rub its behind a little bit. You have to be patient until he hunkers down—the signal that it worked. It's neat when it worked. I'd think 'YES—now I can go inside!'

"Prince is a tiger cub we raised. He now weighs about five hundred pounds and is the second biggest tiger in David's show. I have pictures of him as a cub lying in bed next to me and a picture of us playing on the couch. I also have pictures of that cub nose-to-nose with our ten-pound domestic cat!"

The Tetzlaffs routinely engineer smooth transition for cubs being hand raised in the house to living with their peers in the park. Nancy looks out her office window and smiles, watching the caracals and servals (twenty-pound wild cats) in their enclosure. Gazing beyond them to the cascading magenta bougainvilleas, the delicate pink flowers of the power puff bush, and the orchid trees' purple flowers, she thinks back to another fun time.

"During the day the litter of two or three would take the ten-minute car trip to the park with us. For the day they were out in a playpen full of their toys. It was eight feet long, eight feet wide, and four feet tall. The pen was upside down, so it had a roof. We kept it outside the office area so the cubs could get used to people and to the park noises. As they got older, we walked the cubs on leashes. When it was time for them to be at the park full time, they needed their own area, but we still gave them attention. They had a nice changeover from the different homes.

"For a couple of years we had circuses in the backyard too! Imagine being ten years old and wanting to raise money for World Wildlife Fund. How about having a circus in your backyard? That's what David decided to do when he was ten.

"Our kids were dressed up in outfits like lion trainers and clowns. Our fenced backyard was the performing area and the audience had to be outside the fence. One of our trainers came over from the park with a couple of animals—whichever ones David or Tim could handle. We'd have a young chimp, a cub, a bird, or any of the small animals or snakes. Both the kids and their moms thought it was great. In one summer show the boys raised close to one hundred dollars in twenty-five cent admissions."

Today, family life remains entwined with animals that, through the years, have been an intricate part of their extended family. Even after Larry's passing, the Tetzlaffs, now including David's son, Sasha, dedicate their lives to and share their love for the zoo animals.

Shara Pendragon Smock

SHARA PENDRAGON SMOCK wrote the books *Living with Big Cats and Hooking the Reader: Opening Lines that Sell*. She has written for numerous magazines and newspapers. See her work at www.sharasmock.com

A Letter to Daisy

An old man stands on a pier overlooking Saint Augustine's Matanzas River. Drawing a neatly folded paper from his pocket he begins to read the words he already knows by heart: "To whoever finds this note let it be known that I have left this earth of my own volition. No one pushed me. I've had a good life and now it is my time to go. My Daisy went two years ago and it's been a lonely place ever since. So, now I'm going up to be with her. Sorry if I've caused anybody trouble by my actions."

But, the old man, Charley Coggins, had been drinking when he wrote that note the night before. Now, he was sober and the river looked cold. His eyes brimming, he tore the paper into pieces and watched them float down to the dark water that swirled around the pier's barnacle encrusted pilings. He gazed after them as they floated downstream until they were lost in the sun-dappled surface of the Matanzas. Perhaps he would write her a letter tomorrow. Perhaps that would ease his loneliness.

The following afternoon found him seated in the small gazebo that stood on the pier, scant yards from the spot where, yesterday, he had planned to end it all. On his lap was a yellow tablet. On the seat beside him, a brown paper bag contained an almost empty bottle of whisky. For a while he just sat there, gazing into space. Then he fished a ball-point from his pocket, clicked it open, rested the pad on his knees and began to write.

Hi Daisy,

I don't know exactly how to start this letter. I've never written to an angel before. It seems silly to ask how you're doing. Obviously, you must be doing just fine - after all, you're in heaven and from what I've heard it don't get much better than that. I made plans to join you yesterday but, to tell the truth, I lost my nerve. I don't suppose you had anything to do with that – did you?

Actually, I'd sure like to ask you about that place; heaven, I mean. I miss you, but I'm not sure how well I'd fit in up there. I mean, the idea of walking on streets of gold isn't exactly my idea of fun. I should think it would be hard on your eyes on sunny days, (and I expect every day is sunny up there.) As for loving everybody I bump into ... well, Daisy, that's gonna' be one hell of a big leap for me. But, I suppose that sort of thing takes care of itself once a person gets up there. (By the way it is UP, isn't it?)

Enough of asking you about things I don't know about. Why don't I tell you what I've been doing to keep from talking to myself? Actually, I find I do talk to myself when I'm alone and I'm frankly amazed at how much I know. I wouldn't admit this to anyone else – but I've begun to answer myself! Dumb stuff, you know, like last week when I missed the entrance to Home Depot and found myself muttering; "Now, why in hell did you do that, Coggins? You've turned into that place a thousand times." And then I find myself answering, "You old fool, if you'd been paying attention instead of getting all wrapped up in what Rush Limbaugh was talking about you'd be in the store by now instead of riding around the neighborhood looking for the back entrance!

Remember how, when we first moved into the new house I spent half my time running to Home Depot? Now I go there to pass time as much as anything else. I usually bump into old friends while I walk the aisles, admiring things I have absolutely no use for. You'll be happy to hear that I've taken your advice and now let the young clerks do the lifting when it comes to putting heavy stuff in the trunk of the car.

~

The old man gave up writing for a moment to gaze out over the river. Two large pelicans coasted along just above the surface, their wings fixed in the unique airfoil that allows them to glide endlessly. With their huge, bizarre bills tucked back between their shoulders they somehow managed to look quite stately in flight. He gave some thought to including profound theories on their aerodynamics, but thought better of it. He could almost hear Daisy's voice, "Charley, why do you waste your time telling me such stuff, which half the time I don't understand. Aerodynamics indeed! Pelicans are just big ugly birds that are kind of cute and fly that way because that's the way God intended them to fly.

~

He resumed writing.

I've been thinking about driving over to the animal shelter and bringing home a cat to curl up in my lap when I fall asleep in the lounger or listen to my ramblings when I feel like talking. Most cats are good listeners, or so I understand. Anyway, old girl, that's all I can think of for now, except I sure do miss you. I hope they're treating you right. On second thought, the way you make friends I don't think it could be otherwise. I'll bet you look real pretty in your wings and if I know you, they'll probably have lace on them somewhere.

Well, Kiddo, I've about run out of words – take care of yourself and know that I still love you.

Charley x x x

He knew it was a silly thing to do: writing a letter that had no chance of being read by the one it was meant for. Even email would fall far short of reaching that far into space.

He opened the paper bag, removed the bottle and drained the last several swallows. He felt the warmth spread inside him and then just sat there, holding the empty bottle. As he looked at it, an idea took shape, Of course! He could send it to her in a bottle! Not that it would ever reach her, but neither would it be taken home and buried under a pile of dusty papers on the corner of his desk. No, it would float out to sea, always for him to wonder about, never to be forgotten –somewhere out there, just bobbing along.

He tore off the yellow pages and rolled them into a tight cylinder, the written characters facing out. He slipped them through the neck of the bottle and gave them a tap as they slid in, to uncoil like a spring their cursive writing pressed tightly against the inside of the glass just begging to be read. He screwed the cap on, his old, blue veined hands gripping the bottle and lid tightly. The knuckles turned translucent as he applied the force he knew it would take to keep out the seawater during the bottle's long journey.

Satisfied, he left the gazebo and shuffled to the edge of the pier. His arm came back and the bottle went sailing out over the river. He watched it hit the water –a splash and it disappeared, then resurfaced downstream. It was hard to follow as it floated, so little of it broke the surface, but from time to time he would see a momentary flash, the sun glinting off a reflecting facet as the bottle turned in the current. The tell-tale flashes faded, then stopped as the sun continued its afternoon descent. Charley turned away and he walked the long causeway, back to where his car waited. An evening breeze off the ocean began to whisper in the reeds and he wondered if there were some miraculous way, beyond our ken, where people who had been close for so long could communicate from beyond the grave? A lot of people had tried it but, to the best of his knowledge, no one had ever managed to cross that great divide. But, if anyone could do it, it would be his Daisy. She could be one persevering woman when she wanted to be. A smile slowly spread across his face as he climbed in his old Buick. If he hurried, he could reach the animal shelter before it closed.

William Plumb Barbour

WILLIAM "BILL" PLUMB BARBOUR began writing at 76, when normal people have been retired for five or six years. He is of the opinion that short stories and novellas are the Alka-Seltzer of the literary world, providing quick relief for jaded readers, singular little vignettes to wear in one's buttonhole.

Excerpt from published novel "Harry – the Old Man in the Gazebo" published 1955

Sarah's Relief

For miles around it was known as "The Old Barbour Place." Most Valley people couldn't remember anyone but a Barbour ever having lived on that mountain farm. Now the big cow barn stood empty. Not a sound echoed within its white-washed interior save for the rustle of mice bedded down in a pile of hay that lay in a corner of the calf pen. A dirt road ran past the barn's big sliding door and wound its way upward until it was lost from sight where it entered the woods.

Across the road from the barn, and a goodly ways away, stood the modest house that had sheltered generations of Barbours. A gravel path led to the house. A huge, worn-out tractor-tire lay on its side in the middle of the lawn. It was full of with dirt and overflowed with flowers that had survived the early frost; a riot of red and gold marigolds soaking up the afternoon sun. The working farm house was sheathed with weathered shingles and used low-ceilinged rooms to keep the heat down low where it did the most good, defying winter's icy winds as they roared across the mountain and pried at the windows.

A spacious porch extended across the front of the old place, and on it was an old metal glider. On the glider sat an elderly couple, dressed as if going to church. It was early October and the sprawling mountains surrounding the farm were ablaze with the red and gold of an early Pennsylvania fall - a warm, soft afternoon that carried the smell of autumn in the air. The old woman watched as an errant breeze created a small dust devil that danced along their dirt road. She thought about that dirt road, about the way it had always served as a buffer between her family and the rest of the world. Nobody ever came up that road unless it was necessary. Until a few years ago two cars couldn't pass each other, except where somebody had made a "passing place." She thought of the thousands of times Jim had taken milk cans down to meet the milk truck; the years children had walked up that mountain road carrying their school books, rain or shine. And then there was that snowy January night when Laura was born. She could still picture Jim's figure trudging to the barn in the swirling snow to put skid chains on the Chevy before they started down the mountain. She could still see herself waiting in the living room, the pot bellied stove radiating heat as she sat praying for Jim to hurry – hurry, before her time was upon her. And she remembered the trip to the bottom: Jim, with his head out the driver's side window, the wipers beating helplessly against the fast falling snow, watching him jockey the steering wheel, trying to stay on the narrow road already hidden under a thick white blanket. But she remembered as well, the summer things: the honeysuckle that perfumed the sides of the road when she walked down to get the mail and the way the young stock would run over to the fence when they saw her coming. She would long remember that steep mountain road her family had always referred to as "Our Hill."

Her name was Sarah and she sat next to Jim, her husband of 59 years, holding his hand as he sat dozing by her side. Her hair was silver and pinned up in a bun to keep it out of the way. She was a small woman, but she had worked right alongside her husband, through thick and thin, through sweltering summers and freezing winters.

Her gaze drifted to the calf pasture, but there weren't any calves to be fed this day. Instead, the field was full with farm machinery. Tomorrow, equipment dealers and hoards of strangers would be there, kicking tires and checking grease cups. There would probably be a table set up for somebody to sell hot coffee, fresh pressed cider and home-made doughnuts all white with powdered sugar. The men would stand around talking about crops or the weather and most would be smoking corn cob pipes. The young men would be rolling their own cigarettes to show off in front of the girls. The womenfolk would be there too, all dressed up in their best dresses and wearing bonnets or straw hats. Of course, there would be a sprinkling of city folks, looking out of place and once in a while seen muttering to themselves as they tried to scrape cow manure off their shoes.

The city women would wander around inside the house looking for bargains, like her old butter press, and they'd get giggly over the old flat irons and their detachable wooden handles. She smiled as she pictured her kids when they were little, sitting in front of the living room stove on cold winter nights, breaking walnuts on the bottom of those old flat irons. Her husband stirred, gave her hand a squeeze, and resumed his nap. She studied the work-worn hand that covered hers. How strong his hands had been. Now the skin glistened bluish white where it stretched over his knuckles and the veins stood out and age spots marred their surface.

Their "Tabby" strolled onto the porch and curled herself down on the braided rug that used to grace their living room. She remembered when she had braided that rug and thought of all the women's stockings she had saved up before she could start. Now Tabby lay on it, not knowing that tomorrow everything would be different.

The warmth of the autumn afternoon and the humming of the bees working among the flowers that grew alongside the porch had her nearly falling asleep when she heard the familiar sounds of a car laboring up their mountain road. She woke her husband, locked the front door and picked up the cat. Casting a loving eye over this house that had sheltered them for so many years, she murmured, "Goodbye old friend."

Hand in hand, they walked up the path to wait for the vehicle that would take them on the first leg of the journey to a new home. They waited for the taxi as it ground its way up the hill. They gazed at the field behind the barn, the field that had always grown such nice timothy hay. It was late afternoon and the cool of evening was beginning to set in. She squeezed his hand, the silent language they sometimes used when words didn't say enough.

And then they were in the taxi, their battered Samsonite bags in the trunk and "Tabby" curled up in her lap as if the old cat had done this sort of thing all her uneventful life. They didn't look back as the taxi started down the grade. But, as they neared the bottom and drew opposite the field where they had pastured their young stock, the old man asked the driver to pull over and the couple focused their aging eyes on the center of the field and the square acre of land enclosed by a chain link fence. Inside the fence, a series of large pipes and valves poked out of the tired earth. On the fence a sign proclaimed:

THIS AREA UNDER LEASE TO PENNSYLVANIA GAS

AND ENERGY CORP. NO TRESPASSING

The taxi continued its journey down the mountain.

The old man turned to his wife, "Sure we got everything, Mother? Last time I saw the cruise tickets they were laying on the kitchen table. And did you manage to get the PG&E royalty checks fixed so they'd come to our new address at Hilton Head?"

Sarah nodded her head, "Yes."

Then, more to herself than to Jim, she said, "What a relief to be off this damned old mountain for good!"

William Plumb Barbour

WILLIAM "BILL" PLUMB BARBOUR began writing at 76, when normal people have been retired for five or six years. He is of the opinion that short stories and novellas are the Alka-Seltzer of the literary world, providing quick relief for jaded readers, singular little vignettes to wear in one's buttonhole.

Oh Brother, What a Dog

He tossed the stick high into the air anticipating its retrieval by the black and brown pooch. The dog's name was JD and he was Luke's best friend. When those two got together they were inseparable. Their chemistry was remarkable. Every day they were out playing and teaching and learning. JD proved to be an excellent pupil. Upon Luke's command the canine would do a number of tricks. Luke even taught the dog to eat only when he gave the order, and from then his hands exclusively.

High school graduation was rapidly approaching and Luke wasn't sure what he'd do afterward. Some friends were already employed; others were going away to college. Luke's after school job was just for spending money. It was no career move. By chance, he ambled by a recruitment office on a Friday after class. He cupped his hands around his face peeking through the tinted glass front doors when suddenly they opened. He was immediately greeted by a man in uniform on the other side inviting him with a gesture of his hand to cross the threshold.

"Good afternoon, young man. May I help you make the best decision of your life?"

The teen was taken aback by the sergeant's enthusiasm and answered. "I guess so. I don't really know why I came in here."

"Are you interested in the armed forces, son?" the sergeant inquired.

"My father is retired Army and my brother is on active duty. Yes, I'd like some information." he answered nodding his curly brown head.

They completed and signed paper work expeditiously. Luke would be heading off to boot camp shortly after the end of the school year. He didn't want any time to change his mind so he opted for early entry. But when duty called he wasn't afforded the opportunity to say good bye to his family or his best friend JD.

One sweltering afternoon two weeks into basic training Private Bennett was resting on his bunk attempting to cool off from the extreme outdoor temperature. The inside of the barracks was conceivably ten degrees cooler than outside but the air was rife with the perspiration of dozens of marines. The din of conversation in the building was at a low roar. He was daydreaming of home; wondering what JD was doing and if he was being a good boy when Cooper, the duty officer, entered the room.

"Bennett, front and center," the DO ordered.

"Yes sir," he answered. His six foot, lanky frame nearly fell out of the bunk as he bolted to attention.

"Do you know why I'm here, Bennett?" he shouted, his face just inches from the private's face.

"No sir." he replied hesitantly. His mind was saying "But you're gonna tell me. Aren't you?" as he looked straight into infinity.

"Your mother's on the phone. She says your dog's dying. He hasn't eaten in two weeks." The DO hollered in a deep southern accent, arms grasped behind his belt in typical military fashion, pacing to and fro in front of the anxious recruit.

The chatter in the barracks had calmed to whispers at the sound of the duty officer's command. Sneers and snickers could be heard over the taciturn room as the DO defined the situation.

Luke's mind wandered into monologue. Man, am I in trouble. The guys are going to have a field day with this. Whose mama calls her boy at boot camp? How in the hell did she get through anyway? Agh, my ass is grass.

"Bennett. Did you hear me?" the officer shouted.

Startled out of his inner monologue he answered, "Yes sir. My mother called. My dog's dying. What should I do sir?"

"Go talk to your dog," he roared, pointing to his office.

"Yes sir, yes sir," he replied and scrambled toward the office with the DO on his heels. Additional muffled chuckles and chortles were heard throughout the barracks.

Upon entering the office the duty officer pointed Luke in the direction of the phone and instructed him to pick it up.

With a wavering hand he picked up the receiver and began his inquiry. "Mom, how did you get through? What's wrong with JD?"

"Luke, I'm so glad I got through. Why didn't you tell me you were leaving?" she asked in a forceful yet motherly tone.

"Mom, Mom, please! I didn't have a chance. What's happening with the dog?" he cried.

"Oh, honey, he hasn't eaten a bite since you left. You trained him real good. He won't eat anything we give him. We even tried steak. He's starving. You have got to talk to him. Maybe he will eat if he hears your voice command," she said.

"Well, I'll give it a shot. It can't hurt. Put the phone to his ear, Mom," Luke said as he caught a glimpse of the DO with a smirk on his sun wrinkled face. Luke just held up his hands in a "What the heck?" gesture as he cradled the phone on his shoulder.

"Okay Luke, JD's right here and I told him you wanted to talk to him," she said putting the receiver to the dog's ear.

"JD, this is Luke, buddy. You got to eat. Please eat for Mom. Can you hear me?" he asked.

There was a bark on the other end and probably a tail wag.

"Luke, it worked he's tearing into the meat. Oh my God, he's eating. Thank the Lord." Ma was crying.

Luke could hear cheers through the phone in the background. It was music to his ears. Everyone was clapping and yelling. "We love you and miss you. Take care of yourself. We can't wait to hear some Marine stories."

"I love and miss all of you," Luke said softly as he hung up the receiver.

After saving his dog from certain starvation, Luke turned to his superior for some kind of recognition.

The DO looked up from behind the gun-metal-colored military-issue desk and dismissed Bennett with a wave of his hand. A true marine, he showed no emotion. It was his duty to keep his charges in line. There would be no show of compassion for the young boot saving his dog friend or any other silly drama that unfolds during the course of every training camp.

The young private exited the office with a salute. Cooper returned the salute, leaned back in his office chair, reached for the phone, and placed a call to his home in Mississippi.

Christal Bennett

CE BENNETT is new on the writing scene but that doesn't stop her drive to be a better writer. Ms. Bennett lives in Central Florida where she is working on her first book with the working title, *The Names Were Changed to Protect the Guilty*. Visit: www.cebennettauthor.com or email cbennettwriter@gmail.com

Waiting for a Memory

The seats were hard as ice. Cold blue fiberglass curved to hold the average torso, but not mine. It offered neither comfort nor support. If I relaxed, I curved into the shape of a comma with my chin on my knees. If I stretched out my legs, I slipped off like on a slide unless my heels were firmly planted in the worn blue carpeting with my knees, locked. I switched from one position to the other. I even tried sitting upright. I felt like a vulture. I peered down the hall looking for any motion. I was waiting to pounce on the surgeon and gobble up any news about my father. I craved confirmation that he had survived.

It was an important week at work and a bad time for me to be away. The crucial meeting with the Swedes was scheduled for Friday. My left brain prioritized mental lists of incomplete tasks efficiently delegating work and phone calls. Of course, in my day-dream, everything went like clockwork and I was even presented an award.

My reverie was interrupted by the arrival of a surgeon, not ours. We all listened intently, trying to appear that we weren't. The news was not good and the family with pale, drawn faces and moist eyes left.

Dad had been in surgery for over an hour. As our concern grew, the furrows between our eyes showed our tension. We had started our vigil with a prayer. I said another.

I stood and paced for a while to let the circulation return to my posterior. No one wanted to leave the room. We all wanted to hear the news directly, to see the look in the surgeon's eyes, and to read his body language. Unable to wait any longer, I walked down several long hallways to the restroom.

When I returned, there was no change. No one had moved. Nevertheless, I asked, "Any news?"

They shook their heads in a negative.

Sighing, I sat and stared at nothing. Dad taught me to love sports. We would spend hours outside shooting the basketball with the neighbor kids. The basket was a cardboard box attached to the side of the house. It had a hole cut in the bottom. When it sagged or broke, we'd just find ourselves another box.

I whispered to my sister, "Do you remember basketball with Dad?"

"Yes, he'd lift me on his shoulders. While he dribbled to the basket, he'd block out all the big kids with his big body and let me drop the ball in the box to score."

"Those were good times." I remembered … finally. After a pause, I asked, "Do you remember Dad's waffles?"

My brother overheard us, leaned forward and joined in, "I always thought making them was magic. Dad waved his hands over the steaming waffle iron after he ladled the batter and then closed the lid. I didn't know it wasn't magic until I started to make my own."

"I loved the waffle in the shape of my initial." I remembered a sweeping J.

"My favorite time with him was at the ocean. He taught me to swim there." The youngest piped up.

My sister reminisced, "I liked our races on the beach. He could beat us all, but he'd slow down and pretend he couldn't go any faster so one of us could win." We nodded in recollection.

I remembered, "When we walked in the surf, Dad held my hand so that I wouldn't be knocked down by a wave. He knew I was afraid but trying not to show it. I'm glad he didn't let me become irrationally afraid of something he loved so much."

We quieted as each person's memories took them to distant times and places. I tried to remember what Dad looked like in his prime – a tall, slender man with dark wavy hair. He sat leaning back in his chair with his shoulders pulled back and his right forearm in the air. I would imitate him, but couldn't figure out how on earth that could be comfortable. It was comfortable for him.

"What?" I asked with a mumble as a voice entered my consciousness.

"Look at that." My sister stared through the glass door leading down a long hall to the surgical ward.

"What?"

"The coffin." Her voice grew louder as she pointed. The black rounded rectangle on wheels rolled towards us pushed by two men dressed in white. The contrast between the black of the coffin and the white hallway was startlingly out of place.

"It's coming from surgery." She had to state the obvious.

"Is it Dad?" I whispered in dread. My heart was banging in my chest. I thought I was going to need surgery myself.

By now, curiosity moved everyone from those infernal seats towards the glass door. We saw one of the men in the hall push the elevator call button. The man beside me pulled the glass door open, moving us all aside.

"Who's in there?" He shouted.

A shaky, owl-like voice beside me asked, "Who?"

We streamed out the door and down the hallway like zombies driven from sunlight.

"Open the lid."

"No, don't!"

One of the men held his hands up in front of his chest and pushed outward, "STOP!" His deep voice echoed off the walls. We did.

"We're taking a corpse to the morgue downstairs. Your surgeon will notify you about your family. Sorry to disturb..."

The bell dinged as the elevator door opened. With no wasted motion, the men rolled the coffin inside. The door closed. In mere seconds, the hall was quiet and empty. I was appalled. How could they smash our frail emotions like that!

With deep breaths and some sobs, we each made our way back through the glass door to the waiting room. Like a prison, it held our bodies and our spirits. My family huddled to pray before sitting. With linked arms and fervent voices we whispered the "Our father who art in heaven…" as hopefully and reverently as we could. Others joined in. As the huddle grew, we each added something at the end before the group AMEN – for a steady surgeon's hand, for a good recovery, for God's grace and enfolding love…

Families around us separated to the four corners of the musty little room. A few whispered sporadically. Most just sat reading, staring, or napping with eyes closed. Our thoughts were not in this room, but elsewhere. We were waiting… waiting for news.

Finally, our surgeon entered the room calling our family name. The walls of the square room bent inward as we inhaled collectively and stood up. It was our turn to listen and learn.

The young man dressed in green surgical scrub spoke, "Normally the brain requires 30% of the blood flow from the heart. Pre-surgery, your father's brain received almost 50%. The malformation acted like a sump drawing blood from adjacent areas and starving them. We think that's what caused his seizures. In addition, his body received 20% less oxygenated blood than normal which affected the blood supply to his extremities causing lost feeling in his arms and legs."

"Is he okay?" We asked in one voice. Everyone in the room around us listened quietly.

"We ran a small catheter up the artery in your Dad's neck and released several small beads to clog the malformation. There should be increased blood flow to the rest of his brain, if the beads hold."

"Will the beads hold?" I asked.

"There's a 70% chance that they will."

"He survived, though, right?" I tried to get confirmation, "Is he okay?"

"Oh, I guess I didn't say. I'm sorry. He came through very well."

The exhale was huge since the entire room participated.

"Yes."

"Good."

"Praise God."

With tears of happiness, we circled for a prayer of thanks that included the red-faced surgeon. Then, we let him continue, "Please understand that he did have a stroke. He'll have to learn to walk, speak and button his shirt again. His memory was affected. You'll have to help him remember past events. In addition, he may not remember doctor's appointments, where he put the milk, or your name."

"We can do that." We responded in unison. Each of us sported gigantic smiles.

Dad had taken care of me when it counted. His large, warm hand had covered my entire back for occasional backrubs to put me to sleep when I was afraid of the dark. He had doctored me through colds wrapping his itchy wool scarf around my chest covered with Vicks Vapor Rub. He even faithfully attended all of my school plays and ball games.

Now, it was our turn to take care of him. We would become his memory. It would hurt, but I'd even remind him of my relationship to him, when necessary. I hope he won't have long waits for bits of memory to visit and smile in his mind.

JENNIFER BJORK

JENNIFER BJORK, as a youngster with no television or radio for entertainment, crafted stories around a fireplace. She recently published her first picture book – *Penelope Morris, Of Course!*. Born in California and raised in South America, she now resides in St Augustine. Check out her website: www.jenniferbjork.com

Christmas Chaos

Sue Ellen Mastrogianakos is my best friend in the world. We met long ago when we were in law school. We moved to the same town after we graduated, whereupon she promptly married into a large Greek family. I, however, remained an unclaimed flower for quite a few years—fourteen, to be precise.

Sue Ellen's home quickly became the focal point for Mastrogianakos family gatherings. I liked the Mastrogianakoses; they were friendly, accomplished and interesting. Sue Ellen's parents lived in the same town and were usually included whenever the Mastrogianakoses got together. A retired college professor, he and his wife were involved in a number of worthy charitable and educational activities.

One year, when Sue Ellen called me to discuss Christmas plans, she was particularly insistent. "You have to come for Christmas this year."

"How come?"

"You just do," she replied.

"You'll have to be a bit more specific. You know how crowded my social calendar is," I joked.

"Well, uh, we're going to have all of the Mastrogianakoses this year...."

"You always have all of the Mastrogianakoses," I responded.

"Not all of them. One of them has been out of circulation, so to speak, for several years."

"Oh? Who are you talking about? I thought I had met all of them."

Sue Ellen filled me in on the missing link: Nick, one of her husband's cousins. The last family gathering Nick had attended was his own wedding. Right after the reception, he and his new bride robbed a bank at gunpoint. Nick spent his honeymoon in jail and the last eight years in prison. His wife's sentence had only been three years. She was now his ex-wife and had moved on to greener pastures. Nick was scheduled to be released shortly before Christmas and he and a number of distant Mastrogianakos relations were planning a big reunion at Sue Ellen's. She wanted my moral support in dealing with the anticipated chaos.

I told her I would be there, but that I had already invited my parents and my granny over for Christmas, so the invitation would have to include them.

"Fine, fine," she said resignedly. She had met my family and knew they were a bit on the quirky side. "They can come too. Just, please, don't desert me in my hour of need," she wailed. "Oh, I almost forgot, my parents have invited some students from Algeria so they can experience an American family Christmas. Ask your dad to bring his fiddle so he can play Christmas carols."

I agreed, but I wasn't wild about the prospect. Everything Daddy plays on his fiddle, including Christmas carols, winds up sounding like hillbilly hoedown music. He usually makes me accompany him on the piano and is rarely satisfied with my efforts. I don't do hillbilly very well.

After Sue Ellen hung up, I started thinking about her guest list and the challenges it would certainly present. My granny would certainly be a problem. She had no concept of tact and had embarrassed me—and everyone else in the family—countless times. Short of muzzling her, I didn't know what we could do to keep her mouth under control. I phoned Mama and filled her in on the situation. She liked both Sue Ellen and her family and was happy to go along with our plans.

"There's just one thing, Mama," I cautioned. "Sue Ellen's husband has a cousin who's been in the slammer for a few years. He's getting out right before Christmas and he'll be at Sue Ellen's for his first big reunion. Sue Ellen isn't exactly sure who else he's invited. We need to be certain Granny understands the situation and doesn't say anything embarrassing."

Mama insisted on hearing all the details of Nick's history, so I filled her in as best as I could. I even briefed her on the students from Algeria. Mama is a teacher, so she always supports learning and cultural exchange. "That's just fine," she said. "We'll do our part to make them feel at home and learn about American holiday traditions." I had seen Daddy interact with folks from other countries at the university and I knew what to expect from him. He figures that anyone who speaks with an accent will understand his English better if he kicks it up a few hundred decibels.

However, I was much more worried about Granny. She lives in Starke, a small town fairly close to Florida's largest state prison, Raiford. Starke experienced a small boom when the legislature decided to make Raiford the home of death row and the site of its lone electric chair, Old Sparky. Any time the governor signs a death warrant, Starke's diners, motels, and fast food restaurants make a killing, so to speak.

Granny believed in being tough on crime and thought that capital punishment was too good for most crooks. She remembered the old days when public hangings took place immediately after a verdict of guilt was rendered. "It don't make no sense to drag things out like they do nowadays. Punishment oughta be swift and severe!" I had to keep her away from Nick.

~

Cars were parked for several blocks around the Mastrogianakos home by the time we arrived on Christmas Day. Sue Ellen already looked frazzled when we walked through the door. As she took Mama's congealed salad from my hands to place it on the buffet table, I asked her to point out Nick. She nodded toward a rough-looking fellow who appeared to be about forty years old. He had brought quite a few rough-looking folks with him. The women had a hard, brassy look, the men looked grizzled and reeked of stale cigarette smoke, and the children resembled street urchins.

"Who are all of those people hanging around Nick?" I asked Sue Ellen.

"I don't even want to know," she whispered.

When Sue Ellen rang the dinner bell, she called on her dad to say the blessing, which he did in his usual gracious manner. He had hardly finished the "Amen" when Nick and his sidekicks stormed the buffet. Sue Ellen hung back with a pitiful, long-suffering expression on her face. I stood by her side and told her to bear up. I was there to help her get through it.

After the meal, Daddy took out his fiddle and waved his bow, signaling for me to go to the piano. He rounded up all of the Algerian students and announced, "My daughter and I will play some traditional Christmas music for you. This number is called 'Silent Night.' it's about the night when Jesus Christ, the son of God, was born."

I had no clue as to the students' religious affiliation, but I had a pretty good idea it wasn't Daddy's brand of old-time religion. I gritted my teeth while Daddy tapped out the tempo on my head using the tip of his bow. Mama, relieved that I got stuck with piano duty instead of her, was dozing in a comfortable chair on the far side of the room. She was supposed to be keeping track of Granny but was clearly neglecting her duties.

Granny was roaming about, asking everybody who they were and why they were there.

After about ten carols I was beginning to perspire. It seemed like the students had multiplied and they were crowding around me. One of them turned away to sneeze and I caught a momentary glimpse of Granny headed straight toward Nick. I struggled to free myself from the piano but was hopelessly trapped.

"Daddy," I gasped. "Granny's headed over toward Nick!"

Daddy turned around just in time to see Granny lean over Nick, grab him by the knee, and adjust her dentures by moving her lips in and out a few times. I may have imagined it, but I thought I could see beads of sweat breaking out on Nick's brow.

Everyone noticed that Daddy and I had stopped playing and the room went quiet and still. Mama opened her eyes and gave a start when she saw that Granny had cornered Nick.

You could have heard a pin drop.

"Well," bellowed Granny, her face within inches of Nick's, "I understand we used to be neighbors!"

"I'm sorry, lady. I don't know where you live," Nick managed.

"Starke," Granny proclaimed.

"I ain't never lived there," Nick answered.

"It's right next door to Raiford. Didn't you do time there? I heard you got sprung for the holidays."

Mama rushed up behind Granny and grabbed her by the elbow. She yanked Granny away from Nick and dragged her across the room.

After twenty years, I can still hear Granny's plaintive protest. "I was just trying to be neighborly!"

MARY WOOD BRIDGMAN

MARY WOOD BRIDGMAN, a lawyer and native Floridian lives in Jacksonville. Her work has appeared in national and local publications. She regularly reads her essays and short stories on "In Context", WJCT 89.9 FM, at 7 a.m. and 3 p.m. on Saturdays.

Growing Up Without Ken

My mother really tried to raise me right. It's not her fault how I turned out. Well, not entirely her fault. Lord knows, Mother did her best. It wasn't easy being stuck in a little southern town with three children. There was very little to break the monotony of endless housework and childcare.

One thing our town did have to offer its womenfolk was a very active Woman's Club. The Club had its own little building, which doubled as the public library. Once a month, local matrons would gather for luncheon, gossip, and edification on some topic deemed worthy of their attention. Early on, I realized nearly all of the lectures would bode ill for my siblings and me. The topics uniformly involved something that the matrons should not permit their children to do or have. One month, a podiatrist spoke about the hazards of sneakers; consequently, I never had a pair until I was required to wear them for junior high physical education class. Another speaker pilloried TV and comic books. Of course, rock music took a liberal beating. Kool-Aid and similar sugary drinks were banned from our pantry. To my knowledge, the Woman's Club never undertook a craft fair, a charity drive, or a historical preservation project. It was all about persecution and preservation of the family unit and good Christian morals.

I dreaded Mother's monthly forays into home and child improvement. I never knew what privilege or luxury would be suddenly revoked, not that we had many of them. The TV only got two stations and one of them was the educational channel; reception through our roof-top antenna was spotty at best, so we didn't count on it. We enjoyed reading, although the children's section of the library covered only two small shelves. We sometimes played outside on sunny days. However, my sister and I thought playing with Barbie dolls was the best.

Barbie is the shapely eleven and one-half inch doll that burst onto the American scene during the late 1950s. I was five and my sister was seven when we got our first Barbies and we were enthralled by them. They had identical bubble-cut hairstyles and one-piece red bathing suits. Only their hair color was different. My Barbie was blond, ash blond to be precise, and my sister's Barbie was a brunette. They each came with a pair of red plastic stiletto heels, which were impossibly tiny and very hard for chubby little girl fingers to manipulate.

We were each given one outfit for our dolls and no other Barbie accouterments, of which there were many thanks to the ingenuity of the Mattel people. Not to worry, our imaginations supplied all of the other items that we needed. Our parents had given us identical small suitcases, so those served as Barbie houses. Toothpaste and shaving cream caps were drinking glasses; boxes became pieces of furniture. We fashioned additional clothing from scraps of fabric left over from Mother's sewing projects.

As we grew older, we were mesmerized by advertising that illustrated all of the other Barbie dolls that became available. Our next acquisition was Midge, again ash blond for me and brunette for my sister. Midge had the same wicked figure, but a sprinkling of freckles across her plastic cheeks. She had a two-piece bathing suit, quite a fashion statement and a tad risqué in those days. Mother borrowed a pattern for doll clothes from my best friend's mother and presented us each with a shoebox full of clothes for our dolls. We were in heaven! I was enraptured by a beautiful wedding dress that I found in my shoebox of homemade Barbie clothes. Of course, my sister and I immediately began to plan an elaborate doll wedding. Only one problem, though—what to do for a groom?

Everybody knew Barbie's main squeeze was Ken. Muscular and all-American, he, like Barbie, possessed terrific fashion sense and had a God-given ability to accessorize. We immediately put in our requests for Ken dolls so that the planned nuptials could take place.

Unbeknownst to us, Mother had already heard an anti-Barbie lecture at the Woman's Club. Prior to Barbie, girls played with baby dolls—there were all kinds to cradle and nurse, but no grown-up dolls. Barbie put a resounding end to that. She made a flamboyant appearance with her impossibly pointed bosom, tiny waist, hips, and feet perpetually frozen in stiletto position.

The self-appointed expert, who addressed the Woman's Club on the subject of Barbie dolls, opined that Barbie and her ilk would make little girls grow up too fast. Apparently, it was because Barbie herself was grown up. However, the games we played with Barbie were exactly like the games of "house" that we played with our baby dolls and each other.

Enlightened as I now am by the women's movement, I know that Barbie dolls are supposedly responsible for the average American woman's low self-esteem and poor body image. Puleeze, give me a break! Did anybody ever notice that Barbie's proportions are pretty much the same as those of all of the female images plastered on billboards, prancing across TV and movie screens, and bedecking the pages of magazines? Our body images never stood a chance, even without Barbie. At least she wore tastefully tailored apparel and abhorred exhibitionism. She never showed a nipple (actually, she didn't have one) or a hint of cleavage.

Mother never allowed us to have Ken dolls, or any type of male doll for that matter. Our Barbie dolls were progressively married off to stuffed animals (dogs and rabbits) and our brother's Johnny West "action figure." We just made do with what we had, although we grew tired of explaining to our friends why Mother wouldn't let us have a Ken doll. Actually, we didn't know why Mother had barred Ken from our dollhouse. We usually got by with Mother's favorite explanation, "Because I said so." Sometimes, in an effort to cut the questioning short, we intimated that Ken was against our religion.

Long after we outgrew our Barbie dolls and put them away, we badgered Mother until she finally told us about the anti-Barbie talk she had heard at the Woman's Club meeting. What we couldn't understand was why, in light of the talk, she let us have any Barbies at all. It seemed that Mother had adopted the "no Ken" stance as a sort of "split the baby" type solution. She reasoned it wouldn't be quite as bad for us if we only had the female Barbie dolls. Go figure.

After I was grown, I pointed out to Mother that promoting bestiality was at least as bad as letting her daughters grow up a little too fast. Our Barbies and Midges were forced to marry stuffed dogs and rabbits until Johnny West came along. Johnny was a poor substitute for Ken. His clothes were made out of plastic and painted onto his body. No matter what the occasion, he always looked as if he was headed to a rodeo. I could only imagine how much that pained Barbie.

I suspected that I had been permanently damaged by lack of a Ken doll to complete Barbie's family. I never dated until I finished law school, and I was forty years old before I managed to snag a man and drag him down the aisle. I have, however, always been fond of rabbits and dogs, including the stuffed variety.

I struggled with my unfulfilled dreams and social handicaps until one magical day during my mid-thirties. My boss walked into my office and announced that I had a new job, one that came with the title "Vice President." I was elated. I called my best friend who had, of course, been married for quite a few years. She insisted that I meet her for a celebratory dinner at one of our favorite restaurants.

My promotion entailed a substantial salary increase. As I drove to the restaurant, I couldn't help but think of how I would spend it. I also thought about the fact that there were only two other women VPs in our company. Like me, they were both single. They probably hadn't had Ken dolls either.

There was a large Toys R Us store on the way to the restaurant. When I saw it, my life flashed before my eyes. Without thinking, I steered my car toward the store. I got out of the car and marched through the doors directly back to the Barbie section. I quickly found what I wanted, a box that contained Barbie's beloved, Ken himself. At long last, I felt a sweet rush of satisfaction. After selecting a few appropriate outfits for Ken, I took my purchases to the cashier. As I slapped them down on the counter the cashier remarked, "I see you've been shopping for some lucky little girl."

"No," I replied in my best executive tone, "these are for me."

MARY WOOD BRIDGMAN

MARY WOOD BRIDGMAN, a lawyer and native Floridian lives in Jacksonville. Her work has appeared in national and local publications. She regularly reads her essays and short stories on "In Context", WJCT 89.9 FM, at 7 a.m. and 3 p.m. on Saturdays.

Previously published in Fashion Doll Quarterly, Summer 2009

A Second Chance

If anyone had told me I'd be attending my own funeral as a guest, I'd have said they had a few screws loose. Yet here I am. It must be my funeral because my entire family's sitting in the first two pews; I'm the only one missing. Why else would they be here? Funerals and weddings, that's all they come to church for. It's a wonder the roof hasn't caved in.

My granddaughter's in the second pew with a great looking dude. Must be the fiancé I never got to meet. Looks like I'll miss her wedding—bummer.

That must be me in that stupid, tiny box. I admit I consented to being fried, under duress. It was the cheaper way to go, but I never liked the idea. One third of me is probably lying on a dung heap somewhere. Not that it matters now. At least I haven't gone straight to Hell, though a few people suggested I make the trip.

I don't know what I'm doing here; I must have a mission or something before I receive my "sentence." I wonder—does everyone get to attend his/her own funeral?

Aww, my granddaughter's crying. For real—who knows? She did

that at one of my weddings, too. She was seven when I married number four. She sobbed uncontrollably. If I could have foreseen the future I'd have been sobbing too, or at least running out of the room. Somebody asked her why she was so unhappy. "Because Mimi's moving away," she sobbed—a little drama queen even then. In truth she thought I was quite the pain in the ass when she was growing up.

It's a pretty nice turnout considering most of my generation has already hit the dirt, so-to-speak. Oh—Father just announced the eulogy. Now, who? Oh. Joe's getting up. Joe's my son-in-law, a really nice guy. (My son's husband. Does the term dysfunctional family come to mind?) I get to hear my eulogy; how cool is that?

"All of you here probably know that Mom was a writer, that she realized a dream when she published her first book. Yet I wonder how much you know about the woman that she was." Uh-oh. Here it comes. "Her book, to me, was just another step in an incredible life, because sometimes our dreams can obscure the reality that surrounds us daily and sometimes we need to see ourselves through the eyes of another."

Mom had a very tender heart; some might even call her a "doormat." Yep, my mother's words, well, not exactly; horse's ass was her usual description. She seemed unable to utter the word "no," and gave far more than her share of help. Mom evolved from the "Greatest Generation" that formed much of the woman she was. If I had to reduce her to words it would be something like, she exuded refined elegance, was very genteel and proper." Wow! He never saw me in my finer moments. My husband would cringe at the occasional scatological expletive and remark, "My sugar is so refined."

"But she was also very worldly, "Other worldly" now. open-minded to a degree and incredibly curious. Some might call it nosey.

"Her life was a testament to the power we each possess to face our own challenges and still be able to dictate how we generally live our lives. I also believe that she served as a valuable reminder to all generations, that you are never too old to follow your dreams, as dreams are what propel our future. That was her motto: "It's never too late." It's a bit late now. She was the foundation that anchored her family together. Nice metaphor.

"We can learn much from Dahris, because like those of us in the HIV community, she lived with very real challenges in her life, yet she never let her health deter her from attaining her dreams.

"I have spoken before on how I believe that each of our lives represents a tapestry, with different threads that carry our traits and weave the lives that we live. Each person in our life weaves his own thread through our living tapestry and in doing so they form additional bonds, some briefly, others forever. Dahris was the thread that wove through our 'family,' intersecting, influencing and continually weaving her 'thread' through the tapestry that we have become—the thread that anchored our family, and as such, she will always remain the thread that binds. I can think of no greater legacy."

For once I'm speechless. I never knew Joe felt that way. Uh oh. Show's over; they're filing out now— Suddenly I feel very light, as if I'm floating—I am floating—They're getting farther away. Good bye, good bye—I love you all. They can't hear me. What will happen to me now?

~

I suddenly found myself in another place. I looked around for someone to help me "cross over," a member of my family, maybe, but I appeared to be alone.

"Where am I?"

"You are in Limbo."

The voice came from behind me. I turned to see a man in a white suit. He wore his gray hair on the longish side, piercing eyes, but not unattractive.

"Oh! You startled me."

"I'm sorry."

"Limbo? Purgatory I expected, but Limbo? I thought they did away with that one."

"If they have, the news hasn't reached me yet."

"Who are you, the Ghost of Christmas Past?" I regretted the quip as soon as it left my lips.

"You may call me Peter."

"Peter? THE Peter?" Oh, Lord. Me and my big mouth. "Should I kneel or something?" I sank down on my zipper knees without a thought as to how I'd get back up. I'd say his laugh was heavenly, but I realized this was no joking matter. He reached out his hand and drew me up.

"No, just an underling."

"Is this the usual procedure for the dead?"

"Not for everyone."

"Then why—?"

"Many times in your life you have expressed the wish to live your life over."

"That's because I screwed it up the first time. Wait a minute—you heard me?"

"It's in your file in the Book of Life."

"It's moot now, wouldn't you say?"

"The Powers that Be have decreed that your wish be granted."

"Are you kidding?" He looked much like an indulgent parent with a naughty child. I sobered. "No, of course you're not. You mean, I actually get to go back and do it right this time?"

"The choice will be yours."

"Hot damn." I clapped my hand over my mouth. "Oops, sorry. I slip once in a while."

"We've noticed."

"I suppose that's in the Book of Life, too. Where do we start; I mean, how does this work? I don't seem to have a body, at least not one I can see."

"You will have a body when you get there."

"Peter, is your last name Jordan?" I half expected Claude Rains to pop out from behind a cloud. Peter was inordinately patient, but apparently had no sense of humor. They probably don't have TCM in Limbo.

"Shall we get started?"

"We? Are you going with me?"

"I'll escort you to your destination. The rest is up to you."

"How far back are we going?"

"How far would you like?"

"I'd like to be young and single again, with all my options open."

"Your wish is granted."

"Will I be the same person? I mean, with the same talents as before?"

"You will be you."

"I can't believe it."

"There is one condition."

"I knew there had to be a catch."

"You will have no memory of your previous life."

"Whoa! That's not fair. Suppose I make the same mistakes?"

"You have the opportunity to relive your life. How you do it is up to you."

I figured I'd better not look the proverbial gift horse in the mouth. "Will I see you again?"

"I'll be around."

~

"She's opening her eyes." It was a male voice. My vision was blurred, but he looked familiar.

"Where am I? What happened? I feel—funny."

"You're in the parish hall. You fainted." It was Steve, the main attraction at St. Mary's Minstrel Show.

I remembered then. We were in the show together. That's where we met.

"I never fainted before."

"You were only out for a few minutes. It's hot in here. I think I should take you home."

"I don't want to be a bother. My dad is picking me up at 10."

"We'll save him the trip. Come on, I'll help you up."

His arms felt comfortable as he lifted me off the floor. He was so thoughtful and so cute.

"Look, it's early. How about we stop at the Milk Barn on the way and get a Sundae? Get to know each other better."

"Actually, I feel much better. Maybe, if we call my dad." I couldn't resist the beautiful smile, the wavy brown hair. And he was the star of the show. "Okay, I'd like that, Steve." He held my arm as we walked out of the hall. We passed a nice-looking older man as we went out the door. He looked at me and smiled. He seemed vaguely familiar. Oh well, probably looks like someone I know. He said something odd as he stepped aside to let us pass:

"Oh, Lord. Not again." He shook his head and walked away.

Dahris H. Clair

DAHRIS H. CLAIR is the author of the novel, *The House on Slocum Road*, numerous essays, short stories and articles for various publications and newspapers. She is the founder/writer of an online magazine for writers. For info: www.dahrisclair.com.

Mother Goose

My grandparents owned a summer bungalow on Long Island when I was growing up. A favorite family outing was feeding the ducks and swans at a nearby lake.

After I moved into my own home on the Great South Bay, feeding wild ducks, swans, and geese came naturally. Before long, domestic ducks moved in. One day, three orphaned Canada goslings mysteriously appeared.

In the spring of 1980, three small yellow and brown balls of fluff huddled in my duck pen at the head of my boat ramp. I approached slowly, responding softly to their whistles and peeps. Too young to be on their own, they sensed safety and promptly imprinted me as "Mother Goose."

When a local nature preserve told me no goose would take in another's babies, I was thrilled to raise them myself. I named them Dana, Terry, and Sammie, neutral names because I didn't know their genders. But I did know their faces and personalities. They followed me everywhere. Days were spent foraging in the yard, their diet supplemented with the same feed and minnows I gave my domestic ducks. Nights were spent safely in a box in my bathroom.

The goslings grew quickly. Their squat downy bodies sprouted brown, black and white feathers, and their black legs became long and lanky. They matured into three personable girls.

Swimming lessons were easy. We marched down my boat ramp; they went into the water while I stood on the bulkhead, my presence reassuring them. Eventually they were content to swim with my ducks.

When they were ready to fly, lessons were trickier. My domestic ducks couldn't fly, and I had neither wings nor an ultralight. But my girls were smart and had watched wild geese and ducks take to the air. I walked along my bulkhead offering encouragement. After much honking and jumping about, instinct kicked in. They went airborne! My heart soared with pride.

They reveled in flying and skiing in for a water landing. By November they were confident enough to venture beyond my sight but always returned safely.

Winter approached and hunting season was in full force. Gunshots echoed across the bay, and the wild Canada geese and mallards grew more nervous as they prepared to migrate. I didn't know how strong my girls' instincts were. I prayed they would stay with me; I hadn't raised my babies to lose them to the hunters I cursed with every gunshot.

Sammie was the first to disappear. By Thanksgiving, Terry and Dana were gone, too. My stint as Mother Goose was over. I didn't know if I'd ever see them again.

Four long months later, on April 7, 1981 at six a.m., I heard Terry and Dana's distinct honks announcing they were home and hungry. I was elated, thankful they'd survived, but a hole in Dana's foot proved the dangers they'd escaped. I worried about Sammie who had yet to return.

Terry and Dana checked out the old neighborhood. Not long after, Dana brought home a potential mate to meet Mom. I named him Andy. Dana's Mother's Day gift to me was the nest she started on the bulkhead. However, another pair of geese harassed Dana and Andy until they gave up on the nest. Frustrated, Andy left, and the sisters became close again, staying home until June. To my relief, the free spirits returned in August, Dana's foot fully healed.

A few days later, Sammie arrived home at last with a mate I

called George. Although they both ate from my hand, Sammie wasn't overly friendly.

Another winter closed in and all my girls migrated south. Once again, I prayed they'd be safe from hunters and would return home the next year.

By Valentine's Day in 1982, Terry, Dana and I shared another happy family reunion. This time it was Terry with a hole in her foot and a limp, proving how close she'd come to being killed by a hunter. Anger shot through me. I fed my babies and encouraged them to stay close to home. Sadly, Sammie didn't return, and I never saw her again.

A week later, both girls brought home mates to meet Mom. I named Dana's guy Sonny, and Terry's, Sam, after my lost Sammie. Geese mate for life, so I welcomed these two as permanent members of my extended family.

Geese are also territorial, and in March, the couples fought over the home front. Only one of the pairs could win. Sonny was the more aggressive of the two males. He chased Terry and Sam every chance he got. I felt sorry for Terry, the more timid of the girls, and I began a refereeing marathon. In the end, Terry and Sam acquiesced to Dana and Sonny.

By April, Dana and Sonny were building a nest on the bulkhead. More than happy to help, I brought them grass and weeds. They stayed home round the clock, perfecting the nest and honking for food. Dana didn't mind my counting her eggs through the chain link fence that kept my young children away from the deep water. But Sonny didn't like my snooping and rushed to protect the eggs from wherever he was. Out of six eggs, only three hatched. Sonny finally relaxed, and Mother Goose was joyful over the new additions.

Three days after her goslings' debut, Dana "adopted" a fourth from a pair of geese that happened by for food. Dana apparently wanted a larger family and proceeded to collect goslings. By late afternoon, she had eleven and ignored the two pairs of desperate parents who tried to reclaim their babies, only to be pounced on by Dana or Sonny. The next day only nine remained under Dana's wings. The anxious parents had somehow reclaimed two.

Heartbroken for the parents, as well as for the babies who were too young to know where they belonged, Mother Goose stepped in. I told Dana she couldn't keep goslings that weren't hers. Since each brood was a different size, I could easily tell Dana's from the others. I scooted the kidnapped goslings into the water and successfully reunited most with their parents. Dana however held onto three. She was now the happy mother of six.

So much for "no goose will take in another's babies."

The goslings were almost fully grown by August. Terry and Sam came home, and she and I reconnected. Sonny still chased them, and Dana was jealous of any attention I gave her sister. Thankfully, by fall everyone was getting along, and for the first time, all stayed through the winter.

In February 1983, Sonny began chasing away his six mature offspring to make way for the next brood. The kids didn't understand, and Mother Goose felt their pain. I refereed again. In March, Sonny got into a beak-pulling fight with one of the boys who refused to leave. Like father like son, I thought. Stubborn and tough.

Sonny's chasing duties continued throughout the month, although father and children united once to scare off a lone goose that happened into their camp. The truce only lasted a week.

In mid-May, Dana hatched six more goslings. But joy soon turned to grief. Sam came by alone, telling me in his own way that something happened to Terry. I knew she was dead and it broke my heart.

Dana, on the other hand, was up to her old tricks. She stole two babies, though one eventually died. By July, Dana and Sonny's family numbered fifteen.

The following year I realized I'd have to move, and sadly, I decided to discourage Dana from nesting on my bulkhead again. I wouldn't be there to protect her, and I didn't believe the home's new owners would welcome a yard full of vocal Canada geese. I wanted her to nest someplace safer, but Dana refused to leave as long as I was there. By the time I moved in the fall of 1985, Dana, Sonny, children and mates were a family of twenty-one.

Missing my geese, I went back a few times to look for them, but they were gone. I guess without Mother Goose, they had no reason to hang around. To this day I cherish my time with them.

KARLENE CONROY

KARLENE CONROY is a writer, editor, artist, singer/songwriter and small business owner. She has written three novels of her own, and co-written two with colleague, *Mia Crews. Their latest, The Don Quixote Girls,* is a southern women's fiction with romantic elements. See Karlene's website: www. karleneconroy.com.

My Brother, My Burden

Shadows from the raised tombs grabbed at me as I raced past statues of angels guarding the long dead. Taking a shortcut through Lafayette Cemetery on Halloween night might not be the wisest thing to do, but I have to find Harvey before he does something stupid.

Harv's my younger brother, and although he's always been a little strange, I guess I'm responsible for what happened tonight. Not that it's anything new. Harv's always been different, which is why the kids at school pick on him. More often than not, he comes home blubbering his eyes out. Mom always babies him, telling him it doesn't matter what other people think or do. "You're a very special boy," she tells him. "One day you'll be famous and make us all proud."

Halloween is Harv's favorite holiday. Maybe it's because he can act out his fantasies and blend in with the other kids. We didn't have money to buy fancy costumes, but Harv had found a ratty old hunting coat and cap in a garbage can. He announced he was going trick-or-treating dressed as a big game hunter. He taped a piece of pipe to a hunk of wood he cut to look like a rifle stock. He really was good with his hands.

My Brother, My Burden

That afternoon I watched as he put on the coat and hat, grabbed an old pillowcase to hold all the candy he expected to harvest, and got ready to go knocking on doors. But he never got the chance.

He was acting creepy as usual, waving his gun in my face and pretending to shoot my head off. So I yanked the silly rifle from his hands and threw it in the yard. Harv started screaming about how he hated everyone and was going to kill himself. He picked up his fake rifle and ran off toward the river. Mom came out of the house about that time, slapped me across the head, and told me to go find my brother.

I knew the spot where Harv liked to sit on the edge of the old wharf and watch the barges slip by. That's why I cut through the cemetery on a night so sticky that heat lightning crackled across the sky. Perfect for Halloween. On Toledano Street I saw ghosts and goblins roaming in packs, calling out to each other in excited voices.

Finally, I reached the wharf and strained to see my little brother through the mist descending over the waterfront.

"Harv, where are you?" I yelled, but the slap of the Mississippi against rotten boards was the only answer I heard.

Standing at the edge of the wharf, I called his name over and over. Nothing. I was about to move on when the cloud slipped past the full moon for only a few seconds, but it was enough. A slash of light from the moon reflected off something floating in the muddy water. I stared into that inky trough, a feeling of dread rising in my throat.

"Harvey!" My scream sounded foreign to my ears, blood-curdling, filled with horror.

As I watched, the form rolled over and I saw a thin arm rise from the river holding a make-believe rifle. I leaped into the water without thinking, splashing toward the shape wearing a ragged old hunting jacket. I was still feet away when he slid below the surface. Frantically, I dove toward him, thrashing at the water like it was one of the nightmare monsters roaming the streets of New Orleans that night.

Please, God, I prayed, help me save my brother. At that moment, my fingertips brushed against soggy cloth. I grabbed the back of Harv's jacket and dragged him on to the riverbank.

In the hospital later that night, the doctor examined Harv then came out to talk with my mother. "He'll be fine, Mrs. Oswald. Don't you worry."

Together, we watched him sleep. He was so small in the hospital bed, so still. It was a close call, but I had saved my brother.

Tears glinted on mom's face when she embraced me and called me her little hero.

"Everything happens for a reason, Robert." She put a hand on Harv's head, one arm still wrapped around me. "We don't know what the good Lord has planned, but I know there's a reason he was spared." She leaned down and kissed him on the forehead. When she straightened, mom looked at me and with a catch in her voice, said, "Believe me, one day, we'll all be reading about your famous brother, Lee Harvey."

Victor DiGenti

VIC DIGENTI, a FWA Regional Director, is asked many questions about publishing. The most frequent by his wife who daily asks, "When are you going to get a real job." DiGenti has three published novels, several short stories and eighty-two rejections to his credit www.windrusher.com

Previously published in The Florida Palm, 2007

Bonita's Birds

With a rush of wings, a familiar noise, and a fishy odor, a flock of geese landed on the surface of Joshua and Marge Flanders' farm pond. Bonita counted; there were twenty-two. Their landing stirred the breeze where Bonita sat in her wheelchair nearly hidden by a mossy oak near the edge of the water. They fed and rested. The time seemed a few minutes, although she sat for nearly half an hour. A barely perceptible change in the energy on the pond and Bonita sensed that the geese were ready to move on.

Their migration would take many more days on an ageless call. Bonita Flanders, three months into her fourteenth year, was comfortable on her grandparents' farm. She savored that the plump birds knew exactly what they are supposed to do; fly south before coming cold weather, and back when it is warm. There was a wistful down turn at the corners of her mouth. Bonita glanced into giant clouds and imagined how it would feel if she could fly. At that moment, geese began to lift from the water in ones, twos and larger numbers. A few stragglers roused from peacefulness and joined the rising swoosh.

The flock circled, waiting for the latecomers. A noise intruded into the quiet beauty of the autumn afternoon. Bonita was startled. She glanced toward a clump of cedar trees at the far end of the pond. The nearest neighbor's house was two miles away. Wind, birds and scurrying animals were natural. This noise did not match the sounds she knew.

Bonita shaded her eyes with the notebook she carried to write her thoughts and feelings. She squinted into the northern sky. Geese were soaring, scattering with the air currents—west, then south. A few turned north, the direction from which they had come.

She heard rustling from the windbreak of cedars across the pond. Bonita turned her wheelchair, its motor barely audible, straining to find the source of the sounds.

This was the fourth season, two springs and two autumns that Bonita had watched the geese fly from Canada, over the farm on the trek to places that Bonita had never visited: Florida, Jamaica, pictures in her grandfather's books.

Since the accident that took the lives of her parents and left her unable to walk, she had come to live with her father's parents in the glacial moraine of northern Wisconsin. The countryside was nearly the same as her home across Lake Superior in Ontario. The clear colors and clean-scented air made the move to her grandparents' home less painful.

Doctors said that Bonita's legs were healed. They saw no reason for her two years' paralysis. "Psychological," Dr. Breedin said. The electric wheelchair with its wide tires gave her access to much of the farm, and her grandparents were the best anyone could ask for.

After several moments of calm Bonita felt there would be no more geese today. She turned the wheelchair for the short drive to the house when the sound of a newly-arriving flight caught her attention. She looked over her shoulder. A flock of the gray-black and white birds, families of adults and adolescents, began to settle on the surface of the pond.

Explosions broke the air. The geese abruptly rose, squawking from their aborted landings. In the confusion Bonita heard pain-filled cries. Geese fell with flat splashes onto the water, unmoving. A few struggled skyward, faltered, then plunged into the dry quarry at the edge of the field. Companions left the flight to hover over stricken comrades, and then flew haphazardly in panic.

Bonita was startled by raucous laughter from the short, broad bushes on the far side of the pond. She maneuvered her wheelchair in the direction of the laughter, rolling toward the grove as fast as the electric motor would take her. She rounded a clump of shrubs at the beginning of the woods. Two boys squatted, emptying the chambers of their shotguns. They were grinning.

"Stop it! You monsters!" Bonita yelled. "Get out of here. You're killing my beautiful geese." Tears of shock and anger changed her happy face. "Stop it, stop!"

The boys, not much older than Bonita, were surprised by the oncoming wheelchair and her words. They struggled to their feet, ran toward the fence that bordered the woods and the little-used country road, vaulted it and climbed into a waiting pickup. Speeding away, one boy, whose upper lip was beginning to grow a mustache, leaned out of the window and yelled, "It's fun, kid—fun, that's all."

"Bonita, Bonnie..." A voice came from behind the distraught girl. Panting as he ran, a man with shoulder-length white hair flowing behind him continued to call, "Bonnie." Reaching her, his voice changed to a hoarse whisper, "You...you're walking."

Bonita looked at her hands. She was standing, gripping the weathered fence with one hand. The other was a tight fist, shaking at the receding pickup. Her wheelchair was several feet behind. Feeling the earth beneath her feet, a connection she had not known for two years, tears of anger changed to tears of joy. Bonita moved one foot then the other against the clover-filled grass.

"Gramps--Oh--Gramps," she said. She tested forgotten sensations in her legs and feet. Tentatively, she lifted one foot and stamped the ground. She faltered and her grandfather reached to hold her upright. "I...I need practice," Bonita said. She yelled toward the disappearing geese, "I can walk! Look geese, I can walk!"

Her grandfather bent to pick up a shell casing. Nearby, a metal object glinted. He picked it up and absently dropped it into his pocket with the casing. He lifted Bonita and ran to his house.

Bonita's grandmother heard Joshua's voice as he ran up the steps, "Marge, Bonita can walk. Blessed be." Trembling, he stood the slim girl on her feet.

Bonita told her grandparents, "They were shooting for fun, not even for food. 'Fun,' the idiot said."

Her grandmother wiped Bonita's face with a warm Jasmine-scented washcloth. She hugged her husband and Bonita. "I believe it was your love for the geese. They know you love them. They brought you a healing gift."

Joshua pulled from his pocket the objects he had found in the grass. "This is a high school class ring from right here in the county. I know who can help us; Mr. McConnell, the high school principal."

Marge grinned and gave her excited granddaughter two thumbs up. "We can walk to the pond every day from now until winter," she said.

"Cool," Bonita said, "And skate when it freezes." Her smile was as broad as the wingspan of one of her geese. In the distance she heard the last flock of the day calling to one another, signaling the way home.

GWENDOLINE Y. FORTUNE

GWENDOLINE Y. FORTUNE is author of *Growing up Nigger Rich,* "Outstanding" in *Dictionary of Literary Fiction, 2002, Family Lines* and other published stories, essays and poems. Her novel *Weaving the Journey: Noni and the Great Grands,* is in pre-publication for Fall 2009. Her website is http://xenarts.com/gunr

Life Flight

Lightning lit the night outside the helicopter, the fierce gale buffeting the craft so that it stuttered. Alice unbuckled her seat belt and leaned toward Jamie. Her child lay motionless on the stretcher, the oxygen mask almost obscuring her small face.

"No!" the medic shouted above the helo's noise. "Stay strapped in! We'll be out of this soon!"

A beautiful sunset filled the horizon when the medical helicopter took off, the sky's streaming reds and golds, glowing hope as they headed up the coast to Jacksonville where Alice's six-month-old daughter would get a new heart. Then the storm hit. The pilot told everyone to put on life vests and moved out over the Atlantic, trying to circle the weather, but the maneuver hadn't worked. The helicopter pitched wildly, rising as if lifted by powerful hands and dropping what felt like hundreds of feet, the high winds tossing it willy-nilly.

The engine went silent, and the helo pitched sideways and down, the lightning-lit waves reaching as if hungry to grab it.

This is wrong! Alice's mind screamed. First I lose Jim in Iraq before he even saw his baby, now this chance to save her....

She wrestled her seatbelt off and knelt to untie the straps holding Jamie in the stretcher.

"What are you doing?" the medic yelled, rocking to his feet in dropping helo.

The crew chief stumbled from the front, shouting, "I'm going to launch the raft! Prepare to jump!

The medic knelt in front of Alice and pulled a strap from under her seat.

"I'm going to strap your baby to you," he yelled, "and you're going to hold her as tight as you can. We'll jump together, and I'll help you into the raft! Pray!"

He put Jamie in her mother's arms and strapped mother and child together.

The crew chief opened the door, but before he could launch the raft, the helo pitched ninety-degrees sideways, sending him into space. Alice and the medic slid after him, and Alice hit the water.

"Help us, Jim!" she screamed.

Alice opened her eyes. She floated in gently lapping water under a full moon in a clear sky. I must have passed out.

She frantically checked Jamie and smiled at feeling the little heartbeat. A small dolphin rubbed her arm, and something grabbed the collar of her life vest. Alice twisted her head to see what it was. An adult dolphin held the jacket in its teeth.

What? Am I still passed and dreaming?

The dolphin pushed her gently forward, her pup beside her.

Alice laughed. "I thought dolphins saved people only in Greek myths. Jamie, wait till I tell you about this when you grow up. This must have been your father's idea. He liked dolphins."

Clutching Jamie in the soft motion the dolphin made pushing her forward, Alice dozed. A sound, the lapping of waves on a shore, woke her.

"Jamie, we're safe!" she cried, but the bundle she held was limp. She felt for the heartbeat, for any sign of life. But Jamie was gone. All Alice's life was gone. Her daughter, her husband—all.

"No!" She screamed at the moon. "No!"

Holding her daughter with one arm, Alice unbuckled the strap holding Jamie to her and released the buckles on the life vest. She shucked the jacket off and brought James tightly to her breast. She looked at the sky.

"Jim, we're coming. You'll meet our beautiful child, and we'll all be together."

The dolphin nudged Alice, a tear in its eye. But Alice smiled and shook her head and slipped beneath the water.

ROLLENE GANNETT

ROLLENE GANNETT is a retired English and debate teacher. She has published a YA novel, *Flying Wheels*, and many short stories and essays. Historical fiction and fantasy are her favorite areas. She is active in community and writing groups.

A Tyrant's Birthday

April 20, 1945, Hitler's birthday. We'd spent the night in an abandoned German Army barracks, seven kilometers east of town—Dad, Mom, Aunt Mia, my little sister, and I. We'd pushed our loaded bikes there. Our dachshund Waldmann had valiantly kept up, his short legs a blur as he motored along.

We shared the barracks with several women, children, and elderly men. We'd all become refugees when we abandoned our homes to escape the allied air forces' bombs. In addition to being afraid of the daily bombings, the battlefront drew closer.

Dad was a civilian, and until a few days earlier, he'd been designing dive-plane indicators for the German U-Boat Navy. No longer needed, he was released from his duties and told to go home. Civilian or not, though, the fanatical SS would have pressed a rifle into his hands or hung him as a deserter if they spotted him. He had to avoid them.

A pale April sun found its way through the grimy barracks windows. Everybody was up, preparing to move on. The place was part of a German military installation. It may have been abandoned, but strafing American fighter planes might see it as a target.

The door opened and slammed shut as people hurried to and from the latrines. My nine-year-old sister Ursula pointed at them. "They look like pigeon coops, Daddy."

"Yeah, I guess so," he said, "but we need to go there, too."

He searched his pack for toilet paper. Having found none, he tore an old newspaper into rectangles. He kept a few for himself and handed the rest to Mom to distribute.

The latrines were wooden stalls built over a long pit. Because of the stink, I couldn't stay in there long enough to finish my business. I ran out, gasping for air.

When Dad came out of his stall, he waved me to him. After looking around, he said, "You and I are going on a secret mission."

"A secret mission?"

"Yes, a secret mission."

"What is it?"

"It's a secret."

Mom, Aunt Mia, and Ursula returned from the latrines. We washed our hands and faces under the outside taps and ate a hurried breakfast of brown bread with ersatz marmalade scraped into its pores. All during breakfast, Dad watched our neighbors. I was sure he did so because of our secret mission.

"We have to wait until they're gone," he said. "I don't want them to see what we're up to." He checked his watch. "I'll ask them what their plans are."

When he returned, he knelt on the edge of the army mattress we'd slept on.

"They'll be gone in a few minutes," he said. "They're planning to cross the Danube on the old rope ferry downriver—if the ferryman hasn't abandoned his post—and then hide out in the Bavarian Woods."

When our neighbors rolled their bikes outside, Dad held the door for them. We waved goodbye and wished each one good luck. Once they were well down the road, Dad went to his bike, and after undoing some straps, uncovered a collapsible shovel and large box wrapped in oilcloth.

He handed me the shovel. "This is for you," he said and held up the box for Mom to see. It contained our valuables—table silver, jewelry, important papers, bank books.

"Klaus and I will go and bury the box," he told her. "While we're gone, get the bikes ready and move them outside so we can leave right away."

"Can I come too?" Ursula asked.

"Not this time, sweetheart," Dad said. "Mommy needs your help."

"Waldmann!" he called. "Come on, boy. Let's go for a walk."

The dog ran ahead of us, sniffing and lifting his leg on every bush and tree. Dad and I walked carefully. The ground was pitted with holes and crisscrossed by deep trenches.

"What about mines, Dad?" I asked.

"Won't find them here, son. This place is for training."

He stopped at a large rectangular hole and peered into it. The hole measured approximately two by two meters and two meters deep, its sides shored up with wooden slats that formed ladder-like walls. There were several such holes.

"What are they for," I asked, but Dad didn't know.

The holes were alike, but Dad chose one whose bottom was covered with leaves and branches.

"This'll work," he said, taking the shovel from me. "Jump in."

When I was in the hole, I brushed the leaves aside and Dad handed me the shovel. I dug while he stood near the edge, keeping watch and smoking a cigarette.

"You can give me the box now," I said after a while.

"It isn't deep enough. It needs to be really deep in case somebody else wants to bury something in this same hole. This is an important box. Want me to come down and help?"

"Naw, I can do it," I said. After all, I was an expert. I'd dug many holes when my friends and I built forts. Besides, I'd be twelve in a couple of months, nearly a man.

When satisfied the hole was deep enough, Dad handed me the box. I lowered it into the hole and covered it with the dirt I'd dug up.

Dad squatted at the rim. "Stomp on the dirt a little, then take a branch and brush away your foot prints."

I did what he told me and covered the spot with branches and leaves, but before I climbed out of the hole, he said, "One more thing. You were in and out of the latrine pretty fast. Did you go?"

"No. I couldn't stand it in there."

He took some newspaper scraps from his pocket and handed them down. "Don't cover it," he said and turned away.

When I was done, I called him.

"Looks perfect," he said. "A real work of art. Now give me the shovel, and come on out."

I tossed the shovel out of the hole and climbed out. When I leaned down to pick up the shovel, Dad grabbed my sleeve. "Do you hear that rumbling? Diesel engines."

"Bombers?"

"Airplanes don't use diesels—it's coming from the river."

We ran toward the sounds. Waldmann bounded ahead, his ears flapping. We crossed a small, tree-lined road and ran up the back of the earthen levee that formed the right bank of the Danube. Dad pulled me to the grass.

I raised my head. On the opposite side of the river, not more than three hundred meters distant, a long column of vehicles rumbled along the road paralleling the water—trucks, tanks, and open jeeps with soldiers in them. The morning sunlight glinted off windshields and armor plate.

"They look different," I said. "A different color. A kind of green. Artillery?"

"American Army," Dad said.

I swallowed to keep my stomach down. I had never dreamed I'd see the enemy up close like that.

Waldmann ran back and forth on top of the levee, yapping at us. He wanted to play.

"He'll get us killed," I said.

Dad called our dog. We slithered down the embankment and, staying close to the ground, ran to the barracks. Mother, Aunt Mia, and Ursula stood ready with our bikes.

Mom pointed at the sky. Like a swarm of mosquitoes rising from a swamp, black dots approached our city from the south. My heart jumped into my mouth. Bombers.

Dad tried to catch his breath. I sank to the ground next to Mom and watched bombs drop from the planes like toothpicks spilled from a box. Orange flames and black geysers shot into the sky. The earth trembled, and smoke obscured the city's steeples and buildings.

Mother clutched her chest. "So many people!" Ursula whimpered. Aunt Mia held her, and Waldmann buried his head under my arm.

"We have to leave," Dad said, but nobody moved.

Mom looked at him. "I wonder if our house is still standing," she said.

Dad touched her arm. "We have to go."

The attack ended, and the planes made a sweeping turn to the south before disappearing over the horizon.

"We have to leave," Dad said again. "The Americans are already on the other side of the river. He pointed at the flaming city. "Today is Hitler's birthday, and I hope he burns in hell for what he's done."

Klaus Gansel

KLAUS GANSEL has written articles about boating and boating safety. He wrote numerous short stories and is a winner of the St Petersburg College Carolyn Parker Fiction Award. Klaus grew up under Hitler's brutal regime and is currently completing his memoir, *A Terrible Time.* You can contact him at: Ganselmagic@verizon.net

Life's Myth

"I'm glad I'll get there earlier than she expects," he said softly to himself as he crossed the Delaware Memorial Bridge onto the New Jersey Turnpike. We have to put this behind us.

What had started as a simple misunderstanding between them led to a confrontation and breakup. As an innocent remark, he said to her, "Bet you wish you had been with her more often."

Cindy's reaction was swift and direct. "You don't know what you're talking about, Robert. I live close to her, not you."

It didn't end there.

Later that day, when everyone had left, she let out her hurt feelings. "You seldom called and weren't even aware of the problems here, taking care of her and all. I'm as busy with my life as you are, you know."

"Oh, come on," he replied. "I remember the times she needed help and worried about how she'd manage. Don't take it so personally!"

There was no way she would accept any criticism like that, particularly at this time. "You have some nerve. I was with her when she was anxious about you. You ignored her concerns."

"Wait a second!" he said, realizing his original comment to her had been thrown back in his face. "What makes you think you're so perfect anyway?"

She glared at him in disgust and left the room crying.

That was the last time we were together or spoke until yesterday.

The signage for the Garden State Parkway came into sight and he figured he'd be home with her in less than an hour.

I'm really looking forward to seeing her again and erasing what has kept us apart. We were always so close.

The more enthused he became to get to the house, the faster he drove.

$\sim$

"I'm sure we can finally make amends," Cindy said, as if the cat could understand her words and offer advice. "He'll be here in less than an hour and I have so much to do." A tense feeling in the pit of her stomach remained even after lunch.

His phone call sounded so apologetic. She played his words back in her mind like a tune from a Broadway show.

"Should I admit how much I've missed him?"

It's as much my fault as his. We were always so close.

"Missy Cat, when he walks in the door, I'll put my arms around him and hug him to death. I won't have to say anything until he does, so I can hold in my tears." She hesitated and added, "We've been apart too long."

"Meow." The purr sounded sympathetic.

The house and his room were in order, just as he would remember.

"Oh, I forgot to get the Merlot—his favorite," she said aloud, disappointed that everything wasn't perfect. "I have plenty of time to run out and get it. Maybe I'll pick up more snacks and Diet Coke as well."

As she drove her Volkswagen back from the grocery store, a detour on Main Street for road work required taking Mountain Avenue; it would add five minutes to the short trip.

"Oh well, if it's not one thing, it's another," she whispered. She grinned at how happy their reunion would have made her mom feel.

At the top of the hill, she moved quickly into the left lane and accelerated to make the turn at the light. In an instant she saw the BMW that turned suddenly and sharply into her lane.

～

The traffic in the one open lane moved slowly as drivers rubber-necked, each taking the expected cue from the car ahead.

"This was pretty bad, wasn't it?" the officer stated, shaking his head.

"It sure was. They were going fast and, since there are no skid marks, neither driver hit the brakes. Both were killed on impact."

"Any identifications yet?" The officer asked, as he flipped pages in an overused notepad.

"Let's see. The male was from Delaware and … the female was local, only a few blocks from here." He continued with a sigh, "Funny coincidence, though."

"What's that?" the officer asked. Nothing on this job would surprise him any more.

"They had the same last name."

～

Pa received the news and waited patiently for Ma, who was off enjoying the glorious sunrise. She arrived on the next cloud, smiling as usual.

"We'll have company today, Ma."

"So soon! Which one?"

"Both of them," he answered, a hint of sadness in his voice.

"Perhaps, it's poetic justice," she whispered.

"What do you mean by that, Ma?"

"Look how long I waited there after you left me. It wasn't easy taking care of them, coping with physical ailments, and everything else. That's what I mean, Pa."

He laughed. "Well, as you and I have said many times before—'til death do us part is simply a myth."

"Exactly right!" she exclaimed. "And thank goodness they didn't have to wait long to be with us." Understanding and compassion were hallmarks of her character. "They could only join us when they forgave each other. So life's myth lives on."

They watched clouds pass by looking like bales of cotton bundled up to clothe the angels.

"Did you see the abused young ones on that cloud?" Pa asked, glancing at Ma.

"Of course, I did," Ma replied, sounding melancholy for only a nanosecond.

"Even the Supreme One feels badly for them," Pa said, recalling His repetitive welcoming message to new arrivals.

"Actually, Pa, His sorrow is not so much for those children; after all, they occupy a special place here. The Supreme One personally conducts the tour for them to see the splendor of the universe close up."

She reflected on His presence and added, "Every lost soul causes Him to be dejected and openly grieve."

"Isn't that the truth!" exclaimed Pa. "Those poor souls just made the wrong choice."

They observed another sunrise full of faith, hope and charity, symbolizing the arrival of His gift to all people on Earth.

"Look who's coming," Pa said beaming.

"Well I'll be," Ma said. "They look so happy, holding hands and waving to us. Just like old times."

"Hello, Mom and Dad. We're all together again." Robert smiled at his parents and his caring twin sister.

Ken Gorman

KEN GORMAN moved from Morristown, NJ to Ponte Vedra Beach, Fl upon his retirement in 1997. He has written a political drama, *The Atkinsen Ticket*, published in 2008, and In Honor of Justice, a novel of international intrigue. His website is www.justiceonamission.com

Bonding

There are few things I enjoy as much as eating a fine Sunday dinner and heading for my favorite place…a hammock swinging between two shade trees in the back yard.

That was right where I was heading when I passed through the kitchen. Instinctively, I knew I had made a mistake. Sure enough, my wife, Linda, caught me just as I was almost through the door.

"Oh, there you are," said Linda. "I was thinking that you ought to take Jimmy and go fishing today. It will be great fun, just the two of you. I'll finish cleaning up the kitchen. It will be a good chance for you two to have some time together."

"Well, honey," I stammered. "I was kind of looking forward to a little nap in the hammock. Why doesn't he go and play with the Thornton boy?"

"Because the Thorntons have gone to the beach today, and Jimmy has been moping around the house all morning," she replied.

"But, honey," I began . . . Then, one look from Linda told me that I was beaten.

An hour later found Jimmy and me at our old fishing hole. Looking for a shady place to lie down, I said to Jimmy, "Now, you go ahead and start fishing; I'll be right here watching you."

"Daddy," said Jimmy, "will you help me bait my hook?"

Arousing myself from my lethargy, I replied, "Of course, son."

As I began to bait his hook, he asked, "Daddy, why do you put the worm on tail first?"

"So you won't have to look at his face," I said.

Jimmy looked up at me and said, in that captivating way of his, "Aw, Daddy." Then he looked up at me with a serious look on his face and asked, "Daddy, does it hurt when you stick the worm?"

"Naw! Only if you stick your finger."

Again, he looked up at me, grinned, and said, "Aw, Daddy." As he watched his cork bobbing in the water, I lay back down thinking that would keep him busy for a while. As I closed my eyes, he asked, "Daddy, where do water lilies come from?"

"Oh," I mumbled, "they just come up, unexpectedly." I sensed right then that it was not a very good answer.

Soon enough, he asked, "Daddy, where did I come from?"

You know, your mother has a wonderful story to tell you about that," I replied.

He was quiet for a few moments and then he asked, "Daddy, why do fish eat worms?"

"Well, I guess it's because they're hungry; and if you don't catch some fish pretty soon, I guess we'll have to eat those worms for supper."

His eyes twinkled as he said, "Aw, Daddy...Daddy, you don't mind if I ask questions, do you?"

"Of course not. How are you going to learn anything unless you ask questions?"

He thought for a moment and said, "Daddy, the teacher told us about a very smart man named Einstein and she said he had a theory about relativity. What does that mean?"

"Why, it means that you can't trust relatives," I replied.

Jimmy broke into a wide grin, saying, "Aw, Daddy."

"I don't mean to make light of your question, son; I just love to see you smile. Actually, most grownups don't know much about Einstein's Theory, either. It has to do with space, time and mass. Someday, you'll know more about it than your old man ever did."

He was quiet for awhile; and by and by, he caught a fish. He was so excited and proud of his catch. He watched the little fish 'pant' and struggle for a minute and I noticed a touch of anguish on his face and a tear in his eye. Looking up at me, he asked, "Daddy, can we put him back?"

"Of course, if you want to, son."

He looked relieved. By that simple act of kindness, it told me what I already knew: My son had a good heart and feelings for living and helpless creatures.

As the day wore on, I began to study my son. You know, sometimes we look at our loved ones without really seeing them. For the first time, I realized how much my son looked like me. Why, he was the "spittin' image" of me when I was his age…the unkempt hair, the tattered shirt, the rolled-up pants and that goofy fishing hat. As I gazed, enraptured, at the boy, I realized that here was my own flesh and blood, and I was just about as proud as I could be.

Later, as we sat on the bank having a little picnic, he gazed up at me with those sparkling blue eyes and said, "Daddy, I'm so glad we came fishing today."

With a tear in my eye, I said, "So am I, son…so am I."

"Daddy," he said, "we don't have a fish to take home to Mom. What are we going to do?"

"Well," I said, "I guess we'll just have to eat those worms." Once again, the boy looked up at me and said those magical words, "Aw, Daddy."

It was a day in which my son and I truly bonded, and one that will live in my memory forever. That was many a year ago. Now, my son has moved far away and has a family of his own. These days, I have plenty of time to lie here in this old hammock and recall those precious times. My joy would be complete, could I but once again, look into those big, blue eyes and hear those sweet, childish words, "Aw, Daddy."

As someone so aptly put it:

"A small child can be a pain in the backside, when he's around; a pain in the heart, when he isn't."

JIM GULLEDGE

JIM GULLEDGE was born in Ft. Pierce, Florida, in 1927, which makes me a "Florida Cracker," an endangered species. His wife, Linda, attended school in Miami with him. He began to write short stories as a hobby in 1995, and has a book coming out shortly.

I am Oliver, and I am a Cat

Oliver is my feline mentor, advisor, and all round patriarch. Well at fourteen a cat deserves to be honored as a patriarch, as I am honored to be a member of his family.

"If your pets could write about you, what do you think they would say?" He was lecturing me in the interval between my awakening and filling his food dish. This was obviously a direct challenge for me to ask what he would say.

"You'd have to tame a cockroach to write for you, like Mehitabel has," I replied, trying to confuse him.

"I don't need an Archie, I have you."

"Touché." I paused a second; after all I still wasn't quite awake. "How do you know about Archie and Mehitabel?"

"I am Oliver, and I am a cat. As you should know, that makes me omniscient. I can trace my family back to the ancient Gods of Egypt. Can you say the same?"

"Well, they had to be ancient in those days, didn't they?" He glared at me and scooped up another piece of food with his paw. I gave in. "So what would you say?"

He carefully chewed and swallowed before replying.

"My owner loves me; he would do anything for me, as long as my tail is cut off, my ears cropped for his vanity, my toes declawed. Oh, and he cut my balls off."

"Oliver! No one has touched your ears and tail."

"I speak for us all," he said, with a condescending tilt of his head.

"If you speak for all pets," I said, "Perhaps you should say, 'She stayed by me in the hurricane and risked her life for me? Or he shares my food because he can not afford anything else, and he will not abandon me.'" I thought I had him there because he ignored me, so I went on. "During Hurricane Katrina, FEMA didn't allow people to take their animals with them. Half of those who stayed behind in New Orleans did so because they wouldn't abandon their pets, even when their own lives were in severe danger."

He sniffed. I had obviously bested him with that reply, so he ignored me.

"My direct ancestor Mafdet was the first Egyptian feline goddess." It was as if I hadn't spoken. "But the most famous was Bastet. She was not only a household goddess, protector of women, children and domestic cats, but she was also the goddess of sunrise, music, dance, pleasure, as well as family, fertility and birth."

"She needed her God-like powers to prevent being overwhelmed with obligations," I quipped.

"Don't be facetious. Anyway, she made sure that the penalty for killing a cat—even accidentally—was death. If a house caught on fire, the cats were rescued before the people, just as it should be!"

"Not all Egyptian Gods were cats. What about Anubis?"

"That jackal-headed dog? Elevating him to divine status was idiotic. But that happened before they realized that the first cat was daughter of Isis, and the goddess for the moon and the sun. They even, very wisely I might add, built a whole city for cat worship, Bubastis, in honor of Bastet."

"So why did medieval Europeans believe cats were in league with the Devil?" I said. "Cats were burned along with witches."

"Some of your ancestors weren't so bright."

"Wasn't Bubastis that depraved place where thousands of pilgrims sang silly songs, drank wine, prayed, and showed their wild behavior at an annual Bubastis Oktoberfest?"

Again he ignored my comments.

"Unfortunately, this city was destroyed by the unthinking Persians in 350 BC," he said.

"You left us with a dubious legacy. Young humans have adopted the behavior of Bastet's worshippers. We call it Spring Break."

His tail twitched reflecting possible annoyance despite his outward appearance of calm control.

"In America, in 2009, I admit we at last recognize that our relationship to our pets, to you, has undergone a profound change. We are no longer merely owners."

"You never have been." He sounded a little petulant. "At least not where we cats are concerned."

"May I remind you that we let your more recent ancestors into our homes? We of all the animal species have developed a close relationship with other species. We have created the human-animal bond."

"The animal-human bond was a mutual arrangement. But it is often bondage—for the animal. Some you keep in bondage to raise for food; some to work. And some you support only for vanity. Those are the ones you call pets."

What is a pet? I mused. A pet is a domesticated animal kept for pleasure rather than utility, and we should note that the verb, to pet, expresses fondness, or means to stroke gently or lovingly. It is said that it can also mean a fit of peevishness, sulkiness, or anger. At first I thought that was just propaganda, but after listening to Oliver I was no longer sure.

He went on without waiting for a reply. "Dogs and cats are the only two animals that you let freely into your homes, and allow to become members of your families. Farm animals, birds, or exotic pets are still captives. "

Pets do reflect the ying and yang of our special relationship with species other than our own.

They highlight the best and the worst of human behavior. Just as we need ugliness to appreciate beauty, sin to appreciate good, hate to appreciate love, so we need our special relationship to our pets to provide us with a mirror to our own soul. Who of you can you look into your pet's eyes and deny this? I daren't admit this to Oliver. Not just yet.

"We cats domesticated you."

"Your ancestors joined us to feed on the vermin in grain silos."

"They were pests surrounding your homes."

"What?"

"You had a filthy existence until we took over vermin control for you."

"Well, dogs developed a symbiotic relationship with us, guarding us and hunting for us in return for food and shelter." I didn't want to add that this relationship is so close that the dog breeds we have so diligently bred cannot exist without human friendship—anymore than we can exist without theirs—but Oliver beat me to it.

"Your family house-cat can fend for itself, hunt for food, and adapt to a wild environment. Can you see a Shi Tzu, Pug, or miniature Yorkie doing the same?"

"You have a point," I conceded.

"And you should bear in mind," he wagged his tail for emphasis. "There are as many feral cats in this country as those in your houses."

"Feral cats are a damn nuisance."

"If you got rid of them, the country would be overrun by rodents."

I quickly changed the subject. I didn't think it polite to talk about trapping his distant relatives. I do have some sensitivity.

"We view our bond differently now, and use terms like companion, guardian, and steward, instead of owner," I said. The loss of human and animal life during Hurricane Katrina helped us recognize this need. "On October 6th 2006, President Bush signed the PETS Act (Pets Evacuation and Transportation Standards), into law," I said. "States must have animal evacuation protocols in order to get disaster preparedness funds from FEMA, and allow FEMA to pay for shelters, for both animals and their guardians, in an emergency. "

The Fritz Institute predicted that the PETS Act would save thousands of animal and human lives. It has already. Before Hurricane Gustav, the authorities in New Orleans organized the Louisiana Mega Shelter that housed more than 1000 animals—cats, dogs, rabbits, lizards, snakes and turtles. Ninety-five percent of evacuees—1.9 million people—were able to take their pets with them when they left.

Oliver interrupted my train of thought.

"It's time for a nap." He leaped onto the windowsill and gave a grunt, meaning I should move things so he could lie in the sun.

"What I do for you," I said.

He stretched, rubbing his face on the sill to claim ownership, and sighed with Tuna-baited breath.

"One last thought I might write down for you. I think it's about time you learned the truth about us," he said. "And a bit about dogs. Puppies and Kittens are really alien invaders, sent to subjugate Earth. Their role is to win your affection, and overcome you with love. Then the puppies grow into dogs to police you, and the kittens grow into cats to govern you."

The alien thing seemed far-fetched, and I thought I saw him wink, but the rest of what he said had a ring of truth.

"You can leave me now," he said. "It's time for a nap."

I crept quietly away so as not to disturb him. I had to write his thoughts down before I forgot them; after all, he doesn't have an Archie.

Transcribed, at his whim, by his guardian

BOB HART

BOB HART, a veterinarian, has been published in a dozen magazines from *Horse and Hound* to *Private Pilot*, contributed to *An Incomplete History of London's Television Studios*, at www.tvhistory.co.uk, and authored *Hart's Original Petpourri, Volume 1, Miscellany, Fact, Fancy, Trivia, and Whimsy about Pets, their Veterinarians, and their Owners*.

Previously published in "The Florida Writer", Volume 3, #1, Page 20.

Larry and the Cat

Larry awoke in the middle of the night. He could drown the cat! He groped on his nightstand for a cigarette, found the lighter, and sucked in a lungful of blessed smoke. Blessed smoke? Damned smoke! Pills, patches, and hypnosis over a period of three years had cost him plenty. Fact was, Larry didn't want to quit smoking. Hannah wanted him to quit.

Hannah also didn't like cats.

And Hannah wanted to get married.

He slid himself up and smashed the cigarette out in the ashtray. The cat leaped onto the bed, landing in the middle of Larry's belly.

"Crap!"

Brushing the animal aside, he swung his legs out from under the covers and staggered to his feet. "Damned cat. Now I gotta pee."

While he stood at the toilet, Larry considered how best to drown the cat. Put him in the toilet and hold the lid shut? Damned cat would probably out-wait me. I'd lift the lid, and the thing'll spring out in a lightning flash and lose himself in a closet for two days.

Nah. Whatever he decided, it had to be quick and permanent. Take him out in the boat and drop him overboard? Nice and clean.

No one'll ever know.

Larry flushed the toilet, hit the light switch, and made his way to the kitchen.

"Sixty-seven damned years old, and I got some old woman telling me she don't like cats or smoking. She'll move in, and next thing she'll be moving the furniture around and telling me when to go to bed and when to get up. Bitch."

He pulled a can of Old Milwaukee from the fridge and took it to the living room. After shoving aside a pile of newspaper, he flopped on the sofa, hit the remote, and punched in the TV Guide channel to see what good old movie might be playing in the middle of the night. While the programs scrolled up the screen, he went to his bedroom for the cigarettes.

"C'mon, Oscar," he said to the cat. "Let's watch some TV while I work out a solution to our little problem."

The tabby jumped from the bed and followed Larry to the sofa where he curled up on Larry's his lap and purred.

Oscar's a happy cat, Larry thought. And easy to take care of. Eats whatever's put in front of him.

Kept the rat population down around the trailer, too. Larry hadn't seen one in the four years since they'd found each other in the road.

"But you gotta go, boy. I want Hannah to move in here, and she don't like you. Says she's allergic. Hell, she just plain old don't like cats. She's a mighty fine cook, though, Oscar. And a lot more cozy in bed than you."

Oscar purred.

Larry tuned to a 1940's war movie. "Propaganda, Oscar. Nothing but propaganda, but they sure make you proud to be an American. All that flag waving. Marines on the beaches, fly-boys and soldiers saving our asses. Come to think of it, Oscar, Hannah ain't much fond of war movies, either."

Oscar purred.

"My check comes today, little buddy. We can get some gas, and I'll go out on the lake, catch us some fish."

Larry fell asleep while Hollywood bombs dropped on extras pretending to be the enemy.

The telephone woke him several hours later. Larry grabbed his cigarettes and the phone, answering before the answering machine came on. "Whatcha want?"

"Larry, it's Hannah."

"I can see it's you, Hannah. I keep telling you, I got that caller ID thing. What're you calling for so early?"

"I decided today is the day we should take Oscar to the shelter. They'll find him nice new home, and…."

Larry snapped his lighter and took a drag on his cigarette. Oscar, sensing his owner was upset, jumped to the back of the sofa and reached out a paw to stroke him.

"Larry! Hannah said. "Do I hear the sound of you smoking?"

"No," he lied.

"Just imagine the delicate flavor of my homemade French toast with butter and syrup. When you quit smoking, you'll be able to taste everything. Life will be so much better. You won't cough. You won't stink of ugly cigarettes. I can't wait for us to be a married couple, a real family."

Larry stared at the TV screen. Two soldiers stood at a ship's railing. They smoked and laughed.

"And with that cat out of the house, we can clean it up. No more litter box odors. No more cigarette odors. It will be heaven."

Larry imagined himself not smoking, eating French toast with butter and syrup.

Heaven, Larry thought. Heaven. But he currently weighed around one-fifty, and it wouldn't be long before he'd be up to two-fifty.

He brushed the cat's paw aside. Oscar, undaunted, licked the paw and reached out again.

"Hannah," Larry said. "I just had an idea. Maybe you'd like to go out in the boat with me this morning. Before we go to the pound. I won't even bring any cigarettes along."

Veronica H. Hart

VERONICA H. HART is an FWA Writing Group Leader in Daytona Beach, Florida where she also operates her own interactive murder mystery company. Her musical, *Murder in Morocco*, won several awards from the NY State Theater Association. She is currently working on a humorous suspense novel as well as a young adult novel.

Washing the Dishes

"I'm not doing the dishes. It's not my turn!" Sean's voice was louder than he intended, but he was serious.

"Dad said you were supposed to help me," I argued, my voice escalating as loud as his.

My brother and I were having the same argument that recurred like clockwork every Sunday after our family dinner. It was winter and because he wasn't helping Dad out in the fields or in the barn, Sean's job was to help my sister and me with the dishes.

"I don't have to help, na na na na boo boo."

Sean and I both looked at our little sister, Jeannie, in disgust. Because she helped Mom set the table, she was exempt from this distasteful chore. Mom made lasagna and, of course, it was the best lasagna in the world. It also left the messiest dishes to clean. I was always the washer while my siblings cleaned the table, dried, and put away.

"If we had a new dishwasher, we wouldn't have to worry about it," I yelled loud enough so my parents could hear me. Dad was watching a Browns football game and Mom had her nose in a book.

"We have three dishwashers that work perfectly well without costing a thing," Dad yelled back.

Sean and I rolled our eyes at each other. Jeannie chimed in again, "I don't have to help, na na na na boo boo."

Sean chased her out of the kitchen, and her squeals brought an unwanted reaction from Dad who was missing a touchdown. "Dang it, I told you kids to clean the kitchen, now be quiet and do it."

He meant business, so we worked quietly for a short time, right up until Sean threw an unscraped plate into the sink. The red tomato sauce rose in rivulets in the dishwater.

"Sean, scrape the dishes better!" I elbowed him in the side.

"Don't hit me!"

"Then do it right!"

"I did do it right. You just don't like the way I did it. You think you're Mom and can boss everyone around."

The argument got louder and louder and escalated into flipping dishtowels and throwing soapsuds. Totally out of hand.

Dad walked into the kitchen, his face was red and angry. Sean and I both stood at attention at the definite look of displeasure in Dad's expression and knew that we were about to be toast. He had definitely had enough.

"I told both of you to be quiet and do those dishes. There is no reason why a fifteen-minute job should take an hour of yelling and screaming and fighting. I…"

Off came one of his smelly socks. "Have had…."

Off came another sock, "ENOUGH!"

To our utter horror, Dad stuffed one of his icky sweaty socks in my mouth and the other in my brother's. "Now, you will keep those in there until every one of those dishes is done."

We both nodded our heads and did the dishes in record time with extraordinary unity and efficient teamwork, despite the gagging, hacking, and tears streaming down our faces.

Another memorable argument over doing the dishes, but probably not as fondly remembered, was a Sunday later in the spring when Mom made fried chicken. That particular battle was between my sister and me.

Dad and Sean left the table to work in the barn. "Make sure you get the skillet, too," Mom said to Jeannie and me as she walked out of the kitchen.

"Okay, you're washing this time," I said to Jeannie.

"No way! You always wash. You're the oldest," my sister protested.

Despite being five years younger than me, she was stronger and scrappier. She could cause serious bruises, and we both knew it. But I stood my ground.

"Not today. Today you have to be the washer."

"I am not going to wash these dishes by myself," she said. She put her hands on her hips and put on her bully face. "And you aren't going to make me."

I looked at the iron skillet Mom cooked the chicken in and knew it would be a nasty mess. I knew I wasn't going to make my little sister wash the dishes, either, no matter how much I tried to pull the older-sister card. And then I had the idea.

"Okay, I got an idea. Wanna hear it?"

"What is it?" Her brown eyes looked at me suspiciously.

"We can make a game out of it, and whoever loses has to do the dishes all by themselves.

Wash, dry, put away, the whole bit."

"What kinda game?"

"Tug-o-war! We could play tug-o-war and whoever wins can do whatever they want.

"We'll put the rug sideways and pretend it's the mud pit, use the dishtowel as our rope, and then we'll tug. Whoever steps on the rug first will have to clean the kitchen by herself," I explained. Her eyes sparkled with expected victory.

"Yes, I think that'd be great. Let's do it."

Each of us stood on either side of the rug. Jeannie's brown eyes met my green ones. We flexed our fingers and wrists and my sister even rolled her head around and hunched her shoulders. She planted one foot in front of the other, and I did the same. She handed me one end of the towel and got a firm grip on her end.

"Ready. Set. Go!"

Sis pulled hard. I realized I needed to put my all into it pretty darn quick. I pulled with everything I had and I was getting nowhere. I heard my sister make a sound between a grunt and a karate "ya-ha" and felt her pull even harder. It didn't take long to realize I had made a big mistake. I was the underdog. I felt the tug on the towel and my feet started to slip. In the next second or so, I would step on that rug and those dishes would be all mine.

It was a reflex. Honest. I was sorry for it later. I let go just as my sister was giving it her final victory pull. I watched in horror as she tumbled backwards in what seemed like slow motion. She was on her feet for a while, doing that slipping-on-ice dance with her arms flailing in the air. I actually thought she was going to make it for a second. The next thing I knew, she went through the window of our old farmhouse kitchen with the loud crash. Her knees and feet were bent over the windowsill in the kitchen, and her bottom landed firmly on the back porch. I ran to the broken window and our eyes mirrored the shock of the moment, which got worse as we heard Dad running in from the barn and Mom from the living room.

"You are really in trouble now," my sister whispered just before she conjured up some big tears.

"It was all her fault, Daddy! She wanted to play tug-o-war, but I was winning and she let go," she wailed. I figured that being quiet was the best course of action at that time, so I didn't even try to defend myself.

After inspecting my sister for injuries (there were none), Dad pulled us both inside. His finger pointed at me first and he used my middle name, always a bad sign. "Dawn Ja'net, you are going to clean this kitchen alone."

My sister grinned at me and stuck out her tongue. Dad caught her and said, "And you, Jeannie Renee, are going to clean up all the glass and help me put plastic on the window until a new one comes in." It seemed we both lost, but I still had to do the dishes by myself.

Those dish battles are some of our fondest memories. We all have children of our own now and they have similar battles. The other day, while talking to my sister on our usual Sunday phone call, I could hear her kids in the background.

"It's your turn to empty the dishwasher."

"Nuh, uh! I did it last time."

I could hear the frustration in my sister's voice as she told them to quit arguing and just get it done. I said, "Hey, Jeannie, why don't you take off your socks?"

DAWN SMITH HEAPS

DAWN SMITH HEAPS began writing for the sole purpose of entertaining family and friends and discovered her passion. She has written for *Chicken Soup for the Soul: Divorce and Recovery,* and other articles and short stories. Feel free to say hello at heapsd@bellsouth.net.

The River

Chris Wintermute stumbled out of a plowed drift at the edge of Teoga Street, Forest City's main drag, and just missed getting clipped by an eighteen-wheeler stacked to the gray skies with pulp logs. He could see his breath in the noon air. Granules of ice crunched between his socks and the inside of his blue and yellow jogging shoes. It felt like an icicle was being screwed through his head. He drew the zipper of his tattered insulated jacket tighter.

The narrow, rotted walkway across the decrepit Forest City Bridge was to be avoided. Wearing a brave smile, Chris drew erect and rerouted himself down Juniata Street, past the mansions, for the river.

The headaches had grown worse since last week, when his woodshop teacher had let him have it for leaving his bench a mess at the lunch bell. He hadn't cared about the mess, or the unfinished tool cabinet either. What was the point of his dad's Christmas gift now—who would be home to admire it?

The pain got so bad today in the cafeteria; he'd pushed away lunch and grabbed his jacket from the sixth grade homeroom. Three weeks into January and he still couldn't believe his dad had let Christmas pass without a package—or a single word.

Before him—long and broad—stretched the river, piled shore-to-shore with ice from the intense cold of an early winter. Thick ice that seemed a safe enough short cut to the bridge a mile downstream; there the interstate zigged close to town before disappearing behind Dorn Blazer Mountain.

With luck, he might find his dad at the stone yard out by the inter-state—trucking blue stone to Boston, Texas, or maybe the Carolinas. One of the Joes at the yard might know where Dad was running; he'd hitch a ride. The woodworking award safe in his pocket, he'd get a job in a furniture factory. The police—or some big dude like Mr. T—would help him find his dad.

Like a frosted loaf, Dorn Blazer loomed from the far shore—hemlocks stiff as sentinels, the red shale face of White's Leap encrusted with rime. He was suddenly crying and wiped the tears from his cheeks. The wind kicked up little boils of snow all around him.

Near the ice that jammed the river bank, Chris headed for the shelter of a giant black oak. The pressure of his jacket against the bark warmed him, and his thoughts flew back to the hot summer two years ago—to Scottsville, a magic place on the river his dad called "old country." Late in the afternoon they'd hiked to the secret cove in old country. With stone-caddies whisked that morning from Kasson Brook, they'd hunkered down to fish out the day. Dad hooked a feisty one right off and played the thrashing young pike in through the shoreline weeds, then tossed him back. Strangely, the little pike had hung for a moment in an eddy below their perch: fanning his gills and grinning, before exploding away in a sudden green flash.

"...Dad, where do they go in snow time?"

"They don't go nowheres, sonny. They drop deep to the quiet and feed off the bottom—"

"Dad...I mean what happens under the ice. How do they breathe?"

"Air's mixed into the water. You got too many questions, boy—don't worry over them fish."

Chris still smelled that tasseled field of corn cooking behind them in the August sun, heard the zzzz of the locusts through the buttonball trees.

The branches above were thrashing and creaking in the wind. He slipped down the snowy bank toward the jumble at the bottom—thick cards of ice flung one atop the other, like some giant of the North had lost his cool playing Flipsies. Chris jammed his hands, red and wet from his tears, into his jacket pockets and leaned against a block of ice and thought about his life.

Mom and Dad didn't see much of anything eye-to-eye, especially when it came to money. Way before the blow-up, mom was waiting tables in Forest City. Johnny's Hotel was okay for tips...sometimes; that's why she stayed nights as part-time barmaid.

"Your father's away from me now, Chrissy...weeks at a time. If I don't earn the living in this house, how're you gonna have nice things like all your friends at school?"

"But, Mom...you're never home now either..."

His mother wouldn't think so much of his friends if she heard them brag over their Christmas gifts in the school cafeteria: Carl Barr got a new dirt-bike, and Ronnie Stroka had a radio-controlled model airplane. His father helped him build it.

From the Baptist church down by the McCune County Courthouse, 3:30 chimed faintly. It seemed only minutes since he'd left the cafeteria. The wind turned the chimes all sour and tinny: like notes off a warped tape. Chris brushed a hank of blonde hair from his eyes, heart pounding in the sweat of clambering through the floe. He unzipped his jacket and ducked behind a chunk of ice to catch his breath. Getting to the bridge was hard work...harder than he'd imagined.

Chris slowly worked his way across the river's ponderous silence. The afternoon sky was clearing, sun settling behind Dorn Blazer Mountain. From around the big island, he caught the shimmer of moving water: a thin greenish-white riffle winding its way only to be lost again somewhere beneath the ice.

As he worked toward the far shore, the pulsing in his head started in again. Friday before Labor Day, his dad had driven in after a month on the road—slept a whole day before mom lost her cool:

"Dammit, the dryer's broke again! And I need shelves put up in the bathroom."

"...New dispatcher don't give me no sleep."

"More likely, you're wore out chasing the little tarts you seem to find everywhere!"

Words flew. Chris left the burnt spaghetti on his plate and went up behind the house to check on the rabbits; one of mom's men friends from Johnny's Hotel had dropped them off last Easter.

When he'd come back, Mom was still at the table, Dad on his feet, face beet-red.

"It's me, or them!"

"I can't give up the bar tendin'...not money enough in this house to feed the rabbits—"

"I'll fix the freakin' rabbits!"

His dad had yanked the 12-gauge shotgun from the broom closet, jammed two shells into it, and strode up the hill—blasted the two white rabbits into hamburger.

Still clutching the shotgun, his father had gone for the truck.

"...Well, sonny, I guess you're man of the house now..."

How could he be man of the house when his mother kept bringing new ones home?

"...You'll be home Christmas Day—won't you, Dad?"

"Christmas..? Yeah...sure. Still usin' that leather thing you give me last year. I'll bring you something nice."

"See you then, Dad..."

On the ice, he found himself at the lower end of the open spot— raw current hissing against one blue edge of the floe. A rosy dusk had settled in, the dying rays of the sun piercing one last bank of clouds and drilling into his eyes...it came before him in one stray gust of wind, framed against a billow of pinkish snow flakes. Anytime that scene floated back, the headaches hit worse—if only she'd kept her damn mouth shut...

Mom there at the kitchen table, holding the hand-tooled leather pouch he'd made last Christmas for his dad—for his truck papers— miniature lock still on the clasp, case grimy.

"You took it outta his truck!"

Her long face never flinched. "No, Chrissy... it lay under the back seat of the car—all this time. Shoved way under, where he thought nobody'd notice." Her words dripped hatred and shame, down a sorry billboard of betrayal....

Chris felt faint; he slipped out of the stiff Pumas, stripped off the wet socks, and pressed his bare feet to the ice.

The torment was ebbing when he spotted the pike daintily balanced in a jade eddy to one side of the main floe: rows of glistening little teeth in a precise smile, gills pumping, fins back-pedaling in a ballet of friendship, the bright-ringed pike eyes buoying his resolve.

Chris stooped and tucked the socks into his running shoes. He placed them neatly together, just at the edge of the ice, then stood upright again. For one painless moment, he lingered where the water dove quietly beneath the floe.

Hands at side, straight and tall—a slight push of the toes…

A dark shadow flashed beneath the floe.

There was just enough residual heat to stick the blue and yellow jogging shoes to the ice. If the river cut no deeper through the jam that night, they would still be there in the morning.

Richard Ide

RICHARD IDE has been a professional actor, a Wall Street broker, and has driven long haul trucks nearly a million miles over North American highways. Richard currently lives and writes in the Endless Mountains of northeastern Pennsylvania.

Previously published in Fox & Quill ezine in 2008 and again in Volume 4, Issue 1, in January, 2009.

Every Difficulty Along the Way

For more than fifty years, I've dreamed of finding my birth family. To this day, my earliest memories are seared in my mind—black and white images of two dim rooms separated by a cloth curtain, shadowy figures, and the sound of a faucet dripping.

When the shouting started, I fixed my eyes on the single light bulb in the center of the ceiling, sometimes certain it was getting brighter.

I remember a baby crying.

I wasn't yet two years old as our country entered its last year of involvement in World War II, but I must have known even then that the crying was coming from my younger sister.

My whole life is punctuated by the images and sounds of those days and nights during which I rarely ate and was eventually found alone at home, severely malnourished and void of a child's zest for living.

As time went on, and my residences changed, the images took on color and movement—-a foster brother playing with his spinning top, my cringing when a foster father came home from work, and then, while traveling to the next foster household, imagining the car's wipers forming a water-beaded clown hat when they came together in the middle of the windshield.

By three, I'd been in six foster homes and was labeled difficult to adopt. Prospective parents would have to deal with chronic tonsillitis and an urgent need for surgery to remove the lumpy birthmark on my chest. Men terrified me, which presented another problem. I'd stopped eating, and it was thought I might not live through the trauma of transition again.

The orphanage found a family willing to take on the challenge. Experience in dealing with problem children, a degree in nutrition, and the home's financial soundness sealed the deal.

Still, change didn't happen overnight. I remember pleading, "Mommy, do I have to eat every day?" She told me to sit in my highchair until I finished the oatmeal she'd put before me, and more than once, I watched the sun set through the kitchen window, the oatmeal untouched.

My new father was away on a business trip when I arrived, so there was time to adjust to my surroundings before being introduced to him. Before long, though, I was climbing in his lap while he tried to read the evening newspaper.

They adopted me and said I was chosen and special. My new parents were both scientists with practical views, and strict, afraid I'd become spoiled if treated too well. They tried their best to make me their own, but I never really felt like their child. Though grateful they'd taken me in, a shield went up when I was told I could always be sent back.

I was forbidden to cry aloud, so I retreated time and again to my room, burying my head in a pillow to release my anguish. That pillow became my solace, my friend.

As the years passed, memories of the foster days haunted me, and the longing for knowledge about my birth family increased. Not wanting to hurt my adopted parents, who were sensitive about not being able to have children of their own, I secretly wrote to the agency that placed me for adoption and learned I had two sisters—-one older, one younger. No names, just dates of birth.

My search began. Little by little, I collected information and learned first hand about scam artists and how they give you hope and take your money. I experienced a range of emotions during these years—-enthusiasm, exaltation, disappointment, and devastation. But I couldn't give up.

Every Difficulty Along the Way

After my adopted parents died, I found my adoption papers in their safe-deposit box and learned the names of my birth parents. An attorney tried to help me get more documents released from under seal, but he wasn't successful. My natural father had a military record and a social security number. New hope.

I hired a private investigator to find my father and prepared for our meeting. What would he be like? Would he even want to meet me? Would he be a con artist like some of the people I'd run across in this odyssey? Could he be in prison? Or would my prayers be answered, and he'd be the father of my dreams?

The investigator traced my father's death certificate, only to learn that he had been found alone in his home, just one year earlier. I'd prepared myself for every scenario, but not this one. Not death. He was sixty-one years old. If only I'd looked sooner.

I now mourned the loss of two fathers, the one who had reared me and the one I'd never known. I was devastated. I'd search no more for ten years.

In January 1994, a friend told me about The ALMA Society, a computer-based family search organization. Renewed hope. I joined and two weeks later received a phone call. They'd found my younger sister Joanie. She'd joined ALMA two years before.

My heart leaped. Was it true or a cruel mistake? Fear mixed with jubilance. If true, would she be the sister I'd yearned for? One I could love, who could love me? I'd searched so long, I didn't think I could handle more disappointment. My protective shield clanged into place, but curiosity, faith, and longing drove me forward.

When my sister and I spoke to one another the first time, it was as though we had the same body, the same mind, the same heart. Our conversation was so natural, relaxed. But nervous, too. We couldn't talk fast enough. There were so many lost years to recover, comparisons to make, information to exchange, and this breathless exhilaration to share.

A month later, at last, I met the baby whose cries I heard so many years before. What a day that was. She had my curly brown hair, my thin lips, my pointy chin. We were the same height, wore the same size shoe. We had the same tastes in practically everything, were both more creative than brainy, but what we shared most were the tears and glow of exquisite joy.

We grew up less than ten miles from one another.

~

It's been fifteen years since I met my precious sister Joanie, and we are as close as two human beings could be. We're building new memories, ones to cherish, like our giddy visit to the mall when we were in our fifties, to see Santa for the first time.

My journey has shown me the resilience of the human spirit and has proven that persistence in acting on our dreams brings reward, despite every difficulty along the way.

This story is not finished. We'll never meet our father, and because of age considerations, we assume our mother has also passed away, but Joanie and I have discovered that we still have an older sister and older brother out there, somewhere.

Joanie's satisfied with finding just me, but at sixty-six years old, I pray I live long enough to be reunited with the rest of my family.

Even if success proves elusive, I'll continue to search. I'll continue to dream.

COCO IHLE

COCO IHLE has just completed her first mystery novel about how two long lost sisters reunite and nearly lose their lives searching for a treasure and a murderer in a Scottish castle. She is working with her agent before presenting it to publishers. She may be contacted at: cocoihle@gmail.com

Learning to Say the 'C' Word

I have breast cancer. I have to tell my kids and Mom.

How do I do this? How do I say the word? I can't call and say, "Hi, it's me, I have news," all chipper and cheerful. I can't even talk without a waterfall.

I can't think straight. I'm knotted all over. Fear's done that.

I don't want to worry anyone, but I know I have to call. I'm sobbing. Where is my self- control? I'm stronger than this.

Delaying Mom, I call the kids first. Tina's a registered nurse. Even so, it takes me a few tries to get the "C" word out.

Her no-nonsense personality kicks into high gear. "Read me the mammogram report," she says. "Who have you talked to? What type of doctor did you see? What's the plan?"

I can't talk. I hand the phone to my husband Woody. He reads the report while I cry.

I call Jody next. She's finally entering nursing school. A mother of four children under ten, her nurses' schooling's been put on hold despite her intense interest in medicine. Her youngest daughter turned three this year, so Jody feels now's the time.

My tongue stumbles twice before I can say, "cancer."

She, too, is full of questions. I don't have the answers to any of them and can't talk for crying anyway. Woody takes the phone again.

Richard's a truck driver. When I call, he's at a customer's warehouse, waiting for a load. The "C" word trips but straightens on the second go. I tell him what we know, proud I can talk now without tears. He's quiet for a full half minute.

"Well, that's not good news, is it?" he says. "Why didn't you just get pregnant or something easy?"

I want to laugh but cry instead. Woody takes the phone while I use up Kleenex.

Charity's my youngest girl. She holds nothing back.

"What?" she screams through the phone. "You've got to be kidding! Mom, no!" She's in tears. That gets me started again. Charity isn't usually concerned about medical stuff, but her best friend's mother was diagnosed with breast cancer last week, so she fires questions. Woody takes over. When he hangs up, he holds me.

We can't reach Jason, my youngest son.

I'm emotionally exhausted, and I have yet to make the most difficult call. For a few minutes, though, I need Woody's strength. I don't think to wonder how he can be so strong. I just know he is, and right now, I need to cuddle.

I make the call.

"Hey, Mom, how are you?" I ask in a voice that doesn't sound natural even to me.

She says, "What's wrong with you? What happened?" Moms always know when something's not right.

"I have a lump in my breast, and they think it's cancer."

I'm weeping again. I learn later that when she heard these words, she felt God telling her everything would be all right.

"Well, for heaven's sake," she says, "how in the world did you get that?"

I can't help it—I laugh. Of all the things she might have said, I never expected that.

"Guess I'm the first in the family, huh?"

"No," Mom says, dropping a family skeleton into my lap. "My aunt had breast cancer and a double mastectomy about fifty years ago."

"What? Why didn't anyone tell me about it?"

"Well, you were too young when it happened. And it wasn't

appropriate conversation back then. Later, I guess we didn't talk about it anymore."

I always thought I'd have heart disease or diabetes, the things that run in our family. Not cancer.

"I didn't know any blood relative had cancer except Uncle Merlin," I say. "But his colon cancer's over, isn't it?"

Mom's quiet for a moment. "Well, he finished his treatment. I guess he's okay. We don't talk about it."

"So, how important do you think all this cancer in our family is?"

"Mom, cancer didn't kill Aunt Callia Susan, did it?"

"No, she died at ninety-four. Her body just wore out. You still might have a long life. When they look for cancer, they mean immediate family. I don't think they count aunts and uncles. You need to talk to God. Trust Him. I love you," Mom says.

"I love you, too."

We hang up.

"Talking with Mom wasn't as hard as you thought, was it?" Woody says.

"No. She made me feel better."

Woody nods and smiles.

"I need to call friends," I say. I think I can talk now. I learned I can say the "C" word.

Though I wonder how much talking it'll take to make breast cancer feel real, to accept that I'm now a statistic.

CHRISSY JACKSON

CHRISSY JACKSON is vice president of Florida Writers Association, vice president of Florida Writers Foundation, and president of Chrissy Jackson and Associates, Inc., a property management consulting firm. She has published over thirty non-fiction books and hundreds of magazine articles on customer service and real estate management. chrissyj@earthlink.net ~ www. chrissy-jackson.net

Photo during chemo taken by Michelle Korinko of Chicago.

Specter of Sam

My cousin and I strolled into the old section of Calvary Cemetery, the rusted gate creaking shut behind us. She headed left while I turned right, both of us seeking certain ancestral graves.

Faintly carved creek stones dotted the slopes. Many were tilted; others had broken off and lay hidden in the weeds. Still others were missing entirely. Ambling along, looking for the family name, my shoe caught the edge of a stone and nearly pitched me forward.

Muttering under my breath, I examined the piece of granite. And there it was; Uncle Sam's tombstone. Born 11 January 1871, died 25 January 1898. Only twenty-seven years old at his death. I knew from my genealogy research that there had been no death notice, obituary, or family Bible record giving a cause of death.

Though the stone's shape was plain, the ornamental carving showed the gates of Heaven. Based on my grandmother's tale so many years ago, I wondered about that carving. I sincerely hoped it had been the gates of Heaven that swung open to greet him.

With the sun beating down and the breeze sighing through the graveyard, my thoughts wandered back to my childhood days.

"It was the durndest thing," my grandmother had said one afternoon over her usual cup of coffee. We often sat and talked—my grandmother, my mother, and me. Of course, as a little girl I usually just drank my milk and listened. Grandma told fascinating ghost stories.

"We were visiting some cousins," she said. "This was my momma's sister's family, y'know. I remember somebody saying little Christine had seemed fine when they took her to Uncle Sam's funeral, except they noticed she was awful quiet. Folks notice things like that, if sometimes a little too late." She eyed me through her thick glasses when I gave a small sigh. I had heard this story before and knew what was coming.

I sat quietly at the table, my piece of gingerbread lying untouched beside my afternoon glass of milk. Mother glanced one of those motherly "just checking" glances at me before getting up for more coffee. She never approved of Grandma's ghost stories and maybe she thought I, like that other little girl, was being "awful quiet." So I picked up my slice of gingerbread and Grandma resumed her story.

"They said it was right after the family filed past the casket that Christine let out a shriek that would wake the dead. And then later she was afraid to go into a dark room."

"How do you know that, Grandma?" I prompted. It was the first time I had ever interrupted her story that I can recall, and it must have caught her off guard.

"Well, Lord, girl, I was there," she said. "It was Uncle Sam's funeral, like I said. It was late and the visitors had left. It was time to close up the house for the night but Christine didn't want to go into the dark. See, the house was laid out so you could go all the way around, from the kitchen to the parlor, the hallway, the living room and back again to the kitchen. The hallway door always let in a draft during the night and they had to shut the doors to the other rooms so the house wouldn't cool down too fast. It was still winter, you see, and it was her job to shut all the doors before going to bed."

Grandma paused, dunked her gingerbread in the hot coffee and slurped a bite. "I was just a kid, too, but I'll never forget. Y'know, in those days, friends and relatives used to go with the bereaved family to their house after a funeral, and some stayed the night because of the long ways home. Well, we were stayin' the night, and I sat there listening to her folks laughin' at the bang, bang, bang echoing through the house. It scared me, I can tell you, 'cause I didn't know what was going on. Then her mother led Christine up the stairs to bed. Then several weeks later we visited again."

Grandma paused to shove her eyeglasses up on her nose. They were always sliding down and she was forever pushing them up.

"Then what happened, Grandma?" I asked, already knowing the whole story.

"Well," she went on, "Christine and me played together all afternoon but about the same time of evening when supper was finished and we all sat around talking, her folks started saying it was time for her to shut the doors. It was her chore, after all, they said. They sat there, sorta chuckling. My mother either didn't understand or didn't remember from the last visit, and so she asked what was going on. Well, seems after Uncle Sam died, Christine thought his ghost followed her through the dark rooms. They had to coax her into doing the simple task of shutting the doors every night. And she had to do it. They'd keep at her until she did. In those days, children were taught to respect and obey their folks. So when she did it, they laughed at hearing her footsteps running from one room to the next, banging the doors behind her.

"See, what I remember of Sam was the shape of his face. It was long and sharp and looked like the paintings you see of the devil himself. Far as I know, there was nothin' ever happened with him, it was just the way he looked. But his looks scared her, I guess. This particular evening, her folks coaxed and coaxed and she just sat there looking kinda pale and afraid, and holding my hand tight. Well, I was a little older and I felt sorry for her, so I said we'd go together. I figured with two of us, and me being an outsider, if there was a ghost he'd leave us alone.

"I was wrong. The first room we went into was the old parlor where he'd been laid out. They did that in those days, y'know. Folks out in the country couldn't always get to the church and they didn't have funeral homes, so they used the house for visitation. Anyway, that night the smell of funeral flowers was real strong there in the parlor. The room was durn near pitch black, not even the moon shining from outside. We was about halfway through, tiptoeing across the worn rug, when I felt her stop and turn. She gave a little squeak and started racing toward the hall, holding tight to my hand and pulling me along. She had me believing she'd seen something and I just couldn't help it, I had to turn and look. Well, I wished I hadn't. He was there all right, Sam's evil-lookin' face shifting and wavering in the dark. His eyes glittered and he was grinning, like it was a great joke to scare the crap out of little kids.

"I can tell you, we both ran and kept running, slamming every door behind us as if that would stop the ghost from following. 'Course, it didn't. He was there until we got to the lighted kitchen where the adults were holding their sides and laughing their heads off, and us both standing there crying and shaking."

Grandma slurped her coffee and went on. "Guess it never occurred to them to find out if something really was chasing us. You'd think since I was scared, too, they'd figure something unusual was going on. But, no. Guess they thought Christine's imagination affected me, too."

My grandmother's tale sighed away on the warm summer breeze, leaving me staring down at the weathered stone. Such stories can make you wonder.

I shook my head at my own nonsense. My grandmother was a great story teller and no doubt she embellished a great deal. If the children had been frightened, I placed the blame where their parents had, on their own imaginations.

One thing about cemeteries—they're lonely and quiet. When I felt a tap on my shoulder I nearly jumped over the tombstone. Jerking around to look behind me, I half expected to confront the ghost of Sam. I laughed at myself. It was my cousin, full of apologies for startling me.

"Hey, you found Sam's grave," she said. "Did I ever tell you about Sam? My grandmother used to talk about how his ghost chased her when she was a little girl . . ."

CAROL A. JONES

CAROL A. JONES writes a twice-monthly column on behalf of Freedom Public Library in the *South Marion Citizen* newspaper; quarterly features in *Freedom's Flyer*, the Friends of the library's newsletter; and has completed two novels. View some of her work at www.jonesyworks.blogspot. com

Hope Everlasting

The phone rings. I answer.

"Mom?"

It's my eighteen-year-old daughter, Allie. My heart races. I take a deep breath. "Is everything alright?"

"Yeah, I guess." Her voice sounds doubtful. "I'm in Ybor City with Samantha and the other bridesmaids." Samantha is a school friend engaged to be married this summer. "We had lunch at the Columbia, sort of a bridesmaid bonding event. The food was really good. You should go there."

I wait, knowing there has to be more. My memory is scarred by phone calls like this. There was the phone call after her car was rear-ended exiting school. Another time, she was stranded on the interstate. The most unsettling were when she had an abusive boyfriend. The late night call came from a police station, her refuge after he became violent. Another, from a parking lot, her body bruised and battered, a new dent kicked in the fender of her car.

Allie continues, "We saw a homeless man. You know how sometimes the homeless make roses out of palm branches and sell them?"

"Yeah, my aunt and grandma used to make roses out of the palms we got on Palm Sunday. Go ahead, you were saying..."

"Well, this homeless guy had a bicycle with a basket full of the roses. He was selling them. When he took one to a car, a kid stole his bicycle. He tried running after him but the kid was faster."

I detect something in Allie's voice. "He... he couldn't keep up." She sounds choked, like she's fighting back tears. "He stopped running and just stood there, shaking his head. The kid stole his bike and all the roses. He's homeless. That's all he has." She starts to cry.

She's still there, the sweet sensitive child I used to know. She disappeared for a time when womanly beauty and popularity took over her persona. Recently, Allie has been all about the right look, hanging with the right crowd and making appearances in the right places with little concern for grades, religion, or doing the right thing. I'd been feeling like a failure as a parent.

"Oh, honey. What did you do?" I ask. "Did you give him money?"

"No." She sniffles.

I hear her friends laughing in the background trying to make light of the situation, probably disturbed by what they saw. I remember that she rarely carries cash. Instead, she uses her debit card and my credit card. I run through other options. The police wouldn't be helpful and it wouldn't be safe for a group of teenage girls to run a vigilante mission to find the thief in their flip flops and tank tops.

"Honey, I don't know what to say. I'm so sorry. Sometimes, life isn't fair." I wish I was there with her. I wish I had a million dollars. I wish I could buy the man a house. The story saddens and disturbs me, yet something in her despair lightens my heart.

As a parent, I had many aspirations for my child. Before I named her Alexandra, I looked up the meaning of the name: helper of mankind. I want a lot for my daughter, but mostly I want her to have compassion. I want her to spend her life trying to make a difference.

There's still hope.

Ruth E. Jones

RUTH E. JONES' stories have appeared in *The Healing Project's "Voices of" series*, *The St. Petersburg Times* and *Cup of Comfort for Adoptive Families*. Visit her website at www.ruthejones.com.

Castles and Kings

I pour the last of my late breakfast coffee into my cup. Need to get busy soon, take advantage of Presidents' Day off. Lots to do—weed the flowerbeds, catch up on laundry, and clean our bathrooms until they sparkle.

Our fourteen- and fifteen-year-old daughters straggle back into the kitchen to say goodbye. They're spending the day with friends.

"Be home in plenty of time for dinner," I say.

They roll their eyes. "We know the rules, Mom," the oldest says.

Their departure brings rare quiet. Our home is usually filled with loud music, ringing phones, girlfriends, and lately, moon-eyed boys. Life seems to revolve around their schedules rather than ours these days.

I sit with my coffee for a minute, enjoying the silence. A loud thumping shatters it—the front porch swing's hitting the house.

I go to the door and poke my head out. Our five-year-old Henry's slouched almost horizontally on the swing, his feet on the floor pushing the swing hard.

"What are you doing, young man?" I ask.

"I'm soooo bored," he says. "Katie and Deb have something to do. I don't."

"Why don't you play with Jason?" Jason lives three doors down. "Ask him to come here if you want."

"He went with his parents someplace."

My listing his favorite play-alone games brings headshakes.

"Tell me a story," he says, dropping into a puddle at my feet.

"Oh, honey, Momma has all kinds of chores to do."

He grins up at me. "Do them later, Mom. I love your stories."

"Okay, a short one. I need to get at least some things done today."

"Oh, boy!" He jumps up and hops back on the swing, making room for me. "Make it about knights in armor fighting fiery dragons. Leave out all the stupid girl stuff, though. No princess or people going to a ball in masks and dancing."

Ah, but the stupid girl stuff is my favorite part, I think. Elegant ladies wearing jewel-colored gowns and sparkling tiaras. Castle walls hung with tapestries woven from the finest silk thread. The rogue of a king, tall and handsome, kissing the hand of a scullery maid who's caught his eye. An ending that always goes "…and they lived happily ever after."

"Can I put in a wart-covered frog prince?" I ask.

Henry shakes his head. "No, 'cause then you'd have some stupid girl there to kiss him. No icky stuff."

I sigh in dramatic resignation. "Okay, you win," I say, and we high-five to seal the deal. "No icky girl stuff, only manly things like knights and dragons."

Settling against the swing's back pillow, I close my eyes and see the story unfold. It's an epic tale, one sure to capture the imagination of the most discriminating five-year old.

Smiling, I describe the kingdom envisioned in my head. A huge fortress of rough-hewn gray stone. Rafters in the great hall made from giant oaks. Thick battlement walls, bristling with hundreds of the king's finest archers preparing for the attack. Big black cauldrons of boiling oil ready to dump on the enemy below should they dare approach. Snorting stallions paw the ground in their stables. Knights in shining armor feast in the great hall, boasting of victory to come.

"Mom, get to the good stuff. You know, the battle and sword fights." Henry looks up at me, wide-eyed and eager.

"In the morning, the king's men practice their skills," I say. "The clang of sword against sword rings out across the courtyard." Henry wraps an arm around my waist, and we snuggle. I ruffle his blonde curls. "They need to be ready," I whisper into his hair. "The Black Knight plots evil." I lift Henry's chin and look into his face. "He wants to take over the kingdom."

"Don't let him!" Henry shouts, jumping to his feet. He grabs the old broom in the corner and waves it above his head like a mighty sword. "We must get all the lords from the far lands to help us!"

I, too, jump to my feet. "We'll send out our fastest horsemen with the message, sire. Pray their journey's successful."

Young Prince Henry nods and smacks a fist into the palm of his other hand, his lips pressed together. "They won't know what hit em."

We sit in the swing again. "The kingdom rang with the excitement of an historic imperative," I say. "The lords of the land have arrived, summoned to the king's aide." I look at Henry. "The knights are ready to leave, sire. Do you have any last commands?"

He shakes his head.

"The brave horsemen ride out through blistering heat. They ford raging rivers. They encounter a band of evil trolls in the north woods and battle for a whole day before they claim victory. They press on. They pass a castle, a fair damsel in the east tower waving her handkerchief at her young knight's dwindling figure—"

"Uh-uh, that's icky girl stuff," Henry says. "You promised not to do that, Mom."

"Wait! I'm not finished! A scaly green dragon swoops down on the castle and bites her head off."

Henry shouts, "Hooray! Off with her head! Chew it up and spit out her teeth!"

My darling little boy, I think, when did you become such a bloodthirsty tyke? Where did you get your love of battle? We never let you watch such things on TV. No gory video games are ever allowed though our door. Just where—?

Henry tugs my sleeve. "Mom, what's happening to the king and his knights?"

"Once again the brave king and his men battle onward."

Henry's tummy growls louder than a dragon's roar, and his hands go to his belly. "The warriors must have food," he says. "They grow weak and cannot hold their swords." He moans, sliding off the swing to the porch floor. "We need food and drink."

"Yes, my lord, at once."

I leave him brandishing his broom-sword at the encroaching foes and put together a kingly feast for both of us of peanut butter swirled with grape jelly on enriched white bread. Some raw carrots and an oatmeal raisin cookie—Henry's favorite—on each plate, and tall glasses of cold milk to wash it all down.

While we lunch on the porch swing, the milk on the side tables, Henry begs the story go on. Between mouthfuls, I describe the fierce battle that rages for three days. Henry eats in silence, entranced. After lunch, he leans his tousled head against me, his broom-sword forgotten at his feet. He struggles to keep his eyes open.

I slide my arm around Henry and pull him into my lap. I kiss the top of his head.

"Hey, no icky girl stuff, Mom," he mumbles but snuggles with a soft sigh.

I picture him grown, a young father with children of his own. I wonder if he'll take the time to tell stories. Will he weave tales of magical kingdoms and far away places? Will he sneak in a golden-haired damsel in distress, or will he still think girl stuff's icky?

Humming an old lullaby, I rock the swing back and forth, watching the day pass as I sit holding my youngest while he slumbers on my lap. He makes a laugh-like sound in his sleep, and I know he's dreaming of castles and kings.

Leaning down, I whisper in his ear. "And they lived happily ever after."

M. E. LANDRESS

M. E. LANDRESS wrote *Sour Grapes* and *One Bad Apple*, both part of the Marvella Watson series. She was editor and feature writer for *Cedar Key News* and now contributes to several local publications. See her work at: www.sourgrapes. mysite.com.

Published online in a longer version by "The Westside Story Contest" as 3rd Place Winner, 2006 Fiction Contest.

Broken Chains

Tears of joy stream down my cheeks tonight. For years I berated myself for my lackluster performance as a mother. I still know in my heart I should have done better. There ought to be an eight-hour exam one must pass verifying one's willingness to sacrifice all for your children before you are permitted to incubate an egg.

It would prevent the likes of Octo-mom, Casey Anthony, and Susan Smith. At twenty-two I still endeavored to conquer the world, to discover new lands, to sow my wild oats. Changing diapers, midnight feedings, and colic were not on my agenda. Sowing those wild oats brought a quick halt to my agenda and selfishly, I resented the loss of my freedom. My husband's selfishness topped mine; he abandoned us while the baby still grew in my womb. I muddled through the early years, regretting my lost opportunities. So wrapped up in my own little drama, I lost the chance to experience the awe, the wonder of watching a new life unfold before me—years and experiences now lost, never to be regained by either of us. This loss I regret and apologize for, it is why I consider myself a poor mother.

One day, I stood nose-to-nose with an angry son, high on drugs, cursing me for providing less than he desired. Where had the years gone? Why didn't I know this boy before me? His hopes and dreams, his deepest desires, all lost behind arguments over bedtime, messy rooms, and brushing his teeth. Sometimes the arguments centered on homework, Nike's versus generics, and unfinished chores. Where were the memories of success? Of obstacles overcome? When had I lost his love?

That day changed both our lives forever. I accepted my failure and searched for help. I found the Florida Sheriff's Youth Ranches. After multiple interviews and months of biting my nails, they finally accepted him into the program. The day he left for Live Oak we both cried tears of sorrow, loss, and pain. For two years they nurtured my son. He grew strong and valiant with four loving house parents and seven house brothers. They all worked together as a family unit, learning respect for each other, for those beyond their group, and ultimately for themselves. During this time I learned as well. I took parenting classes and workshops, shamed to realize all the years I'd wasted, years that can never be replaced.

∼

Upon his triumphant return, we began a new path together. His teachers loved his new attitude of "yes sir, no ma'am" and he easily graduated with great grades. It wasn't easy and there were numerous setbacks. Setbacks I wasn't sure how to overcome. When his stepfather was killed in a horrific motorcycle accident, my son spun out of control. Not long afterward I discovered he was hooked on prescription pills, a mood enhancing drug called Xanex. He began taking it to mask the pain of his grief and quickly became addicted. Lost in my own grief, I failed to notice the initial changes. The ensuing years became a struggle of ups and downs, failures and successes as we both fought our demons.

∼

After dropping out of college, he began a job and has never failed to work. Girls came and went but none he really adored. When he turned twenty-six he renewed a friendship with a high school lover. Aware of his addiction, she loved him enough to stand by his side and became his sentinel during his weaker moments. I am proud of his success against addiction, knowing of his constant struggle.

But now he has another reason to strive to succeed. Five months ago his wife bore him a daughter. The joy on his face as he held her in his arms gave me faith in his ability to overcome all odds. I regret that I missed that joy when he was born. The tears of joy I cry tonight are due to my realization that the chain has been broken. He will love and protect Jennifer June all the days of his life and she in turn will give him the reason to maintain his sobriety. I wasn't a complete failure after all.

DONA LEE

DONA LEE GOULD, Editor, Author, Book Store owner, leader of Florida Writers Association, Manatee. I write fiction and nonfiction. Currently editor of *Plotting Success*, a monthly newsletter for Sarasota Fiction Writers, an 80 member local writing group. I write for the local papers on writing and the art community.

Snips and Snails, and Puppy Dog Tails

Recently I joined a family of seven, six of the male persuasion. Now, raised in a small family with only two sisters, this has been a most awesome adventure. It seems there are some serious differences aside from those of the anatomical variety.

I have discovered boys can truly turn any object into a gun. At sunrise, the two youngest stumble to the breakfast table—one picks up a banana and bang, you're dead! The other boy, not to be outdone, quickly takes a few bites out of his pop tart, takes aim, and bang, bang…his brother's dead in an explosion of crumbs. And the fight begins. Escalating from slurs of "Shut up, you idiot, I killed you," gear up to punching and kicking when the shouting doesn't work. And shouting never works.

I'm rather baffled by it all, as no one ever wins either the shouting matches or the physical fights. From a girl's point of view it all seems so pointless.

And whoever labeled girls as moody never encountered a pack of boys. I've seen the younger ones go from sunny smiles to red-faced, door-slamming rage in less than fifteen seconds.

And etiquette? Forgetiquette! Sheets are used for drying off after a bath, towels are for snapping each other, and shampoo is for making bubbles in the bathtub. Toilet seats are the least of the problems. The brothers have yet to master the little lever on the tank for something called flushing.

Ten minutes after arriving home from school they have raided the kitchen for an afternoon snack. The spotless kitchen now looks like a bomb went off. Every dish is dirty, sixteen dirty cups litter the countertop, and at least one kid is hanging his head in the refrigerator complaining there's nothing to eat. With no clean surface remaining to do their homework, they drag their book bags out to the living room and spread out papers, books, charts, graphs, pens, pencils, and crayons across the floor and begin hounding their father for help with their homework.

Meanwhile, Dad's trying to find enough space on the stove to prepare dinner. Good luck with that. I leave the circus up to him as his experience in this arena far exceeds mine. Needless to say dinner is rarely on time—putting off bedtimes and creating cranky children.

If the circus sounds crazy, it is, but there is an upside too. Delays are occasionally caused when the family attends a banquet honoring one of them for deeds well done. They have many things to be proud of, and I enjoy watching their sheepish grins when one of them nails a performance, or learns to play a new song, or creates a phenomenal dessert, an amazing sculpture, or a provocative story.

Watching the love shine through when they hug their dad goodbye or follow in his wake like little ducklings behind papa duck, or see their enthusiasm when they beat the next level on a video game makes it all worthwhile.

Then at the end of the day, I realize these children will one day rule the world.

 # Dona Lee

DONA LEE GOULD, Editor, Author, Book Store owner, leader of Florida Writers Association, Manatee. I write fiction and nonfiction. Currently editor of *Plotting Success*, a monthly newsletter for Sarasota Fiction Writers, an 80 member local writing group. I write for the local papers on writing and the art community.

The List

Robert checked his front pants pocket. Good. It was there. His list. Right where he'd put it. That was a good sign. Maybe he'd stopped slipping. Maybe . . . maybe he wouldn't get any worse.

He pulled the list out. Only one item on it. Jewelry store. He knew when he woke up he had something important to do today. And this was it. The jewelry store.

He slipped into his boat shoes and looked at the bed. Kathleen was already up. He used to get up before her, but nowadays, she was out of bed first. He wanted to find her, make sure she was home.

He walked out of the bedroom. "Kathleen? Kathleen, where are you?"

She stood at the counter in the kitchen holding . . . the round blue thing. She turned and smiled. She was so beautiful.

"Good morning," she said. "How did you sleep?"

How did he sleep? What did she mean? "In the bed. You were there, too, Kitty. Then you got up. I slept in the bed."

She turned back to the round blue thing. A bowl. He remembered now. A bowl. He put his arms around her waist.

"You smell good," he said. I love you so much."

"Oh, Robert, I love you, too. I'm making blueberry pancakes. Your favorite."

His favorite? Yes, she was right. He loved blueberry pancakes.

She handed him something. "Here are the place mats and utensils. Will you set the table on the lanai?"

"Lanai?"

"The screened-in porch." She smiled and gestured with her head. "Right out there, through the sliders."

He took the rolled bundle she gave him onto the lanai. The Marco River was calm this morning, but the sky was gray. It could rain. He should check the boat. Make sure it was tied securely. Robert went to the screen door and turned the handle, but the door wouldn't open. He put the bundle down on the concrete and used both hands. The door still wouldn't open. Rusted probably.

He went back in the house toward the garage.

"Where are you going, Robert?"

"To the garage."

"The pancakes are almost done. Why don't you wait?"

"No, I need…." What did he need? He couldn't remember. He looked at her, but her back was to him. He went to her and put his arms around her waist in a hug. She felt warm against his chest.

~

Kathleen put the plate in front of him. He picked up the spoon and cut a bite of pancake.

"Wait, sweetheart. I heated the maple syrup, the way you like it. Shall I pour it for you?"

He shook his head. "I can pour it myself."

He poured the syrup and ate the pancakes and drank his coffee. He was supposed to do something. He couldn't remember what. He wasn't a surgeon anymore, so he wasn't scheduled to operate. He had something to do today, though, something special.

"More pancakes, Robert?"

He looked at his plate. It was clean. He shook his head. "No, I have to do something."

Kathleen stood to clear the dishes.

"Do you know what I have to do?" he asked.

"No. Today isn't your golf day. That's tomorrow. With Fred and Howard."

Fred and Howard. Two other doctors. Old friends. Golf. Good. He still played golf. He stood and looked at the river.

"That's it! The boat, I have to check the boat."

He tried the screen door. It still stuck. "And I have to fix the door. It needs oiling."

He started toward the house, but Kathleen put her hands on his arms.

"Andrew took the boat to the marina for servicing. It'll take a few weeks to get everything done."

Andy took the boat? His son Andy? "Did I ask him to? I don't remember."

"That's okay."

"Is it broken?"

"No. It just needs some maintenance."

"You're right, Kitty. We always had the Jenny Lynn serviced every year."

"Oh, Robert, you remembered the boat's name. You named it for Jen when she was a baby. Jenny Lynn, Andy's first little girl."

She hugged him tight. It felt so good. He put his hand on her breast and smiled. "Let's go to bed, Kathleen."

~

He woke up. Kathleen was still asleep. He remembered. Oh Lord, he remembered. Sweet Kathleen. His sweet Kathleen. He got up, picked up his trousers from the floor, and tiptoed from the room.

He put on his trousers in the kitchen, then reached into his pocket and pulled out the paper. Jewelry store. He had to go now. But where were his car keys? In the bedroom? What about Kathleen's? He looked around. Her purse was in the dining room. He found her keys. He held the paper and the car keys in one hand and went to the door that led to the garage. The door wouldn't open. He turned the knob again. And again. Mustn't wake Kathleen. But it wouldn't budge. He sat on a chair in the kitchen and put his face in his hands.

"Robert? I didn't hear you get up. What's wrong?"

He looked up. Kathleen stood in front of him, wearing her pink robe.

"I can't open the door."

"Do you need something from the garage?"

He nodded.

"What do you need?"

He shook his head. He hated this. "I don't know."

She knelt in front of him. "Let's check your list. It's in your hand. With my car— How did you—? Oh, you found my purse. Anyway, here, I'll

157

hold the keys. Do you want to show me your list?"

He handed her the list and the keys.

"Jewelry store?"

"Yes. I have to go now."

"Do you need to buy something?"

He looked at her and tried to think. "I can't tell you. It's a secret."

She smiled and rubbed his hand against her cheek. "After that nice lovemaking, I hope you don't have a girlfriend on the side."

He smiled back. Kathleen always made him smile. "You're my only girlfriend, Kitty. I have to go though, before . . . before I forget."

Kathleen stood. "Okay. Let me get dressed, and I'll drive you. Oh, the breakfast dishes. They can wait, I guess."

"I can drive myself. Give me the keys."

"I need to run some errands, too, Robert. I'll drop you at the jeweler's and then pick you up. That will work for both of us."

"No. I don't want you to drive me. I'll drive myself." He stood and held out his hand. "Give me back the keys."

She had a funny look. She didn't look like his Kathleen. "I can't do that, Robert. Doctor Wolfe said you shouldn't drive."

Dr. Wolfe? Who was Dr. Wolfe? "Why did he say that? I can see."

"Oh, Robert, I know. Your vision is fine. But, sweetheart, it's. . . it's your illness. The one that makes you forget things now and then. That's why you can't drive." She smiled. "But you're doing well. You have a medication that helps you. Look, here's your list. You remembered to write down the jewelry store. That proves how well you're doing."

"I want to drive."

He felt like crying. But men don't cry. Men drive cars.

Kathleen put her arms around him, and he cried. She cried, too.

Kate W. LeSar

KATE LESAR is a former health administrator and trainer. She has written numerous international training manuals for health care workers and currently designs and writes marketing materials for small businesses. She is working on her first novel.

Published in "Love is Ageless: Stories about Alzheimer's Disease," 2002

Non-Western Medicine

My pulse quickened when I heard the apartment door open. I knew it was silly of me to worry. Lu-Wen was only an hour late. But she'd been so sad lately, I longed to kiss her and try to bring back the smile I so missed.

I rushed to the hall where I stopped short. Her wide oval eyes stared unseeing into the hall mirror as if looking into the world beyond.

"What is it, honey?" I asked.

Lu-Wen turned, grabbing me with a tongue-thrusting kiss.

Pushing away to catch my breath I noticed a feral glow in her eyes. "Wow! What's going on?"

Instead of answering, Lu-Wen pulled me into the bedroom, tore off my clothes, and led me in wild passion, climaxing with her deep-throated primal scream. She fell immediately into a deep sleep. When I tried to wake her for dinner, she wouldn't budge.

The following morning at breakfast Lu-Wen's face held a benevolent smile.

"What's up?" I asked.

She ran her long painted nails down my arm. "You know how you've been urging me to see a physician? Well, I heard about a doctor from my country who just opened an office near campus. Dr. Oshee and Mr. Woo gave me my first treatment yesterday afternoon."

I smiled my encouragement. "It seems to have worked. Tell me more."

"Dr. Oshee is an old healer, the type I used as a child. Gosh, I feel like I've found a new lease on life."

Her happiness continued to grow as Lu-Wen kept regular appointments. A month later when Lu-Wen discovered she was pregnant with our first child, she insisted that Dr. Oshee was to be her obstetrician.

I had reservations. "What kind of medical training does Dr. Oshee have? Does she have hospital privileges?"

Lu-Wen smiled serenely. "I trust Dr. Oshee. She'll deliver me here in our home. Look, here're the prenatal vitamins she's started me on."

I examined the two bottles she took from her purse. One was a traditional prenatal vitamin. The other had foreign writing. I opened it and shook out a triangular green pill. It had a peculiar swamp-like odor.

After about a month I fished an empty medication bottle out of the trash and took it with one of the green pills to a friend, Tony Lee, a professor at the university.

"This is very peculiar writing," he said, examining the label. "I'll run it through the computer and have the lab analyze this pill. I'll get back to you."

When he called, Tony seemed both excited and confused. "According to our programmers, this writing has never been seen before. What's really weird, though, is the chemical analysis of the pills; unidentifiable compounds with lots of sulfur radicals. Where'd you say you got this stuff?"

When I confronted Lu-Wen in the kitchen that evening she burst into tears. "Dr. Oshee says my pregnancy is coming along perfectly! If you loved me you'd accept me for what I am."

I held Lu-Wen, stroking gently. "Honey, I love you very much. I just want the best for you and our child. Tell you what; I'll come with you on your next appointment and meet Dr. Oshee and Mr. Woo. Since you think so highly of them, I'm sure I'll be satisfied once we've met."

Lu-Wen tensed in my arms. She stepped away and busied herself wiping the kitchen counter. "I'm not so sure that's a good idea."

"Lu-Wen, if this doctor is going to be delivering my child here in my home I'd like to meet her beforehand."

She turned and looked into my eyes. "Darling, you must trust me. Our baby girl is growing just fine."

"How does Dr. Oshee know it's a girl?"

"Oh, it's always a girl."

I grabbed her by the shoulders and looked deep into her eyes. "What do you mean?"

Lu-Wen laughed nervously. "I didn't mean anything, darling. I just meant ... I just meant that I'm sure we're having a girl. Dr. Oshee said so. She is a doctor, after all."

I painted the nursery walls pink, forced into trusting a doctor I'd never met. I also prepared the master bedroom for our planned home delivery. Lu-Wen promised me delivery would be on her due date, so I stayed home from work that Tuesday. Sure enough, early that morning her contractions began.

Dr. Oshee drove up in a white windowless van. Yellow wrinkled skin stretched across her ancient face. In greeting, she ran her long red nails gently across my arm.

Mr. Woo towered seven feet, with strange flattened features and greenish scaly skin. He wore what looked like an oxygen tank on his back, with nose prongs bringing him sulfur-smelling gas. He piled equipment onto a dolly and wheeled the load into our bedroom. Side by side he set up two delivery trays and two basinets, one with a pink blanket, the other with a blue.

"Why are there two of everything?" I asked him.

He didn't answer, just stared down at me with green oval lidless eyes.

"Mr. Woo no speak," Dr. Oshee explained. "He Noo-bop."

"Oh. I ... I'm sorry," I said hesitantly.

"No worry. Not contagious."

Lu-Wen grimaced, holding her belly. "I think she's coming soon, Dr. Oshee."

Dr. Oshee set Lu-Wen up in the bed and handed gowns to Mr. Woo and me. I stood next to him, watching Mr. Woo staring at Lu-Wen in what I thought was a very inappropriate way.

"How is she progressing, Dr. Oshee?" I asked.

"Soon. She deliver baby girl three pushes."

Sure enough, a few minutes later baby Gabrielle entered our world, full black hair, powerful lungs, as beautiful as her mother, with the same huge oval eyes. Dr. Oshee cut the cord, wrapped her in the pink blanket, and handed her to me. I squatted next to Lu-Wen who stroked our baby lovingly.

"Oh, isn't she beautiful?" Lu-Wen cooed.

"Absolutely gorgeous," I agreed.

"Not done," Dr. Oshee said.

Lu-Wen grimaced and Dr. Oshee said, "Push! That it. Push again. Ahh. Now he come."

I turned to look and froze, watching Dr. Oshee deliver a second baby, a male, with green scaly skin. His pointed red tongue popped out.

"Wh ... What's that?" I choked.

Mr. Woo grabbed the baby, wrapping him in the blue blanket and cuddling him closely. Mr. Woo's pointed tongue stretched out and licked the thing, blowing his sulfur breath into the creature's nose.

"What's happening?" I asked feebly. "Is that Mr. Woo's baby? Please someone; tell me what's going on."

Lu-Wen took little Gabrielle and gave her a kiss. "What difference does it make, darling? Look, we have our baby. Isn't she beautiful?"

"Yes, of course! But you just delivered a green monster that another monster shows every intention of taking away with him. I demand an explanation!"

Dr. Oshee shook her head. "Told Lu-Wen. Should warn."

"Yes," I insisted. "You should have told me. Look, I don't care if my boy has some strange disease, but if he's my son I intend to raise both him and my daughter."

"That not possible," Dr. Oshee said. "Baby Noo-bop no can live on Earth."

"On Earth? You mean ... you're all Martians?"

Lu-Wen laughed. "No, silly. We're not from Mars. We were all born on Earth." Then she sighed. "But I do miss Noo-bop. Wait 'til you see it, darling! The flowers are gorgeous! The orange mountain canyons are magnificent. And the purple sunset will take your breath away."

"You ... you're an alien? But ... you're so human?"

Lu-Wen blushed. "Thank you, darling. I'm a half-breed. You see, all the Noo-bop women died in a terrible plague. The only way we half-breeds can birth is to produce two children, a half-breed girl, like Gabrielle, and a Noo-bop male. It's the only way the species can survive. Please understand, Darling. You can tell, just like me, Gabrielle will grow up seemingly human."

"The women live on Earth and the men on Noo-bop?"

"I knew you'd understand. You're Gabrielle's true father and Little Larry's stepfather. Little Larry has to live on Noo-bop, but we'll visit him there."

What could I say? I loved Lu-Wen. I loved Gabrielle. And, I suppose, I loved Little Larry.

So here I am, back from our two-week vacation on Noo-bop. Larry's five years old now, and a strapping young Noo-bopian. Here's his picture in his Bop-ball outfit. Isn't he a good looking kid?

PHILIP L. LEVIN

PHILIP L. LEVIN serves as president of the hundred-member Gulf Coast Writers Association, Gulfport, Mississippi. Published works include the best-selling murder mystery *Inheritance,* the children's fable *Consuto and the Rain God,* and editing of two GCWA anthologies. His next work will be non-fiction *Thirty Years as an E.R. Doctor.* www.gcwriters.org/inheritance.htm

Demise of the Tooth Fairy

The magic of childhood was threatened this afternoon.

"Mom," my seven-year-old said, "there's really no tooth fairy, is there?"

My eyes glazed over and I kept typing, stalling for time, incoherent words filling my computer screen. I thought of the health fair I went to last week and the little plastic baby-tooth holders I brought home for the kids. Kids who believe in magic. Kids who get excited about leaving a tooth under their pillows for the tooth fairy.

"Mom, how do you do it? I sleep on the teeth. Do you come in at night and take them?

Do you leave the money?"

My mind raced, envisioning anger and tears. I didn't want to let the tooth fairy go yet.

I turned to look into the blue eyes that yesterday saw magic everywhere. "Why do you say that, babe?" I asked.

Kira didn't back down. She straightened her little body to its full height, crossed her arms, and looked at me. I felt my cheeks flame under her interrogator stance.

"I think you do it," she said. "I think you take the tooth and leave the money for us."

My mind scrambled for words. Kira locked her eyes onto mine and deepened her voice to replicate my 'I mean business' tone. "Tell me the truth. Are you the tooth fairy?"

I took a breath and nodded.

Kira dropped her arms. Leaning toward me, she put her hands on my shoulders, stood on tiptoes, and kissed my forehead.

Then she smiled, and the sun came out again.

Kira skipped out of my office to go back to play with her friend and their menagerie of stuffed cats and dogs.

I couldn't move. Tears ran down my face. My little girl's growing up, I thought. The tooth fairy's gone, and Santa's next.

But—I smiled—the love behind them is still here.

That's magic enough.

KAREN L. LIEB

KAREN LIEB has had articles and photographs published in numerous magazines, websites, and newspapers. She is FWA's conference photographer and the Melbourne Writer's Group webmaster. Karen serves as President of Florida Writers Foundation (FWF), a 501(c)(3) non-profit corporation dedicated to promote literacy and writing skills. For more info, visit www.karenlieb.wordpress.com.

Dolls for Our Babies

We had the perfect number in our family—four. Dad (Don), mom (me), son (Joey), and daughter (Kira).

A couple weeks before Christmas three years ago, our friend Bruce called. He'd recently married, and he and his wife Ellen wanted to visit. Great idea, especially since we all loved to play card games. Ellen got on the phone. She asked if I thought the kids would like ragdolls.

Thinking back to the beautiful dolls my grandmother made by hand, I said, "I think they'd be a hit. I'm not sure about Joey, unless you have a funny-looking one, but Kira, definitely."

"Wonderful!" Ellen said. "We'll bring some with us, and your kids can choose a couple."

Bruce and Ellen arrived with a semi-closed cardboard box they put on the floor. After Don and I exchanged hugs and greetings, Ellen told us to call our children to the living room so they could pick out their ragdolls.

"Kids," I yelled, "Bruce and Ellen have presents for both of you. Come on and pick yours from the box."

The kids came running and stared at the box Ellen kneeled beside. She opened it and, smiling, tipped it gently.

"Kittens!" Joey said.

"Mom!" Kira squealed. "I love them!"

Three of the critters made for the Christmas tree and climbed it. Two scattered to who-knows-where, and two went to charm my children. Someone, not the ones with the kids, meowed loudly.

"They're cats! You brought cats!"

"Yeah, Ragdoll kittens," Ellen said. "I asked if that was okay. What did you think I was talking about?"

"Dolls! Dolls made out of fabric. These are live critters, and they're everywhere!"

Crash! The tree fell over.

"Mom, help!" Joey yelled from under it. Two hands flailed in the branches, and a sneakered foot peeked out, tangled in a light string.

Don, Bruce, and Ellen righted the tree. Joey lay sprawled on the floor, ornaments all over him, a kitten licking his face. "Mom, this one likes me! He's the one I want!"

Ohmygosh. These are cats. Real live baby cats, and the kids think they are going to get to keep a couple.

Bruce and Ellen rounded up the kitten herd and put them back in the box. Don and I looked at each other.

Kira found the loud meower stuck inside a Christmas stocking that had somehow fallen off the mantle, ending up behind the couch. She held the pink-nosed white kitten to her face, rubbing it against her cheek.

"Mama, I like this one. I'll name her Daisy."

Don arched an eyebrow at me. "We've been had, had, had," I said under my breath.

～

Three years later, Zoom still climbs things, and Daisy still gets herself into places she can't find her way out of. And they chase each other all over the house, knocking stuff over constantly.

But that's okay. They're family.

KAREN L. LIEB

KAREN LIEB has had articles and photographs published in numerous magazines, websites, and newspapers. She is FWA's conference photographer and the Melbourne Writer's Group webmaster.

The Best Damn Radioman

"I want to go home!" he demanded, sounding more like a four-year-old than an octogenarian.

I knew that Dad would never go home, but I also knew he could not possibly comprehend the fact that he was losing his battle with an enemy called Alzheimer's.

It was hard enough to watch my father grow old. It was heartbreaking to see a man who was once brilliant and accomplished forced into a nursing home by this baffling disease.

Dad had conquered enemies before. During World War II he successfully completed thirty-five intense missions with the 390th Bomb Group. On their twenty-first mission, their plane, Cocaine Bill, was shot down in Belgium. Luckily, they suffered no casualties and landed in an area that had just been taken from the Germans.

Now he was reduced to a single bed in a stark room at the end of a dark, lonely hallway, surrounded by fragile souls who were also ravaged by constant confusion. Sometimes his inability to remember what was happening from moment to moment was a blessing in disguise. My father kept asking what hospital he was in and to my way of thinking that beat knowing he was locked in an Alzheimer's unit. I just couldn't deprive him of the hope of returning home.

As is typical with many patients, he could recall certain things clearly, especially things about his past. Unfortunately he seemed to remember his regrets with particular clarity.

"You know I washed out of pilot's school," Dad said, temporarily forgetting his request to go home. After his dream of becoming a pilot was shattered, he trained to become a radio operator and joined the war effort as a Radio Operator-Gunner on a B-17. He had always spoken with great pride about his team, made up of young men with nicknames like Snake, Hap, Tex and Dixie. All of them had been forced to grow up too fast.

Although he didn't talk too much about the war when I was a child, I remember how he described their missions as "terror over the skies of Germany." He said he always knew when they were going on a particularly dangerous bombing mission because their four a.m. eggs would be fresh ones, instead of the usual powdered ones.

My young mind had trouble taking in the few details he shared with me, like the fact that it was seventy degrees below zero outside the plane and sometimes "all hell was breaking loose" on the other side of Dad's little window. He once told me he would never forget "that awful smell"—a mixture of fear, gasoline and gunpowder.

My father wore his inter-plane radio in one ear and received messages from the 8th Army Air Force in the other ear. In the midst of all that the Radio Operator-Gunner had to fire a machine gun when enemy fighters approached as well as literally kick the bombs out of the plane.

Again he repeated, "I washed out of pilot school."

I didn't want him to focus on the one thing he considered his real life failure, so I said, "Dad, you were the best damn radioman in the Army Air Force."

"Where did you hear that?"

"From your crew. The pilot even told me that when we went to your bomber group reunion. They all said you were the best damn radioman ever."

It took timing and a sense of rhythm, plus a great memory to be an efficient radio operator, and Dad had all of those skills. It was quite challenging to remember the transmissions and decipher the coded messages quickly, particularly since the codes changed each day.

"I wanted to be a pilot," he whispered.

"If you hadn't become a radio man on that B-17, your crew probably wouldn't have made it through the war."

"I don't remember that!" he said with a scowl.

I had become better acquainted with some of the surviving members of Dad's crew over the last several years. Dixie had told me the story about my father saving the entire squadron from the distinct possibility of being shot down. We all heard about Dad's washing out of pilot school, but we had never heard about his being a hero. In fact, until Dixie informed me about the incident and the story Dad had written about their brush with death, I hadn't known anything about that harrowing day.

When I discovered the story I read and reread it, soaking up all the details that my father so carefully included, like the fact that weather, enemy fire, equipment failure and post-mission fatigue could make the return trip extremely dangerous. Many times, some of the B-17s would be so crippled that they had to ditch in the North Sea.

"You were coming back from a bombing mission over Chemnitz in February of 1945. Remember Dad?"

I reminded him of the story he had written many years before, A Close Encounter. In it, my father described how their lead operator had turned off his radio like many others in their squadron. When the mission was over they thought they could relax, even though turning off their radios was against orders. But Dad knew those orders were for a reason and in his story he wrote, "The only communication between aircraft was the radio and only essential messages were allowed. But those messages were crucial for the survival of the entire bomb group."

My father wrote that the radio suddenly "crackled alive and a new route for England was given to the entire group." If they followed the original route back to their home base, they were going to encounter massive fighter attacks. Dad tried in vain, but couldn't raise the lead operator. He had to do something. They were about to fly into heavy fire. A twenty-two-year-old kid from South Texas realized that it was up to him to save his comrades from probable death.

"Remember, you took down the entire message in your log in code, and then quickly decoded it."

"Oh yeah," he recalled. "I was good at that. I had a knack for decoding things pretty fast. You had to be able to concentrate with a lot of distractions too."

I had gotten used to Dad's jumbled memories, but it still amazed me that he could recall key facts about his stint on a Flying Fortress sixty years earlier while he could not tell me what century we were living in or the name of the current president. It didn't matter. All that mattered at this moment was the fact that he was remembering something positive about his past.

"You got the emergency information to your pilot, Jack Bouton. He called Lt. Kenny in the lead ship with the vital message and he immediately changed the return route."

"He was a great pilot and leader. He saved the day," Dad sighed.

"No, Dad, you saved the day. If you hadn't been so vigilant, think how many men could have died that day."

I knew that on two previous missions they suffered heavy casualties, losing almost 120 airmen. This could have been even more disastrous, but because Dad hadn't logged out, he heard the frantic call to change routes and their trip home was a safe one.

I patted his withered hand, the same one that used to feel so big and strong to me when I was a child. He wrapped his fingers around mine.

"You see, you were the best damn radioman."

He closed his eyes and smiled. He began to relax his grip on my hand and seemed to drift off to sleep. For a few minutes my father's life was peaceful again, free from the anxiety of being trapped in a mind full of scattered thoughts that came and went like leaves in the wind.

Suddenly he squeezed my hand and opened his eyes.

"You know what? I was the best damn radioman in the Army Air Force during the war. They say I probably saved the whole squadron. Do you want to hear about what I did?"

"Yes, Dad," I answered, choking back the tears. "I'd love to hear the story about the best damn radioman."

MELINDA RICHARZ LYONS

MELINDA RICHARZ LYONS earned a B.A. in journalism from the University of North Texas. Her work has appeared in many magazines, and she is the co-author of *WOOF: Women Only Over Fifty* (Echelon Press). For more see www.woofersclub.com.

Exceptional Love

Kay stood at her Bronx apartment's kitchen window overlooking a park. Couples strolled arm in arm, and children played in the fallen leaves.

It was October 1946.

Without turning, she said, "A month ago, there was no problem. Why all of a sudden has one come up?"

"I don't know, honey," her husband Jim said. "All I know is that it's something they won't tell us over the phone. That's why the appointment Tuesday. To discuss it."

Tears slid down Kay's face. "We've prepared for months, thinking everything was okay. I can't imagine.... Oh, Jim, I'm worried."

Jim took her in his arms. "Everything will work out. It's probably nothing."

The couple married, for the times, late in life, both twenty-eight when they took their vows eleven years ago in October, 1935.

They'd met at the newspaper where they worked, Kay a secretary, Jim the pressroom manager. Fellow employees urged them to date, saying they'd make the perfect couple, both of them kindhearted, fun-loving, and Catholic.

Once wed, Jim and Kay immediately tried to produce a baby. Several of their friends were childless. These friends accepted their fate. Jim and Kay, though, refused to accept a future without children. Children held a special place in their hearts, their desire to nurture a family stemming from events in each of their lives years before they met.

When Jim was ten, he and his younger brother and sister were placed in an orphanage. Their father had lost his job and, in the ensuing months, drank himself to death, leaving a wife and three children and debt. With no means to feed and clothe her youngsters, Jim's mother had no choice but to place them in an orphanage. She yearned for the day she'd return and bring them home.

Two years later, Jim's mother did return to bring Jim and his brother home. Their sister, though, had been adopted, and nothing could be done to get her back. Jim's mother, a domestic, toiled tirelessly to support her boys. Jim, resolute to contribute, found work at a newspaper and dropped out of school at thirteen. He spent his spare time searching for his sister.

Kay's family was more fortunate than Jim's. Her father was a doctor, his office in his home. Because of his expertise in infectious diseases, tuberculosis patients flocked to him. TB, the number one killer in New York during the 1920s, primarily infected the poor. Kay's father turned away no one and never demanded payment from those unable to pay for his services. He earned enough, he said, from patients who could pay to provide for his family. Though he couldn't afford to hire a nurse.

Following graduation from high school, Kay assisted her father. She witnessed the death of many children, praying nightly for them, pleading with her God to stop taking them.

A year later, fatigue weakened every muscle in her body. And she spit up blood, signaling a severe case of tuberculosis. There were no drugs to combat the disease, the only known cure fresh air, rest, and good nutrition. Kay's mother cultivated a garden full of vegetables and pureed them for Kay's meals. Kay's sister took Kay roller skating, weather permitting, every day. Bed rest consumed the remainder of her hours. She continued to pray for all who had succumbed to TB, and for her family, asking her God to watch over them should she die.

Seasons came and went and finally, two years from the onset of the disease, so did the fatigue and coughing. Her father said she'd fully recover. Every morning thereafter, Kay attended mass at St. Francis of Assisi, praying for the families affected by tuberculosis.

In 1943, eight years after their marriage and hope for a pregnancy fading, Jim enlisted in the U.S. Army. He didn't want to leave his wife, but the war stories he printed made him feel useless.

Kay's dream for a family dwindled when Jim left, the void inside her more agonizing each day. With no husband or children to care for, she joined the Women's Auxiliary Army Corp, her assignment, driving an ambulance. When a ship carrying injured soldiers docked, Kay picked up the soldiers and took them to area hospitals.

Kay didn't hear from Jim often. When she did, she cried for days. He'd been stationed at an ammunition depot in England, a prime enemy target.

One day after delivering a soldier to the hospital, she bumped into a doctor she'd last seen at her father's funeral. They struck up a conversation. Dr. Levin, an obstetrician, knowing Kay had married a while ago, asked if she had children. When she answered, "No, despite years of trying," Dr. Levin suggested she make an appointment to see him.

The following week, Kay sat on an examining table waiting to hear Dr. Levin's findings. When the door opened, Kay noted the doctor's absent smile.

"I'm afraid I have no solid explanation as to why you've not conceived," he said. We know the chances of conceiving diminish with age, but we don't know all the long-term effects of TB, and it's possible the disease damaged your reproductive organs. Because you're approaching thirty-eight, I recommend you adopt." He smiled. "Adoption requires an exceptional kind of love not everyone's capable of, Kay, but I think you, and from what I've seen of Jim, are excellent candidates. If you're interested, speak to Sister Mary at the Foundling Home downtown, and be sure to tell her I'll provide a reference."

Although saddened at knowing she'd probably never conceive, Kay knew before leaving the doctor's office she wanted to adopt.

But would Jim?

She didn't write him about her visit with Dr. Levin. Jim's last note said, General Eisenhower, personally, promoted me. He's sending me into occupied Germany to build a Stars & Stripes newspaper plant.

Because occupied Germany meant danger, and the Women's Auxiliary warned of the consequences of sending anything but good news overseas, Kay had to wait for Jim's return.

Ten days before their tenth wedding anniversary, the war in Europe over, Jim walked down the ship's gangplank. Kay ran to him and jumped into his arms.

Kay waited two weeks to share the information she received from Dr. Levin. She held her breath a long time while Jim digested it all, almost three whole minutes. Then a smile spread wide across his face.

"I'd love to adopt," he said, "and I can see from the joy in your eyes that you want to, too."

They met with Sister Mary at the Foundling Home and commenced the long adoption process. The anticipation of beginning a family filled them with excitement, and they bought a crib, bottles, diapers, everything they'd need to care for their newborn.

Then they waited.

On Tuesday, appointment day, Jim and Kay sat across from Sister Mary.

"You applied for adoption a year ago," the sister said. "At that time, we promised you a baby in approximately a year, from parents raised as Catholics. We can generally fulfill this promise because the majority of our unwed mothers are Catholic. The young men involved, too, are usually Catholic. But lately we seem not to be experiencing the norm, and it's possible it could take another year for us to find a match for you. Unfortunately, both of you turn forty next year, and the Foundling Home does not place babies with anyone forty years and older."

Jim and Kay looked at each other.

"However," Sister Mary said, "we have an adorable three-week old baby girl available. Her mother is Catholic." Sister Mary paused. "Her father is Jewish."

Kay leaped out of her chair. "Her father's heritage makes absolutely no difference to us!"

Jim stood and turned his wife to him, his grin wider than Kay had ever seen it. "We are going to have a baby!"

Sister Mary radiated delight. She, too, stood. "And if you want, you can take her home today."

The couple wept. They laughed.

Holding hands, all three sent up a prayer of thanks.

At long last, Jim and Kay brought home the child with whom they could share their love. They named her Karen.

They had a family.

LINDA McGOWAN MALLOY

LINDA MALLOY is a graduate of Cardinal Cushing College and also of Sacred Heart University, where she was inducted into the National Continuing Education Honor Society. She just completed her first children's chapter book, Miss Snapperfin, Memories. Born in the Bronx, married with two children, she resides in Sarasota, Florida.

A Novel Approach to Life

November 2008.

"Yale?"

My Italian Greyhound usually races to greet me, his feet stampede-like across the tiled floor, but today the house was quiet.

I found him on the bedroom floor beside a tangle of sheets, pillow-cases, blankets, and comforter. He looked at me with worried eyes.

"Oh, Yale," I said, reaching down to pet him and let him know everything's okay, "you stripped the bed again."

The messed-up room meant someone had rung the bell while I was at work. I opened the front door, and sure enough, UPS had been there and left a package. When I picked it up, a tingling shot up my arm. It was addressed to my daughter.

I put the package on the hall table and walked away.

Later that evening, thinking, You're going to have to open it sooner or later, I went to the package and looked at the return address. Tears filled my eyes as I unwrapped the box and pulled the acrylic trophy from its bubble wrap.

"Oh, Amanda," I said, "your book award is lovely."

I cradled it against my heart and took it to Amanda's bedroom to place it beside her urn.

~

Twenty-two months earlier.

A special bond can exist between a single mother and her only child, their reliance on each other bordering on co-dependence. We were inseparable. When Amanda played on her school's volleyball and basketball teams, you could find me on the game bus or in the stands doing the stats. When she interviewed entertainers for the regional magazine she freelanced for, she took me along to meet the stars like Jerry Seinfeld, Duran Duran, Billy Squire, and Jethro Tull. When she pursued her master's degree at Wake Forest University in Winston-Salem, North Carolina, I moved from Tampa to Winston-Salem to be nearby.

Amanda had been diagnosed with lupus at age seventeen, and after two decades of battling the disease, it spread to her kidneys, and the diagnosis was end-stage. My initial reaction was to give her a kidney, but the nephrologist said they wouldn't consider me because I was overweight. For twenty years, I'd topped the scales at two hundred ten pounds, but that day I vowed to lose the weight.

For the next seven months, while Amanda endured tests to obtain authorization for a transplant, I tackled an aggressive diet and exercise regime. By the time she was put on the national transplant list, I had lost eighty pounds. I could donate my kidney.

But our blood types didn't match.

Hope left, and fear moved in.

Amanda grew weaker and weaker, no longer able to accompany our Yale and me on evening walks around the block. To keep her involved, I came back with reports of what the neighbors were up to, embellishing to provide much needed comic relief. To my delight, she found inspiration in these tales and used them to write a humorous murder mystery, filling her long hours confined to bed.

That the book was published the day after my birthday thrilled her. She presented me with the Advance Reader's Copy, laughing. "You've always loved Judy Bolton and Nancy Drew, so this book is my gift to you."

Her health worsened, and our small family became a partnership, learning how to set up and administer peritoneal dialysis at home.

She was now confined to bed ten hours a night. Fifty-box shipments of solution arrived monthly. I stacked them in the living room. In December, we arranged the boxes into a pyramid, draping them with strings of red and green lights. Amanda's IV pole held a wreath and stocking. Presents surrounded our makeshift tree. We took pictures, turning them into Christmas cards for patients at the dialysis center. Our house lost some of its oppressive hospital feel.

Amanda become so fond of her twin heroines, she penned a sequel, writing while hooked up the dialysis machine.

"I wished as a child I'd been born an identical twin," she told me. "So one of my characters has my traits before I got sick and the other my personality after I got sick—more serious and cynical."

Her personality traits, even down to her fondness for sock-monkey pajamas, can be found throughout her novel.

We spent evenings in critique sessions, discussing what worked and what needed a rewrite. They were special times of togetherness, and we laughed a lot over the quirky characters and their antics.

When Amanda scheduled a book signing at the South Tampa Barnes & Noble, I evolved from proofreader and critic to publicist, exploring ways to advertise the event. I arranged for the Tampa Tribune to do a feature story and photo shoot of her writing the sequel in her sock-monkey pajamas while on dialysis. They invited her to the Tribune's office to record a reading of her novel's first chapter for Tampa Bay Online.

Her book signing at Barnes & Noble was her last event, a truly memorable adventure together.

~

Today.

I struggled for nearly a year after Amanda died to find a way to say good-bye. Then one day I realized it wasn't really necessary.

I can go to the library and see her in the stacks, her picture with Yale on her novel's back cover. I can visit her at Barnes & Noble on the shelves in the mystery section. I can feel her tireless creativity when I hold the literary award she received posthumously.

And when solitude closes in, I can listen to her reading her novel's first chapter on TBO.com.

Chapter One, 17514 Quail Court. Steve Shelley wasn't much of a man. He beat his wife, exposed himself to the female neighbors, and drank like a fish. Oh, and did I mention that his idol had become the sadist across the street? So it was a sad day for Steve the morning he stepped out of his two-story traditional house, walked down his recently pressure-washed driveway, bent over to retrieve his newspaper, and upon looking up, found himself staring into the vacant eyes of his hero.*

Excerpt from A Beautiful Day in the Neighborhood

TONI MARTIN

TONI MARTIN provided publicity and marketing support for the 2008 award-winning novel *A Beautiful Day in the Neighborhood,* along with editing magazine and newspaper articles by the local author. Visit the FWA Wesley Chapel writers group leader at http://www.ntwcwriters.blogspot.com and http://www.publishedauthors.net/amandalouisemartin.

Down the Altahama to Darien

Miss Evelyn opened the screen door and stepped out on the porch. "You'd best come inside now."

"It ain't hardly dark, and I ain't ready."

"You know what the damp air does to your bones."

"They're my bones, ain't they?"

"Well, I'm the one who has to take care of you."

Miss Evelyn waited as if looking for a reply, but when none came, she went inside and let the screen door slam.

Lamar Williams sat in one of the rockers on the nursing home's front porch, looking out at the broad expanse of brown water across the road. He could almost feel the river's motion, almost hear the men's voices, the logs creaking. Darkness blended the river into the sky before Lamar stood.

"Just once more," he said aloud without realizing it. "If I could just go down the Altamaha one more time."

It became Lamar's habit to sit on the porch each evening, waiting for darkness to claim the river, Just once more a mantra in his head. A mantra the Altamaha seemed to sing to him.

Lamar had spent his life on the Georgia Rivers—the Oconee, the Ocmulgee, and the Altamaha—running rafts of timber down the water to Darien. Days on the rafts in blazing sun or sleet or rain or cold, and nights under the stars when the moon made the river a trail of silver, or moonless times when the blackness so enshrouded, he could hardly breathe. The stories he could tell of river men and alligators in taverns in Darien. But no one in the nursing home cared about Lamar's stories.

It was a small nursing home, most of its residents prissy old women. His roommate had been a lawyer. Lawyers. What did they know about rivers and timber rafts. Lamar was grateful that at least the nursing home was on the river.

Miss Evelyn had given up nagging at him, her last words about it, "If you want to sit there and aggravate your rheumatism, go ahead."

Every year at the end of April, the park three miles upriver celebrated Heritage Day. They put up an old moonshine still, and some of the older women demonstrated the making of hominy and lye soap. The blacksmith set up a little forge and made the old tools, and a small replica of a timber raft that floated the logs down river was tied up at the bank. Miss Evelyn was taking the nursing home residents who were well enough to the celebration.

The night before the festival, she instructed those going to assemble on the front porch at 9:45 to wait for the van.

Lamar Williams was up at first light. He put on jeans and a denim jacket. He'd taken sandwiches from last night's supper. They were tied up in his red bandana, and now he retrieved the bandana from under his bed where he'd stashed it and took his straw hat from the closet shelf. His roommate the lawyer snored noisily as Lamar cautiously opened their door. He scanned the hall and saw no one. Lamar staggered a little trying to place his steps silently, but he made the front door without detection and stepped into the misty dawn air.

It took him more than two hours to walk the three miles to the park. It's funny, he thought. Yesterday my legs was just a-aching, and today I don't feel no pain.

He found the raft right where he knew it would be. It was a lot smaller than the rafts he'd ridden so many times, but it was complete with steering gear and a small canvas shelter. It would do. He stowed his bandana under the shelter and was just untying the raft when the sheriff and his deputy drove into the park.

"That crazy old coot's fixing to go down river on that raft," the sheriff said.

"Shall I go git him?" the deputy asked, getting half out of the car.

"Leave him be," the sheriff said. "That's Lamar Williams, and I reckon he's goin' down the river one last time."

Lamar howled with glee when he shoved off into the Altamaha's current. He passed out of the boundaries of the park. He passed the landmark oak at the bend of the river. When he passed the nursing home, Miss Evelyn was on the front porch with the residents waiting for the van.

Lamar doffed his straw hat and waved it in wild circles above his head.

He waved it all the way down the Altamaha to Darien.

MURIEL McKINLAY

MURIEL MCKINLAY, a veterinary technician, left Connecticut for the life of a "lone woman" in the heart of rural Georgia. Her Georgia stories document the strength, integrity and simple dignity of the people who became "her folks." Her nature column and articles have been published as well as poetry.

The Scrapbook

June 1, 2005.

I step off the WestJet flight from Toronto, Canada and enter the crowded Tampa International Airport. I'm looking for someone I may or may not recognize who may or may not recognize me. Thirty years is a long time. "I'll be wearing a green shirt," he told me. Somehow that did nothing to quell the butterflies in my stomach.

June 4, 2005.

A park bench overlooking Sarasota Bay. A marina filled with luxurious yachts, but what catches my eye is a tiny white boat named "L'il Biscuit" anchored near shore a few yards from me. The palms are swaying in the evening breeze. The water is a floating veil of peach and rose and golden silk. The domes of the high-rise condos along the shore are burnished bronze. His words sound as natural as the bird-song in the hibiscus and jasmine along the path we have just strolled. "I want to marry you." The man in the green shirt has just proposed to me.

March 1, 2006.

I think back to the tiny white boat in the harbor. How intimidated it must have felt in the presence of all the large sail-boats and glamorous yachts surrounding it. Yet there it was anchored bravely in the Bay. I hear the minister say: "I now pronounce you man and wife."

I am immediately anchored in this new land nearly two thousand miles away from all whom I love and all that I cherish, except for the man in the green shirt.

I am still a little dizzy with the newness of my surroundings. The long trail through a maze of immigration papers has finally granted me the status of a "resident alien."

"Alien" is what I feel when I have to go about establishing my new identity with proof of all the things I took for granted for years. Driver's license, bank cards, library privileges. Election Day I have to sit home with no right to vote because I am not yet a citizen.

March 1, 2009.

Another flight is arriving from Canada. My husband and I scan the passengers arriving at the gate. Our faces light up when we see them, the young couple with the little girl in pigtails and the little boy wearing a green shirt. We step forward to embrace my daughter, her husband and little Rachel and Joshua.

"Mommy, can I stay with Grampie while you go get our bags?" Joshua is already clutching my husband's hand.

"Mommy, give Nana her gift!" Rachel looks up with big blue eyes full of excitement. "Later, honey." Mom smiles.

March 2, 2009.

We've had a wonderful day at Disney and been to the beach to build sand-castles and hunt for shells. The "Northerners" are losing their pallor already and glowing through their suntan lotions. The children fall fast asleep with their stuffed dolphins tucked beside them. We settle in to comfortable sofas to unwind and catch up on news. My daughter pulls a carefully wrapped gift from her luggage and passes it to us.

The gift was a scrapbook. In elegant form on the first page Paula had inscribed: "My gift of love to you both." The page is decorated with antique hand-tatted lace doilies. They were mementos from a century-old farmhouse by the Bay of Fundy we'd had as a summer home when she was a child. We'd had several changes of city residences over the years but the farmhouse was the source of our happiest times together and she, along with her sister and two brothers, had always considered it "home."

I had given Paula the lace ten years ago at a time when I had to let go of much that represented our traditional family life. When a marriage is broken, either by death or divorce, the family patterns, delicate and fragile as lace, have to be rewoven. In the initial unraveling, one is never certain if the process will succeed or fail. Paula smiled when she knew I recognized the lace. Our eyes told each other that, despite the hurdles, we'd made it.

In the following pages of the scrapbook Paula had chronicled, through a sequence of photographs and dated captions, significant chapters of my story since I'd married the man in the green shirt.

Getting married when one has four grown children and three grandchildren is not like getting married when one is twenty-one and unencumbered! For ten years I had lived alone believing no man could possibly be right for me and my large brood. Even when their father had remarried and brought a new definition of family to their lives, I could not see me complicating things further. Certainly with my large gang I did not need to take on any step-children or extra grandchildren either. As a registered nurse, I worked nights, weekends, and holidays to alleviate the loneliness. I was doing fine, thank you very much.

Sometimes life finds you even when you're not looking. When a friend told me that a certain widower who knew me years ago wanted my phone number, I thought perhaps a few chats wouldn't hurt, especially since he now lived "way down south." Loving the rugged scenery of Maritime Canada, even with its frigid winters, I knew there was no chance I would ever move far away. Even when he told me how beautiful it was in Florida, I remained unconvinced. Besides, all my family and friends were in the North with me. I had aunts and uncles and cousins along every mile of the roads I drove to work. It was home. "Just come for a visit," he pleaded. I did.

To accept his proposal meant I had to pack up and leave my home, my family, everything dear to me. It meant changing the pattern of my family too. How would they accept him? Me, in this new role? Perhaps it helped when I was able to explain that he wasn't exactly a stranger to them even though they couldn't recall meeting him. He had in fact, once been my family doctor and actually delivered three of my four children. Still the fear of being taken away from my family bothered me. He assured me this would not be the case. "You'll still see your family," he promised.

As we turned the pages of the beautiful scrapbook I realized how much he had kept his word to me. We were looking at reminders of summer days of us boating with the children in Canadian rivers, having picnics looking for treasure on deserted islands, laughing together and roasting marshmallows over campfires when the October leaves were brilliant. We had birthday cake and ice cream with all the grandchildren on their special days, saw them beat us at crokinole games. There we are making snowmen together over the Christmas holidays and huddled by the woodstove drinking hot apple cider. Here they are with us feeding dolphins at SeaWorld and there we are together on the flume ride at Busch Gardens. That's us with the children on the golf cart going to the playground.

There's a page labeled "Soul-Mates." Beneath a picture of my husband and me at the helm of a boat in Sarasota Bay, Paula has inserted a caption that says: "A hard stretch of road is always made easier by a good traveling companion." She knows my story, my struggles. She has heard of the grief my husband went through in losing a wife to cancer and a daughter nine months later. She knows we are good for each other and make each other happier than we could either be alone. She knows I embrace his daughter and there are three little ones here for whom I fill the role of "grandmother." She sees his love for my family and especially an unexplainably deep bond of love between little Joshua and him. I think it's because they both like to wear green shirts at airports.

She tells me it took almost two years to complete the scrapbook and every page I look at is a testimony to Paula's dedication to the project. In addition to the most wonderful pictures, she has painstakingly chosen every detail: the paper, the quotes, the art, the trims, the scripts.

It was a labor of love. It is a gift of love. It tells a story of love— family love that heals and blooms, and like finest lace, is often woven most exquisitely out of darkness.

Phyllis McKinley

PHYLLIS MCKINLEY, author of four books of Poetry, has received multiple awards for her writing. Her fifth book, "Do Clouds Have Feet?" a children's picture book, is scheduled for release this fall. Web site: www.leafyboughpress.com

Beloved

She could hear the whoosh of blood pressure in her ears now that the house was quiet. An unnatural quiet, now that they had all gone and the sirens dwindled to nothing. Braced against the wall, she turned her gaze down the hall. The door to the bedroom was still open.

Alternating between dream and reality, Lena Polacco lurched down the hall like a drunken marionette. She wished it away. She prayed it away. She bargained it away. "Please, Saint Anthony. Please, God. Make it all a nightmare. Let me wake up in bed next to Frankie. I promise my next retirement check – the whole thing. I swear."

Her eyes swept the unkempt room.

"Ahh-hh, no-o-o!" Ragged sobs tore from her depths, knifing open the silent house. Pillows lay skewed like arched eyebrows; a waterfall of bedcovers streamed over the edge of the bed. Ahead, light too brilliant, too cheerful for the night, glared through the gaping bathroom door. Empty pill bottles lay pen, scattered across the counter. Blood congealed on the cold tile floor near the toilet.

"Ahh-hh, ahh-hh, ahh-hh!" Lena fell to her knees on the carpet, then curled into a fetal ball and cried herself into an exhausted, fitful sleep.

Morning burned a line of sunlight through the blinds into her puffy eyes.

The avocado shag carpet had been enough to cradle her sorrow and exhaustion of the night before, but now her arthritic bones were as stiff and unyielding as the floorboards beneath her. The weight of physical and emotional pain held Lena down as the events of the previous night pierced through the fog in her brain.

While she slept, Frankie had taken all his pills in an effort to end the agony of delayed death. Bottle after bottle lay empty on the counter, attesting to the chemical orgy that provided Frankie with his ultimate release, though the final sleep he had anticipated did not arrive as peacefully as hoped. His unceremonious departure came with a bloody, cracked skull when his frail body splayed across the tile floor.

Lena pushed up on knees that cracked like dry twigs, then paused, knowing she'd never make it to her feet without support. With a groan, she knee-skated to the bed, certain that one day her knees would refuse to serve her body. Was there a way, she wondered, to spread the effort among the bones and muscles in her spare frame and avoid injury? If I fell, how long would it take someone to find me? Would I starve to death? When they found me, would I be a half-decayed corpse like Old Mrs. Minna down the street?

Lena shook her head. When I was a kid, I was made of rubber. How did all my parts change to spent elastic and glass? Body parts I never knew I had now pop or sprain. Lena pressed on the mattress and eased to her feet. Her temples throbbed. She swayed in place, waiting until the pulsing in her head subsided. She scuffed across the carpet to the bathroom, stopped at the doorway and stared at the blood, now dried on the tiles.

The scene was etched in Lena's mind, but she tried to erase it with towels. She stared for a moment, taking in the physical evidence of her husband's death, then turned to the sink. The tap squeaked as she twisted the handle.

Frankie never got around to changing that washer, she thought. Cupping her hands beneath the flowing water, Lena rinsed the stale taste from her mouth and splashed her face. She gasped. Like a slap, cold water forced her into reality. She blinked, droplets streaming over her cheeks like last night's tears. The mirror revealed a stranger.

Radiant auburn tresses had faded to a wretched shade of iron with the unmanageability of wire. Whose eyes are those? Mine? Can eyes fade, too? Once an enviable golden brown, they faded into sallow, sagging skin. Her face folded in on itself, drying in ripples like the windswept Sahara. Beneath thinning skin, knobby bones crested her shoulders. Lena thought of them like vultures perched on high limbs, waiting to feast on death's leavings. Gravity pulled heavily on the skin of her arms, drawing it downward, like slack sails on a becalmed boat. Half—or less—what I used to be.

They had kept each other young and beautiful through fifty years of marriage by seeing each other as they had looked on their wedding day. Frankie had charmed her away from a slew of suitors, all clamoring for her favors.

Where did she go—that beautiful girl? Without Frankie, the spell was broken. Without Frankie, her mirror image was The Picture of Dorian Gray. Without Frankie, she was dust. Without Frankie...

Selfish! Selfish, selfish, selfish! Lena pounded the counter with her fists as tears coursed the channels in her cheeks. All he thought of was his pain.

"What about my pain now?" she demanded of the hag in the mirror.

"Show him he won't get away with it. Show him two can play this game", the hag advised. "Two can play this game."

One sweep of her arm brushed the counter clear of caps and bottles. They tickety-tacked, bouncing and rolling across the tile floor. With a defiant glare at the crone in the mirror, Lena yanked open her vanity drawer. One by one she placed her own prescriptions in a neat line on the counter. Methodically, she unscrewed each white cap and set it behind its amber bottle. Six.

"That should do it." Lena raised a glass then set it down with a sneer of revulsion. She had nearly drunk bathroom water from the glass used for brushing teeth. She hawked a derisive laugh, raised the glass and filled it with tap water. Who cares if it tastes like toothpaste?

"Now. Some of each? All of one kind? Does it matter? Don't let Frankie get any further ahead of you." Lena raised her chin and emptied the remains of the first prescription into her mouth. Her tongue sectioned off a few capsules at a time that she swallowed with great gulps of water.

That's strange, she thought. What have I got to smile about? Her image had the hint of a youthful smile. Like a sepia-toned tintype, her hair suggested a bit of color. By the third bottle, her hair darkened to its near-youthful color and her skin responded as though pumped with collagen. Her breasts rose beneath the baggy nightgown.

Lena laughed aloud. "Boobs! My God, I've got boobs again." She stared at the empty containers. "Hey, what a combination! They oughtta mix this stuff together and call it The Fountain of Youth."

The mirror was a blur of colors; green, blue, white, and something—or someone. Lena tossed down the fourth bottle and her eyesight cleared. She could see everything; near, far, in between, just like she'd never had cataracts. Sky, trees, grass, clouds! And a figure in the background. This is getting better by the bottle! She swallowed the few small pills in the fifth container.

There was something familiar about the strong figure and the athletic walk as he approached her.

"Lena, my Sweet! The most beautiful girl in Brooklyn!" He stopped just paces away and held out his hands.

"Frankie! Wait!" She gulped down the pills in the last bottle, clutched the mirror frame, and closed her eyes to stave off the revolution in her stomach. The queasiness ebbed. Lena blinked her eyes open to warm sunlight and a feather-like breeze caressing her face. It's the field in the mirror!

Frankie ran to Lena, enfolding her in his arms and crushing her to his chest. He nuzzled her auburn locks, and she felt him stir to the warmth and fullness of her in his arms. His fingers tilted up Lena's chin. He kissed her tenderly.

"Come; sit with me, sweet Lena. Let me tell you of the wonders I have seen here."

Frankie sat, his back against the ragged trunk of a glorious oak, and pulled her down beside him. Lena's skirt, like a peony in full bloom, flared and settled around her knees, revealing shapely calves. Beneath the sheltering oak, playful kisses punctuated animated laughter and chatter. Neither noticed—nor would have cared—that an imperceptible mending of the torn fabric of their universe was under way.

"My Lena, the most beautiful girl in Brooklyn."

"Frankie," she stroked his chiseled cheekbone, "my beloved."

Virginia Nygard

VIRGINIA NYGARD, former elementary education teacher and Associate Librarian with the West Palm Beach Library, has contributed articles to educational journals, published poetry in an anthology, written book reviews, and short stories. She is an editor with the online journal agoldenplace.com and author of DÉJÀ VU DREAM (2008).

Lucky

The sky purpled like a nasty bruise shot through with streaks of yellow bile. It was going to be a soaking the likes of which Sadie was sure she'd never seen. All about her rumbles of discontent rolled, then bellowed as if the powers of darkness had recaptured heaven.

Deep in her belly the baby shifted and kicked his displeasure with the change in barometric pressure. From conception, Sadie was certain it was a boy. She carried lower, heavier. He wore her out same as caring for a grown man.

Lightning slashed across the sky and disappeared into the woods behind the barn where it coursed through a tree. She heard its bones split and the final, merciful snap of its neck. In the barn the animals murmured their discontent.

Eight months pregnant, and Clem's in town on business. What's more important than seeing to a pregnant wife and two young 'uns? Not to mention the animals. Whenever he's closed-mouth it's so's I won't worry. And that's exactly what makes me worry. Can't make the man understand.

Fat raindrops plopped in the dust at the end of the stone path, and teased the dry grass. Pelting rain was more than the scorched earth could accommodate. The water sloughed off and puddled where gravity called it, which was pretty much away from anything that needed it. A soaking rain was the only thing that would do any good for the hardtack land and dry crops.

Darkness exploded in peach-tinted light that blinded Sadie and prompted an astonished gasp. One hand caressed the swollen girth protecting the precious bundle within, the other steadied her against the strong oak table beside the window. Was he whimpering in the womb?

She turned from the window to the dark hollow where mewling grew to howling. Two tiny, barefooted girls burst from the shadows as they flew down the stairs to clutch at their mother's skirt.

"Mama...Mama...!"

"Hush now, Emily. Hush Anna. It's just a thunderstorm. The lightning hit close by. You're safe babies; you're fine," she crooned as they disappeared in the russet folds of her dress.

At three and four years of age, her daughters were Sadie's mirror image; slight of frame, yet strong and wiry. They would grow up no bigger than their mother who stood five-feet tall. Pregnant almost to term, Sadie felt like a fat Rhode Island Red hen gathering a clutch of chicks beneath her feathers.

Light flickered on the wall. She spun to the window, and the sight confirmed her fear. Smoke seeped through cracks in the barn walls. Plaintive cries from the creatures within reflected the same unspoken knowledge; death owned a corner of the barn and squinted a greedy eye at each in turn.

"Emily, Anna, look at Mama." Sadie forced her voice to convey calm and confidence. "Come, sit in Mama's rocking chair," she ordered, lifting each little one into the rocker. She covered them with a patchwork quilt. "Stay here. You understand? Mama has to check on the animals. Don't move an inch. Promise?"

"Yes, Mama."

"Promise, Mama."

Sadie whipped her shawl from the peg by the door, wrapped it about her, clutching it to her bosom. She tossed a warning look over her shoulder. "Mark me, if you move, you'll get a whuppin'." The wee, wide-eyed girls huddled together, seeming to shrink into a single being.

Sadie shut the door behind her. Assailed by gusts of wind and needles of rain, she pulled the shawl closer. Flames licking at the edge of the barn lit the slick flagstone path. At the end of the path, mud oozed over her leather slippers. There was no time to lace boots. The wind and rain forced her to struggle with the barn door. With every ounce of her strength, one mighty shove popped the bar loose.

Pungent smoke billowed from the open door. At the far end of the barn, the fire flared. She tugged open the sty gate. Squealing pigs scrambled and bolted for the door. Hens and the rooster flapped from the roost and she shooed them to safety. After releasing the two cows from their stalls, Sadie slapped their rumps. The Holsteins lowed their way out of the barn and into the corral. She closed the gate and turned. A cramp knifed her belly. She sucked air, holding it until the pain subsided. Sadie felt the cold seeping through wet clothing. Despite tucking her shawl into her apron, she was soaked through.

In the barn, smoke stung Sadie's eyes and raked her throat. A spate of rain kept the fire down but the horses were in a panic. Their whinnies were pitiable. Nostrils flared and the whites of their eyes confirmed their panic. Micah's hooves thundered in the dirt. Jonah ran to the stall corner and reared, and battered the wall with his hooves. Flames licked at the stall posts and the beam above.

"Easy Micah. Easy Jonah," she cooed to the hysterical horses. "Mama's gonna put on your halter and lead you out of here." As Micah obeyed her urging, Jonah's cries grew shriller. Again he reared and pummeled the stall. With Micah safely tied to the corral railing, Sadie trudged back for Jonah. Mud sucked off one of her slippers. She kicked free of the other and bemoaned the lost time.

Padding barefoot into the barn, she stepped into the stall where Jonah pawed the ground, his breath labored. "Easy, boy. Easy, Jonah. Nothin' to be afraid of. Like I said, Mama's gonna get you out." She sweet talked him and worked on the halter and lead. "There, now. Let's go." Jonah didn't budge. A sinister cracking sound told Sadie a beam was about to give way beside the stall. "Jonah, please...." Her eyes swept the stall as she tugged the stubborn horse's lead.

Placing an old saddle blanket over the horse's head she coaxed him into following her. The beam cracked through and thudded the earthen floor behind them. Jonah picked up his pace. Breathing hard, Sadie barely kept up with him.

At the door, wind whipped the blanket from Jonah's head as ragged lightning found a nearby target. Sadie's belly cramped again and she lost her grip on the coiled end of the lead. The leather snaked about her ankle. Jonah reared and bolted back into the barn.

Sadie was thrown on her back, the breath gusting from her. Jonah, galloping toward his stall, dragged Sadie by the leg until she slammed against an open stall door. Holding fast, she toed loose the braided lead snagged around the opposite ankle. She lay back panting as the horse reached familiar surroundings.

"Jonah!" A burning beam slammed into the gentle horse's back. His screams pierced Sadie's heart and she retched at the smell of burning hide. Her hand slipped in vomit when she tried to stand. The pain in her ankle warned she would not make it out of the barn on two feet. Rising to her knees, she felt her water break.

"Oh, baby, no - not now." She crawled to the entrance and sagged against the door, praying for strength. The hayloft blazed like the fires of hell. Death engulfed the barn and fixed his eye on her.

"No!" She spat. "Not my baby! Not me!" She dragged her weary body to the porch steps and watched the skeleton of the barn waver in the fireball. The contractions were closer now. She had to get out of the rain and the mud! Groaning, she hoisted herself up each step and then slumped heavily against the wall of the house. The baby was coming fast.

She stared in awe as she wrapped him in her torn petticoat. Still encased in the amniotic sac, the baby's body shimmered. Born in the caul! A child of good fortune, destined for greatness, so all the old women said. He may even have the gift of second sight! Remembering that Grandma had pressed Mama's caul to paper and preserved it as an heirloom, Sadie tore another piece of petticoat. Just as the sac burst, she pressed the cloth to the membrane over his face, then peeled it back with care, hoping to make a keepsake of it. She sucked the fluid from his mouth, and rubbed his back until she heard his tiny breaths. Pulling lengths of yarn from her shawl, Sadie tied off the umbilical cord then set him to suckle at her breast.

Hooves thundered into the yard, and Clem slung down from the back of the Appaloosa stallion. By the flickering light of the waning fire, he saw his wife, slumped and still against the house. Something at her breast squalled and wriggled. "Sadie? Oh, God ..." He gathered her in his arms. "Sadie?" The little thing wriggled and stuck its fist in a tiny pink mouth.

She opened her eyes and smiled at Clem. "Our son. Born in the caul. Lucky." She sighed and closed her eyes.

VIRGINIA NYGARD

VIRGINIA NYGARD, former elementary education teacher and Associate Librarian with the West Palm Beach Library, has contributed articles to educational journals, published poetry in an anthology, written book reviews, and short stories. She is an editor with the online journal agoldenplace.com and author of DÉJÀ VU DREAM (2008).

Kudzu's Last Stand

My granddaddy made a dying wish and we carried it out like orders from the President. Right before he passed, he said he wanted Daddy to go out and buy Mammy a puppy so she wouldn't be lonesome when he left this world for cigar heaven.

The day after Poppa's funeral, I went with Daddy to the animal shelter where we found Kudzu, the homeliest mutt in the entire county. Mammy and Kudzu fell in love the minute they laid eyes on each other and remained side by side till the day she drew her last breath.

When it came time for Mammy's final request, she wanted us to take Kudzu and make him a part of our family. It had not been too long since we had to bury Igor, the black Lab who was known all over town for sleeping through twelve straight summers. Since we had not replaced Igor and Kudzu was in need of a family, we did what Mammy had asked of us. It worked out pretty well.

Kudzu took to eating from Igor's bowl, slept like a zombie in Igor's lumpy old bed, and he even took to snuggling up with Igor's leftover raggedy blanket. We had loved that dog even before my grandmother died and afterward, when he came to live with us, he only grieved a few weeks. I think that old dog appreciated us for taking him out of Geezerville so he could get in a few romps around a younger neighborhood.

Mammy added something else to her last wishes. She asked that when Kudzu died that he be buried in the plot between her and Poppa, the space we wrongly figured would one day belong to one of us. At the time Mammy made her deathbed wishes known she was very weak, so we could hardly hear what she was saying. We agreed to everything she wanted.

The reality only hit us after she said, "Good. Now I can die in peace knowing Kudzu will rest beside me and Poppa."

However, we didn't figure on the Greenburg Sanitation Department having its own ideas about where old Kudzu should rest following his lazy demise.

"What the sanitation department doesn't know won't hurt 'em one bit," my brother announced the day Kudzu finally gave up the ghost. Intending to bury Kudzu according to Mammy's last wishes, Scrappy drove us out to the cemetery late one night. "Sanitation people be damned."

I went with him, but I was in not at all thrilled about the whole deal. We couldn't get inside through the front gate because it was locked up tight. That didn't make a lick of sense, I told my brother. "Why bother to lock up a cemetery, Scrappy? It's not like people can't wait to get in there. And the ones who are already there aren't going anywhere."

"People steal funeral flowers all the time. Don't you know anything?"

"Give me a break, Scrappy."

"I'm not kidding. I remember one time my friend Jo-Jo stole flowers off a grave and then gave them to Dinah Fay Rossler."

"That's the tackiest thing I ever heard, Scrappy. I sincerely hope Dinah Fay threw 'em back in his face."

"Nope. She grinned from here to Sunday and told Jo-Jo he was a gentleman." Scrappy laughed out loud. "She said, 'Jo-Jo, unlike some other boys in Greenburg, you have real class.' We just about laughed our butts off."

I didn't find it a bit funny, but then Scrappy and his buddies grossed me out on a regular basis.

"Well," I countered, "it still seems to me like locking the cemetery gates so people like Jo-Jo won't steal the flowers is a bit of overkill."

Scrappy ignored my clever pun. He was on a roll and I could tell he wasn't about to quit.

"Hey, Sis, I bet you don't know that people come in here and dig up graves, do you?" He lowered his voice and tried to sound creepy. "They open up the coffins and look for valuables. They steal them right out from under the corpse."

"No way! What kind of valuables?" I couldn't imagine anybody crazy enough to feel around inside a dead person's eternal bed hoping to find anything of value.

Scrappy laughed, trying to sound like Boris Karloff. "They take rings and necklaces and watches. Daddy told me people get buried wearing their stuff 'cause they think they can take it with them."

He turned off the headlights and we drove around to the side where it was so dark you couldn't see your own tongue if you could stick it out far enough to look. Kudzu was in the trunk, wrapped up like a baby in Igor's ratty old blanket. We parked under some trees and sat in the dark for a few minutes.

Scrappy said, "Come on, Sis. Might as well get it over with. I'll hoist you over to the other side of the fence. You stand right there and wait till I come back."

"Where're you going?" Fear punched me in the stomach.

"I've got to get Kudzu out of the trunk," he said, like I didn't have a brain.

"So I'll help you carry him." No way did I want to stand in that pitch black cemetery all by myself.

"Just wait right over there till I get him, so I can lower him down to you on the other side of the fence. You can hold him long enough for me to crawl over the fence, can't you?"

I felt like slapping my brother into the middle of next week. My eyes were as big as a couple of Yo Yo's, and my mouth was acting weird. It didn't want to close.

"Are you saying you want me to hold a dead dog?"

"Only for a minute. It won't take me long to shinny over the fence, but I can't do it and hold Kudzu at the same time, can I? If he's too heavy for you, just put him down on the ground. Jeez Lueeez!"

That dog could have been the size of a Chihuahua instead of fifty pounds of Southern fried leftovers. I'd still have dropped his butt on the ground where dead dogs belong. We wandered around until we found Poppa and Mammy's gravesites.

Scrappy told me to keep a lookout for the security guard while he dug the hole for Kudzu between our grandparents. I found out later that the guard actually lived on the cemetery grounds, but he was almost always dead drunk by that time of night. We didn't know that on the dark night.

Scrappy dug down pretty deep and wound up covered with sweat and red clay by the time the hole was big enough. He thought of everything, even a Bible. When the dirt was packed down tight over ol' Kudzu, Scrappy said the two of us should jump up and down on top of the grave so it wouldn't look like new dirt. Then my brother pulled out a flashlight and began to read a passage from the Bible. We both said "Amen," and he snapped the Good Book closed.

"First thing tomorrow, we'll come back and plant a big red azalea bush on top of the grave," Scrappy said. "Nobody needs to know that Kudzu can still fertilize azaleas like he did when he was alive and pooping on every bush in sight."

Scrappy turned in my direction for a minute, just long enough for me to see the shiny spot on his cheek. Our eyes met and held for a split second. I squatted down to retie my left sneaker so I could pretend I hadn't noticed his tears.

When we went back to the cemetery the next morning hauling an azalea bush, one had already been planted. And it was in full bloom.

CAPPY HALL REARICK

CAPPY HALL REARICK is the author of five books and presently of two newspaper columns and one e-column, *Puttin' on the Gritz*. Cappy's stories have been included in many anthologies throughout the country and you can read her columns on her web site. www.simplysoutherncappy.com www.lowcountrysun.sc www.griffinjournal.com

Previously published in "Simply Southern," page 89, 2002.

Final Swing

"Don't you run away from me!" His step-father swung again, the bat came around toward him, but the boy ducked in time. A lamp shattered. Shards of glass splashed across the floor, covering his exit path. He scrambled from the room, slivers digging into his palms.

"Get over here, you little…"

Bobby rolled into the hallway, wincing as more glass sliced into his back. He leapt up and sprinted for the front door, slapping the screen door latch. The flimsy door groaned in protest, then smacked outward and against the front of the house. Tears streamed down his cheeks. In two strides he crossed the porch and launched over the front steps. His bare feet hardly noticed as he landed on the hot cement walk.

"Come back here! Right now, damn it!"

The muffled command issued from inside the house pushed Bobby harder as he turned the corner, his stringy hair flopping from side to side.

$\sim$

The bear-sized man filled the doorway. Sweat glistened on his brow and stained his greasy tee shirt. He looked left and right, but his stepson was no longer in sight and had left no clues. No matter. Ron Justice knew exactly where the kid was headed.

∾

Bobby ran as fast as his legs would carry him, his calluses rebuffing the rocks and pebbles underfoot. His exhalations punctuated his flight like a coxswain's cadence, "henh, henh, henh," until his Mom's place came into view. He slapped the mailbox—a habit he couldn't break— then vaulted up and into the weathered clapboard house. He closed the door, locked it, and ran into his bedroom. He locked that door too, before diving under the bed. Scooting back against the wall, he put his thumb in his mouth and waited, breathing hard, spittle running down his fist. He squeezed his eyes closed, wishing–hoping that by not seeing he could not be seen.

∾

Suzy Condon heard the first door slam, then the second. She knew instinctively what was going on. She stopped chopping the celery she was preparing for a dinner salad. Interrupted in mid-stroke, she thought, "Here we go again." She reached over and snatched the cleaver from the butcher block, then headed down the hall and knocked on his door.

"Bobby," she said. "Come on, honey, open up. You're safe now." She looked at the faded drawing taped to the door. It was now two years old, from when he was in third grade: "Private–Boys Only–Girls Keep Out!" A couple more years, she thought, he'll change his mind.

"Bobby, I'm ready for him. Please come out." She waited, then heard something move and guessed he had been hiding again. Next came the soft padding of feet on the hardwood floor. He opened the door slowly.

"Where are you hurt?" It was difficult to keep her voice calm. "What did he do to you, baby?" She didn't see any marks on his arms and legs, and his face was only puffy-red from crying. He's such a beautiful boy. Why should he have to go through this?

"My shoulder," he said. He turned so that his left shoulder faced her.

"Can you take off your shirt, honey?" She tried to calm him by talking softly.

He started sobbing. "It hurts."

"There, there, Honey. It'll be okay. I promise, Bobby, I promise." She couldn't hug him; afraid it would hurt him. "Let me lift your shirt and just take a quick look."

She knelt on one knee and placed the cleaver on the floor. Taking the bottom of the shirt in her hands, she pulled it away from his skinny frame. She lifted it slightly, then turned her head sideways and peered up toward his shoulder. Her eyes stopped on his bruised ribs, painted a reddish-purple the size of a football.

"That bastard!" She released the tee shirt and bent over, steadying herself with both hands on the floor. How could I let this happen again?

A tear fell and mixed with the dust on the floor. Be strong for him. She blinked to stop more from falling, shuddered, then picked up the cleaver and stood.

"Let's get a Popsicle, okay?" she said. She hoped to distract him with the frozen treat.

"Okay."

He stopped crying and wiped his face with his arm. She turned and walked back to the kitchen; he clung to her free hand. Her cheeks burned with rage. Her hand clenched the cleaver tighter. That bastard has got to pay!

In the kitchen she put the cleaver down by the refrigerator and reached into the freezer for his treat.

"How about grape?"

"Sure."

She tore the paper wrapping and handed him the Popsicle. He took it and started licking.

She studied him, but couldn't read anything on his face. He was lost inside somewhere. I have to stop this! He's being destroyed! I have to get him somewhere safer, out of reach of that monster!

A knock at the door startled her. He's trying to get in! Bishhh! Keeghhh. She heard glass skittering across the floor. She jerked her head up. He's coming in through the window!

She snatched up the cleaver. Bobby dashed into the pantry and shut the door.

"Who's there?" She moved to the side of the kitchen entryway, crouching down by the cabinets. She held the cleaver behind her, wavering, unable to hold it still.

"You know who it is, bitch! You can't keep me out of here. Send Bobby out—now!"

"Get out of here, asshole!" She couldn't hold it any longer. "You don't—"

She recoiled as he lunged into the kitchen, swinging wildly. The bat dented the refrigerator. She swung the cleaver with all her might. The blade bit deep into his shin, cutting through denim and bone. He screamed in agony and pitched forward onto the linoleum. As he fell the bat flew out of his hand and skittered toward the pantry. Rage surged through her body like wildfire as she scrambled toward him.

"Never again, asshole!" she swung and shouted.

The cleaver bit into the back of his thigh.

"Aaah!" He rolled over, eyes locked onto hers, his teeth clenched. The speckled tiles turned red beneath his leg.

The pantry door opened. Bobby grabbed the bat.

"Don't! Ever!" She swung with each word, but he kicked at her arm with his good leg.

The cleaver flew out of her hand and clattered out of reach.

"Hah!" he sat up. "You little…"

Whock!

She flinched at the loud, hollow knock as the bat crashed on the crown of his head.

Whock!

"Bobby," she whispered. The rage had depleted her energy. She couldn't speak.

Whock!

John Rehg

JOHN REHG has been telling stories his entire life, but only recently started putting them to paper. He has published poetry and is revising his first novel while shopping a science fiction short. He helps other writers overcome their fear of technology. Learn more at www.writerscyberguy.com.

When Time Stopped

The deuce-and-half truck comes to a bone-jarring stop and I sit waiting for the hueys to show up. Waiting, Christ that's all I do when I'm not being shot at, wait. That and crap details. Thirteen days and a wake up. I can hear the choppers coming up the valley.

My brain already feels like it's melting from the heat. The towel I have around my neck is soaking wet, and all I've done so far is walk from the hut they call a barracks to this truck.

Sitting, waiting, hacking my lungs out with the smell of the diesel. God, I don't need this! Thirteen days and a wake up, then I'm out of here. Taking that big white freedom bird back to the world, back to what I left behind. All those I left behind.

The sarge is screaming at me to get the hell out of the truck. The LT is talking to someone and pointing at the map. He doesn't look happy.

My turn and I'm the last boonie-rat to get in the chopper. My ass is going to be hanging out of the door. Great, just great. The chopper lifts off and my stomach sinks to my ass. The world falls away. The noise is so loud I can't hear myself scream. The wop-wop-wop of the blades echoes in my head.

Looking ahead, I can see the red smoke of the landing zone in the distance. The gun ships are buzzing around like birds looking for a meal, and I can see white tails from the rockets as they disappear into the bush ahead of me.

We're coming in low through the red smoke from the LZ, red damn smoke. It's going to be hot. The chopper banks to the right, I push back against the bulkhead, my feet try to push themselves through the deck and I hold on with one hand as the chopper tilts. I can see the ground, straight down. Thirteen days and a wake up. God, do you hear me? Thirteen days and a wake up.

Small arms fire riddles the side of the huey and the gunner opens up. I can feel the rhythmic thump of the gun as it fires. I see the ground and trees explode with the rounds from the fifty.

The cherry across from me gets hit. His face reflects his surprise. He slumps forward and that red-black color spreads across his fatigue shirt. His head bobs up and down like a doll. He falls toward me and I push him into the center of the chopper. Thirteen days and a wake up. I'm so damn scared I can hardly breathe. How could anybody get used to this? Focus. Stay alive.

The red smoke swirls around the chopper and I get ready to jump out. I already have one foot on the skid. I can't see; the smoke is blinding.

As the rear of the skid touches down, I'm out and running away from the chopper. Mortar rounds start landing, they have the LZ dialed in and the ground erupts all around me. I turn and look back, a mortar round hits the chopper I was just in. Burning, it crumples to the ground. I can see the pilots waving their arms trying to get out, they're on fire. It explodes. I avoid the screaming shrapnel from the exploding bird. I can feel it go over my head. Thirteen days and a wake up.

The mortar rounds keep coming and the ground is erupting up in the air. I stand and run for the bush, any place but out in the open. Can't see anyone else, I don't know if I'm in the middle, the rear, or the point. The small arms fire is fierce and I drop to the ground. The rounds sound like small jets flying over my head. I can see the flash from the weapon firing at me and I fire back. The smoke stops.

Looking up I see the gun ships coming in and the smoke from the rockets. Then I hear and feel the rockets hit just in front of me. Thirteen days and a wake up.

Small eruptions explode in the dirt right in front of me. I try to bury myself in the ground. I can hear someone yelling for me to get my ass up and run forward. Thirteen days and a wake up. Thirteen days and a wake up.

I see two others running toward the bush and I stand. A mortar round lands just in front of me. A wall of something unseen stops me and holds me in space. I see the dirt flying up, out, and hovering in front of me. I can see each grain as it spins in the air. The flash of the mortar follows and I float through the air as if I am a feather that will never reach the ground.

The red smoke of the LZ lingers, unmoving, above me. I don't feel anything. I look up... and I can see the sky. It's blue ...bluer than I have ever seen it. I reach up to touch it but I can't. The gun ships seem to hang in this cobalt sky, their blades move in slow motion. The hueys stand just feet above the ground.

My chest is burning. I can see something sticking out of my chest. It doesn't seem real. Thirteen days and a wake up, Jesus fucking Christ, thirteen days and a wake up.

I try to touch the thing... my hand comes into view. I close my eyes... and when I open them, my hand seems to freeze in one position. I close my eyes again and I open them—my hand is in a different position.

I can't hear anything but the blood pulsing through my head, like a single beat of a drum, repeating slower over and over again.

The doc runs up to me. His mouth is moving like someone that is trying to speak to a foreigner but I can't hear him as he pushes some morph into me. He looks into my eyes and again he moves his mouth. He is shouting but all I see are his lips moving.

I try to speak but nothing comes out.

The world becomes a fuzzy blue light.

Someone else kneels. The doc shakes his head and they leave. I know what that means. Thirteen days and a wake up.

The song White Rabbit is playing in my head. My chest isn't burning any more. It's not that bad to die. Screw you, God. Just thirteen more days and a wake up. Someone picks me up and I'm thrown into a chopper.

The world is growing dimmer.

～

Standing in the drizzle of a rain, the priest stops speaking and the crack of the rifles breaks the silence, startling all of us out of our trance. In his last letter he told me that he would be home in two weeks. He asked if I could get his car running. He wanted to drink a beer with me. I found it odd to think that my son was old enough to drink a beer. He will never be my little boy again.

A stranger walks up to me and hands me ...a flag. A flag! They take my son and give me back a flag. A poor exchange. I'll never see his face, the light in his eyes, or hear his laugh. I grimly take the damp cloth and hold it to my chest, as if it was my child. The two weeks have long passed but no matter how long he lays there, for him it will always be thirteen days and a wake up before he can come home.

JOHN RYAN

JOHN RYAN has been writing primarily fiction for about five years. He is enrolled in the UCF creative writing program and is member of both the Florida Writers Association and SCBWI.

The Promise

Jan stood silently in the pouring rain remembering her last telephone conversation with Paul.

"If you don't like it, take me to court," Paul taunted her.

Jan held back her tears. How she hated those words. For the past five years she had begged, pleaded and fought with Paul for a raise in child support for their daughters, Melissa and Jenny, and each time his reply was the same. Paul knew she didn't have the money to take him to court. If she had the money, she wouldn't need to take him to court. It was a Catch 22 situation.

"You're a liar!" she retorted into the phone. "You just bought a brand new Mercedes. Your new wife's walking around in designer clothes, while your children and I wear hand-me-downs from friends, and you have the nerve to tell me you can't afford $20.00 for a new pair of sneakers for Melissa."

As usual, Paul just laughed at her.

Jan knew from experience that no amount of pleading or threatening would change Paul's mind. She didn't even know why she bothered to humiliate herself this way. Jan was tired. She had just come home from her second job when Melissa showed her she ripped her sneakers at school that day. Even with two jobs and the measly amount of child support Paul provided, Jan still didn't have the money for extras like clothes and shoes.

"If we're finished, I'm hanging up," Paul stated nonchalantly.

"Finished! No. Not by a long run. We'll never be finished. Not until one of us is dead. I just pray you'll die before me so I get the pleasure of spitting on your grave and damning you to hell," Jan sobbed into the phone.

"Yeah, yeah -- I've heard it all before. Tell you story to somebody who cares."

Jan slammed the receiver down before Paul had the chance to hang up on her. Damn him! Damn him! Damn him! Everyday of her life since the divorce she wished him dead.

Now standing over Paul, looking down at the freshly overturned dirt, barely hearing the words of the priest, she suppressed a smile for the sake of her daughters. Who has the last laugh now?

Her psychologist, Dr. Taylor, advised her to confront Paul one last time. "Make your peace with him, or you'll never be able to live with yourself. It's the only way, Jan. Nothing can be accomplished by bottling up your hatred. It's time to let go and move on with your life."

But what did Dr. Taylor know? Dr. Taylor didn't have to see her children do without. Dr. Taylor never saw Melissa and Jenny's sad little faces when Jan told them they couldn't have dance lessons, couldn't join cheerleading, Girl Scouts, or any other activities because they didn't have the money for those little extras most children take for granted. Dr. Taylor never had to contend with the psychological beatings Jan took from Paul every day of her life.

∽

The night of the accident Jan had been at her best friend Nancy's 40th birthday party. Nancy's husband, Tom, had bought Nancy a beautiful new Rolex for her birthday and had asked Jan to wrap it. No one but Jan knew she had set Nancy's new watch a half hour ahead before wrapping it. Around ten o'clock that evening, Jan feigned one of her migraine headaches.

"Nancy, what time is it?" Jan inquired.

"It's almost 10:15 p.m. Why?"

"I have an awful headache. Is it all right if I go lay down in your room for awhile?"

"No problem. I'll make sure no one disturbs you. Are you sure you don't want Tom to drive you home?" Nancy asked.

"No, really. I don't want to spoil your party. If I just lay down for an hour, I'm sure I'll be fine." After locking Nancy's bedroom door, Jan crawled out the window and sneaked to her car she had parked down the block. Jan knew that every Friday night Paul left his house at 10:00 p.m. to frequent one of the local bars.

Her plan was so simple. Jan only waited a few minutes for Paul to leave his house. Then she followed him to Miller's Pass, more affectionately known to the locals as "Dead Man's Curve."

Paul always drove too damn fast for his own good, and the riskiest part for Jan had been pulling along side him in order to force him off the road and down the side of the cliff. Luck had surely been on Jan's side that night, for no other cars were on the road, and her car hadn't touched his, leaving no evidence that she had even been in the area.

The whole process took less than forty-five minutes, and when Nancy checked in on her at 11:00 p.m. real time, she was lying comfortably on Nancy's bed.

"Feeling better yet Jan?"

"Yes, much better. Did I sleep long?" She asked, knowing full well Nancy would take this opportunity to look at her new watch again.

"Only an hour, sleepy head. It's only 11:30 p.m. Do you want to get up now?"

"Yes, I think it's time I rejoined your party."

Jan stayed until the party was over and offered to help Tom clean up and put a passed-out Nancy to bed. Knowing Nancy as well as she did, Jan knew Nancy would be unconscious by the end of the evening. It had been almost too easy to slip off all of Nancy's jewelry and place it on her dresser, but not before she fixed Nancy's watch to the proper time.

～

The police came to Jan's house the next day, as she knew they would. Paul's new wife, Sheila, had been hysterical when she received the news. Sheila had insisted it wasn't an accident and that the police question Jan. The young officer who came to Jan's house apologized for disturbing her.

"Mrs. Brentwood, can you establish were you were last night between 10:00 and 11:00 p.m.?"

"Why at my friend Nancy's birthday party. Why officer? What is this all about?"

"I'm sorry to be the one to inform you, but last night your former husband was in a fatal car accident. It looks like he took Miller's Pass a little too fast. His car went over the cliff."

Pretending shock and disbelief Jan even managed a few tears for appearance sake before she replied, "I was just speaking to him yesterday."

The officer looked down at his shoes and shuffled his feet uncomfortably. It was obvious he felt awkward having to ask these questions. "Yes, ma'am, I know. That's why we're questioning you. His wife seems to think there was some sort of foul play. We understand you had a nasty telephone conversation with him yesterday."

Wiping her eyes on her sleeve Jan replied, "Why, yes, but then we haven't really been civil to each other since the divorce."

"I understand, ma'am." The officer smiled slightly. "I'm divorced myself."

"Oh," Jan replied.

"I wouldn't be too concerned. It appears to be a routine accident, but then we have to check everything out."

"Of course, officer. I understand. You're just doing your job."

"Now, if I can just have your friend's name, we'll check out your alibi. I'm sure I won't have to bother you after this."

～

Paul's funeral hadn't been pleasant. Sheila made a terrible scene in front of their friends and family. "I know you had something to do with this," Sheila screamed at Jan when she, Melissa, and Jenny entered the funeral parlor. "I want you out of here, right now."

Sheila ran over to Jan and slapped her hard in the face. "You're probably glad he's dead. Now you'll get your lousy money you were always hounding Paul about. His insurance policy should set you up for life." Sheila's father grabbed her before Shelia could strike Jan a second time.

"I'm so sorry," he said, "Sheila's just so overcome with grief. She doesn't mean what she said."

"I meant every word of it. Get her out of here. I don't want her here. Paul wouldn't want her here." Sheila screamed even louder.

"Sheila, honey," her father pleaded, "please calm down. Jan has every right to be here. Remember the children. You don't want them seeing you like this."

~

Yes, the funeral had been hard, but it was over now. Jan had waited until everyone left and then came back to Paul's grave. Dr. Taylor had been right. She did have to confront Paul one last time, but not to say she was sorry or ask for amends, but to remind him of her promise.

Spitting on his grave she remarked, "I'll see you in hell, Paul. See you in hell," Jan repeated over and over as she walked off into the rain.

HELEN M. SANSONE

HELEN M. SANSONE has had one short story accepted for publication with Coastal Publications out of Seattle, Washington entitled *Tickled.* Currently, she is looking to have her first novel a political romance, entitled, *The Stuff That Dreams Are Made Of,* published.

Scents of Heaven

The smell of roses captured Vera's attention as she sipped iced tea at the kitchen table in a vain attempt to offset the sweltering Texas summer. At first, Vera noticed a subtle release of perfumed air, but then the aroma soon became thick and heavy. She felt unsettled; her motherly instincts urged her to check on her five-year-old daughter, Anna.

Shoving back her chair with more force than necessary, Vera dashed the short distance to the kitchen sink. Ignoring the toppled white-washed wicker chair, she leaned over and peered out the window to where Anna played. She smiled at the sight of her daughter frolicking under the shower of water sprinklers she set up on the lawn. Anna glanced up, spotted her mother and smiled and waved with childhood enthusiasm. Vera waved back, then shifted her attention to the sky directly behind her daughter. Dark gray clouds gathered where there was blue sky just a moment before.

"Another Texas storm," Vera sighed, "I don't know if I'll ever get used to this sudden weather change." Vera's family had recently relocated to Corpus Christi from the suburbs of New York. In response to the sluggish economy, when her husband's company bid on a large development in Texas came through, they leaped at the opportunity.

The weatherman hadn't mention rain. Anna's going to be disappointed when I tell her to come inside so early. Vera reached the back door and noticed an increase in the potency of the floral scent. Her nostrils tingled from intensity of the smell. Anxious, having experienced this phenomenon before, she flung the door open and dashed out onto the porch.

~

It was the summer of Vera's seventh birthday. She and Grandma Anna had a special day planned. 'Out on the Town' they called it. Lunch at Nielsen's Ice Cream Parlor, then off to Woolworth's to pick out her birthday present. With Vera's mom working, Grandma Anna was Vera's built-in babysitter. She lived on the second floor of their duplex.

"When a-you smell the roses, and see no flowers," Grandma Anna explained in her thick Italian accent, "Angels protect a-you."

"Protect me! From what, Nona?" Vera asked.

"Protect a-you from ….from a falling, fires, anythin'." Grandma Anna flipped a pancake onto a dish.

"Can I see my angel, Nona? I'd love to see mine! I bet she's beautiful, dressed in white with flowing golden hair and wings as fluffy as….as fluffy as snow."

Grandma Anna turned from the stove and smiled, carrying two plates of pancakes. She placed the plates on the table, pulled out a chair, and sat beside her granddaughter.

"Some-a times you see them, Joya mia, but not a-know it is your angel."

"What do you mean, Nona?" Vera held her fork in the air, her eyes fixated on her Grandmother. Vera's recent quest for angelic facts came as a result of a trip to the library the day before.

"Some a-times they look like you and me…you know, like people."

"Wow!" Vera's eyes widen.

"Now, enough-a the questions, Joya. Go, take-a you bath. Okay?"

"Okay, Nona." Vera got up, kissed her grandmother's forehead and put her dish in the sink; she washed it then dashed off to play.

They left the house at noon, walking hand-in-hand, to catch the bus to town. Grandma Anna hummed while Vera hopped on one foot jumping over the cracks in the sidewalk.

"Step on a crack, break your mother's back," Vera sang in a whisper. That's a weird rhyme, she thought.

Just before reaching the bus stop at the bottom of the hill, a faint floral smell reached Vera's nostrils. I smell roses. Angels? Vera wondered. The scent grew stronger. Vera halted, tugging on her grandmother's sleeve.

"Nona! Nona! I smell roses. Is it angels?"

"I don't-a smell nothin', Joya. Hurry, we will miss the bus."

"Nona!" Anna said, frustrated, "I really do smell roses!"

"Maybe the apartment there," Grandma Anna pointed in the direction of a building near where they stood, "plant some a new flowers."

"Maybe." Vera said, unconvinced. Walking past the building, Vera drew in a deep breath. She still smelled the fragrance but said nothing.

The bus stop was crowded and there was no available space to sit on the bench, so Vera and Grandmother Anna stood near the curb. The scent had grown stronger, making Vera's nostrils tingle. No mistake, I definitely smell flowers, Vera thought, let me look. Vera turned and took a step. Suddenly, a woman grabbed Vera's shoulders and pushed her, with force, into an overgrown bush in the abandoned lot.

Vera screamed. The shrubbery caught her fall. In the next split second, an out-of-control car careened through the exact spot where Vera had stood, barely missing her grandmother, then came to rest against the brick wall of an office building.

"Anna!"

"Thank God you moved!" a bystander commented, "Are you alright?"

"You could have been killed!" another replied.

Startled, Vera looked out from inside the thicket and grabbed onto a hand helping to free her from her snare. Vera stood up, glancing around the small crowd that gathered.

"Where…where is the lady, dressed in blue?" Vera asked, "She saved me."

The eyewitnesses looked at each other.

"No one dressed in blue that I remember." A woman answered.

"Me neither." Another replied.

Grandma Anna knelt down beside Vera and hugged her. "My bella! Are-a you okay?"

"Yes, Nona," Vera replied and then whispered, "I told you I smelled roses. The lady in blue, she was my angel, wasn't she?"

"Si, Joy mia, si." Grandma Anna whispered back as tears flowed down her cheeks.

~

A large, black, thundercloud had assembled. Vera called her daughter in a calm voice, "Anna, it's going to rain, come in the house."

"Okay, Mommy." Anna ran toward her mother then stopped. She turned around and ran back to where she had been playing.

"Anna!" Vera's voice cracked.

"I have to get Tabitha."

As Anna bent down to pick up her favorite doll sitting on the grass by the sprinklers, an unimaginable scene came into Vera's view. The menacing cloud had formed a funnel and was approaching at breakneck speed.

"Tornado." Vera murmured. "Hurry, Anna!" Vera shouted, running down the steps. She scooped Anna in her arms and headed toward the house. Large drops of rain pelted them. A powerful wind kicked up, making it difficult to proceed. Vera struggled against the current of air, pushing hard to move forward. Just as she reached the porch, and placed her foot on the first step, the weather-warning siren belted out an ear-piercing shrill. Anna screamed, startled by the unfamiliar blaring.

"It's okay, joya mi, don't be afraid."

Inside, Vera forced the door shut with her back, stopping long enough to bolt it, and then raced through the hallway and down the basement steps, holding her daughter tightly.

Vera recalled that the previous owners said to go to the wine cellar. It was a damp, musty back room. Anna cringed. She hated the dark. Vera turned on the light. Several unpacked moving boxes were scattered about. Vera toed one over to the furthest corner and sat on it, holding Anna on her lap.

"We'll be safe here," Vera crooned, patting Anna's soft brown hair.

"Mommy!" Anna sobbed, "Where's my daddy!"

"Daddy will come get us real soon."

The storm's fury intensified; relentless thunder rumbled, then silenced for a moment. Vera sighed, thinking the storm was over when a deafening sound filled their ears. The single light went out. Anna screamed and tightened her arms around Vera's. The roar of a freight train, passed overhead. Vera covered her daughter's ears with her hands, desperate to stifle the frightening racket.

Fragrance of roses emerged out from the stale air, enveloping them.

"Mommy, flowers!"

"Roses." Vera felt safe. She closed her eyes and hummed a lullaby.

The rain and thunder continued a bit longer, and then dissipated. Vera gently woke her sleeping Anna and walked over to the door.

"Anna, I need you to walk behind me." Vera put Anna down. "Hold unto mommy's shirt."

Vera checked each step's soundness before proceeding. They remerged into the hallway and continued to the living room. The house appeared intact.

Vera knelt down and hugged Anna, "Are you okay?"

Anna nodded.

"Sit on the couch for mommy. I have to go outside for just a moment. I'll be back real fast. I promise."

"Okay, mommy." Anna walked over to the couch and sat, still hugging her doll.

Vera pulled hard on the front door knob to get it to open. She tiptoed out onto the veranda and gasped. Every house in her neighborhood was flattened or damaged, with the exception of her house. She descended the steps to the debris strewn yard and turned to survey her own house.

No damage. Vera's legs buckled under her. It was a miracle. Tears rolled down her cheeks. Kneeling, she looked heavenwards.

"Nona Anna, angels saved me again, me and my Anna."

MARYANN SCIAVILLO-LOPEZ

MARY ANN SCIAVILLO-LOPEZ is currently involved in the writing of a Christian Historical Novel, *Sons Rise*, and has written blog columns for pet grooming and pet care, along with a bi-monthly newsletter for her pet store/grooming shop.

A Tale of Six Chickens

Living with Daddy was a true adventure. We moved from place to place, job to job and laugh to laugh at warp speed, never secure but always landed on our feet. We never knew what was on the horizon.

Life changed with every move – more than just living in a new community - and after pretty well covering New Jersey, moved on to Pennsylvania. I was fifteen and, up until then, we had never lived in the country, and certainly not on a farm. This time we moved to a farm – livestock and all. As with our other family projects, and life with Daddy was always a project, we adapted to this new venture, though with more reservations than usual.

Until we could get into the full swing of farming, Daddy took a job as a salesman with a slate quarry in Bangor, a small town twenty miles away. What he knew about slate was a mystery to us, but he did well, as usual.

One of our first projects was to dam up the little stream that coursed through the property. It ran past the small red barn and across the dirt road where the old farm house stood. During that first summer of fun around and in the stream and pond, Daddy decided to launch his next project. Chickens!

"You can't be serious," I stuttered. "Chickens? What do we know about raising chickens?"

"I have a book," Daddy smiled. We were sitting around the dining room table where we often spent after dinner hours talking. "I read up on it and it looks quite simple. We'll raise broilers." It was those darned books again. We never began a project without proper research found in a library of how-to-books.

He explained that you start out buying day old chicks and put them on the top level of something called a battery. After feeding them for six weeks, moving them down a tier every week, they were called broilers. All you had to do was kill them, clean them, and sell them.

"That's all? Who is going to do this killing, cleaning and selling?" I asked. Daddy avoided that question for the time being.

"Just think," he said, "fresh eggs in addition to chickens."

Of course, some of the work fell to my sister and me. After school, we were the ones who climbed the ladder to the loft, felt under disagreeable hens for eggs they were reluctant to give up, and filled feed troughs and water basins. There was also the mucking out. Yuck! I was not cut out to be a farmer.

Daddy didn't kill a chicken until it was already ordered. That system worked well most of the time. He planned to kill just enough birds to fill the orders – humanely, of course. It might seem strange to say "humanely kill," but after some research Daddy discovered the preferred way to end the lives of our chickens. He hung them from a tree near the chicken house, each by a single leg, in a bunch of about six or eight chickens at a time. Then he took a very sharp knife, opened their beaks and plunged the knife through the roof of their mouths, killing them instantly. It was a better method than wringing their necks or chopping their heads off and it also was supposed to help release the feathers, to make plucking easier.

The slaughtering was done before he left for work. The routine was simple. Mother would bring a large tub of water to boil at the entrance to the storage shed. I would fill another vat with icy water from the stream. To prepare the chickens for cleaning, we soaked them in the hot water, then plunged them into the icy water. This apparently helped release the feathers. Pam and I pulled the feathers from the bodies and mother would to the inside part. Even so, just pulling the feathers was a yucky job.

My sister and I helped pluck the chickens but refused to do any of the internal cleaning. We had to draw the line somewhere, so Mother did that.

One morning Daddy killed six chickens to fill current orders. Then he climbed into his truck and rumbled off down the dirt road, calling out the open window, "I'll be back in two hours to pick up the chickens." My sister went with him that day so it left Mother and me to do the chickens. It wasn't a monumental task, but it made me queasy. I figured I would never be a farmer's wife.

When Mother and I went to collect the bodies for processing, we discovered that one chicken had avoided the knife.

"He missed one," Mother muttered. We stared at each other in disbelief.

"That means there will be only five chickens ready and you need six," I reasoned, staring at the lone fluttering chicken hanging with his dead buddies.

"Yes," Mother said, frowning, "we need six. We have six orders."

"Well, I'm not killing it," I said, retreating from the cluster of chickens hanging from the branch like a bunch of feathered bananas.

"We have to," she said.

"We…?"

"It'll be okay. I'll use the axe." Her face took on the color of an olive left in water too long. And she avoided making eye contact.

"An axe. An axe?" I said. "How are you going to kill that chicken with an axe? It's hanging by one foot."

"We'll cut it down." I noticed that she was still using that "we" pronoun instead of the "I" one.

"If we cut it down it'll run away. They're stupid but not that dumb. He probably knows what happened to the others. After all, he was there."

"She," Mother corrected, as if that mattered. "Get the axe, I'll think of something."

I got the axe as ordered but couldn't imagine what she was going to do to solve this problem.

When I returned with the weapon of choice, Mother had loosened the cord that held the bunch of chickens together. The live one was still attached to the others and struggling madly to escape but Mother had her foot on the cord still tied to his—her leg.

"Take these dead ones and put them in the shed and then hurry back." She ordered. Her face had gone from green to gray.

When I came back she was still standing on the cord, the hapless chicken seemed to have exhausted himself—oops—herself, and was panting and flopping weakly on the ground.

"I've thought of a way."

"How…?"

"I'll carry her over to the chopping block by the shed and hold her while you chop her head off."

"Me!"

"Would you rather hold her?"

"I'd rather be in Timbuktu," I grumbled, but I picked up the axe and followed my mother, carrying the feeble chicken across the bridge to the site of its ultimate demise…we hoped.

We stood next to the chopping block.

"Do it quickly," she said, "we don't want to have to try this more than once. Remember this is the only way and it will all be over in a second."

I wasn't convinced. As I think back over the next series of events, they always seem to play in slow motion. I can still see Mother crouched down, holding the chicken across the tree stump that served as the block. I raised the axe over my head, held it there for what seemed like an eternity, closed my eyes to slits and brought the axe down across that skinny, feathered neck. A shudder ran up my arm the instant the axe hit the chicken's neck and the chopping block. I screamed, tossed the axe in the air and ran. Mother screamed, threw the chicken in the air and ran; we met in the middle of the dirt road clutching each other.

So much for murdering chickens.

I don't even remember finishing the chicken job that morning but it was the last time we ever had to be executioners. Later, we moved on to turkeys and ducks but that's another story.

 ## SUNNY SERAFINO

SUNNY SERAFINO has written nine novels, three of which have won literary awards. She also teaches creative writing, chairs a writer's critique group and is a professional speaker. See her work and activities at www.sunnyserafino.com

This is an abridged excerpt from "Following Daddy."

My Old Man

There's the old man, just like clockwork. Gets off work at the gas company to come watch us practice. Sits in the first row of bleachers behind the plate, never says a word, just watches. Wears that stupid white cap from the gas company. If I had to wear a cap like that, I'd hide under the bleachers. Thank God most of the guys don't know he's my old man. His Levi's aren't bad but, jeez, that green shirt with his "Paul" name tag is like totally gross.

Come on, Paxton, hit the ball. I've been on deck long enough. It's only batting practice, you dork, so Kaminski's lobbing up grapefruits. The grapefruit stuff'll stop as soon as I get in there. Whenever I'm in the box, Kaminski starts throwing like he's in the World Series.

The old man likes baseball. Comes to all the practices and games. Got me started, always throwing a ball to me when I was a pup. Uncle Mike says he was the best player in the state in high school. Had scouts hanging all over him. Could've signed for a nice bonus. Old timer talk. Why'd he quit playing if he was so good? Uncle Mike always says he hung up the spikes right out of high school and never played again. Decided to get married and stay home. Baseball ain't for a married man, always on the road away from home. So he quit.

Yeah, yeah. There's town ball. And what about the semi-pro team over in Racine? Pretty good players who make a few bucks betting on their games. What's the big deal? He couldn't've been that good, or he would've played.

But Uncle Mike never quits. For your old man it was family, church and work. His trinity. But he was the best. Hit nothin' but line drives. Put the fear into pitchers, the way he hit line drives up the middle. Ha! They threw a pitch and ducked! You take that hotshot pitcher on your team, Kaminski. His old man made it to the show, spent two years in the Bigs. Know what? He couldn't get your old man out.

They played against each other a lot. One time your old man almost killed him with a line drive. It would've torn the guy's head off if he hadn't ducked. Next time up, your old man almost took two pitches in the ear. So he stepped out of the box and asked Kaminski if he was afraid to throw a strike. So Kaminski came with heat and your old man hit the ball into the river. I tell you, he should have played in the show.

Yeah, well, why didn't he keep playing? Couldn't catch the ball, or what? Couldn't throw it? Had to be a reason.

Listen, piss ant, nobody around here, including the old timers, ever saw a better center fielder. Said he looked like DiMaggio out there. Graceful and fast, with a rifle arm. But he was a family guy.

Hate to break Uncle Mike's bubble, so I never say anything. But I happen to know I came along five months after the wedding. What does he think, I can't look at a calendar, can't add and subtract? So maybe the Old man was good, maybe he wasn't. But he wasn't all charity when it came to settling down. Maybe having to get married queered him on baseball. Maybe he blamed Mom. She never comes to ball games, can't even stand the sight of a baseball. He could've kept playing. Who's bullshitting who?

There's Kaminski's old man sitting on the other side of the field in a suit and tie. Him and the old man never talk to each other, that's for sure. Come on, Coach. Get Paxton the hell out of the box. He swings a bat like a chimpanzee in a tutu.

Maybe he was a good outfielder, maybe even a ball hawk. He's quick on his feet for an old guy of thirty-six. And, yeah, he can throw a ball hard enough to break your hand. Probably couldn't hit. I don't care what Uncle Mike says. If he was that good, he'd've played. Maybe he just wasn't competitive.

"Paulie, get in there and take your licks!"

"Okay, coach."

Get out of the way, Paxton, and let me hit. The old man says I have a quick enough bat, but I'm not getting around on the ball. Says to open my stance and take a shorter stride. What the hell does he know? He hasn't swung a bat in, what, eighteen years? Uncle Mike says the old man wouldn't even use aluminum bats. Bought his own wooden ones because the pro's use wood and some hitters can't transition from metal to wood. More bullshit. I'll show him how to hit. Look at that jerk Kaminski going into a full windup. Here it comes. Watch this, old man.

Uhh! I'll get the next one.

What're you smiling about, Kaminski? Throw the damn ball.

Uhh! Foul tip.

Kaminski the Dick. Throwing hard and working fast. Here's his curve. There! Clean shot to right. Take that, Kaminski. He'll come with heat now.

Uhh! Popped it up.

Come on, Kaminski, keep it in the strike zone. There! Line drive to right center. Lay it in here, Kammie, so I can pull the damn ball to left.

Uhh! Fooled me with that curve. What kind of crap is that, throwing curves in batting practice? Why's Kaminski coming off the mound? What's going on?

"Give me the bat."

"What're you doing, Pop?"

"Give me the bat."

Okay, take the bat. What the hell you gonna do with it? Look at that stupid cap. Let me crawl under the bleachers and throw up. Throw up and die, if I'm lucky. Why the hell's he embarrassing me like this?

"Open your stance two inches and lower the bat. You hold it so high, you look like you're climbin' a rope. You think your strike zone is over your head? And bend your knees more."

Jeez, he's getting in the box. Somebody please shoot me.

"Pitch to me, Kaminski."

Look at those stupid shoes. Somebody should tape this. Ha! He missed that pitch by a foot. Wish Uncle Mike could see this. Maybe he wouldn't feed me that bullshit any more. Look at that. Missed another one. Everyone's laughing and pointing. What's the old man digging in for? No spikes on those clodhopper shoes.

Bango! Good stinger through the box. Damn near knocked Kaminski on his ass. Kaminski looks mad.

Whup! Liner to left. The old man's gettin' lucky. Kaminski put some real heat on that pitch.

Whoa! Nice shot off the fence in left. Damn, it's quiet. Nobody's saying a word or laughing. Look at Kaminski's red face. Man, he's ticked off! And look at his old man. Looks like he's ready to kill somebody.

"Okay, Kaminski, quit lobbing the ball. Give me some heat."

The old man's crazy. The scouts have timed Kaminski at ninety miles an hour. Here it comes.

Zow! Line drive to right. The old man went with that outside pitch real nice. Kaminski is so pissed he can't see straight. Here it comes. Aw, Kammie, you jerk, throwing at the old man's head! That's bush. I'm comin' at you, man.

"Stay back, Paulie."

Okay, old man, you're on your own. Good thing you hit the deck when you did. That pitch could've killed you. You're too old for this.

"Give me your best stuff, Kaminski. If you got the cojones!"

Now he's pointing the bat at Kaminski. This could get ugly. Kaminski's into a full wind-up. Here it comes.

Wow! No doubt about that one! Way back, back. Over the fence and into the river. Jeez, that must be four hundred and fifty feet! Everybody's yelling and clapping. Holy Smoke! Maybe the old man really could have made the Bigs.

"Here, Paulie. Get in there and hit."

Jeez, how do I follow that show? Kaminski knows it's my Old man, so now he's mad at me, too. Even madder than usual. Open the stance a couple inches, lower the bat. Kaminski's coming with heat, I know he is. Let him come. Here it is.

Crack!

All right! Not in the river, but over the fence. I own you, Kaminski!

"Hey, Paulie!" Coach is waving his cap. "You can hit like your old man!"

Look at Kaminski kicking the dirt and throwing a fit. And his old man in the bleachers looks disgusted as hell. Coach is all smiles and still waving his cap, so I can't help what I say next, it just comes out, and I don't care who hears it, even if it makes me dork of the year.

"He ain't my old man, Coach! He's my father!"

PETER SHIANNA

PETER SHIANNA's first novel, *Take Off*, was published in 2005. His second, *Love Tag*, is scheduled for release in October. Both are from traditional publishers. His shorter works have appeared in the *Kansas City Star, The Rockhurst Review, the Creative Writers' Journal* and in three anthologies. His website is petershianna.com

Previously published in The Second Annual Journal of The Creative Writers Notebook, 2007

Is This My Baby?

I dropped the car keys as I ran to catch the phone.

"Hello, Shara." It was Glenna, my adoption lawyer. We hadn't spoken for a few months. "I have some news for you. A baby boy was born three days ago, on Tuesday."

I took a deep breath and my hand tightened on the phone. "Really?" I said.

This was unusual. The adoption procedure was a thorough plan, telling a couple the birth due date months ahead, giving them time to prepare themselves, other family members, and the baby's room. Larry and I had not received any such plan

"The adoptive couple changed their minds because the baby is biracial. I know we haven't discussed this possibility with you, but are you open to a biracial baby?"

In the late '80s when this took place, the biracial category was not listed on the information form. I also question whether an attorney in 2009 would reveal the baby's location, in Illinois or any other state.

"Larry and I have talked about it and skin color doesn't matter to us, but this is such a surprise. Wow! Where do I begin with my questions? He's healthy? Where is he? When can we see him?"

Glenna jarred me back to the present with, "By the way, we need your answer about adopting this baby on Monday."

"This is amazing, Glenna! An adoption falls through and we get the chance to be instant parents. I can't believe it! I'm so happy we can go see this boy. I know that's how I'll get my answer. We'll look in each others' eyes and know if we are family."

I thought about our hope chest, filled with baby blankets, heirlooms, and even some toys. I giggled a bit, thinking that we didn't have a diaper in the house; so much excitement, so much to prepare in such a short time. I felt the enormity of both the lifetime responsibility and the fun involved in decorating a room for him; I looked forward to baby-proofing the two-storey house, buying the right crib, a rocking chair, and a musical mobile.

Oblivious of the time of day, I called my husband. He was in class lecturing graduate students. I asked his secretary to have him phone me as soon as he got out of class. By the time Larry called, I had concocted a perfect plan. I was breathless while telling him the news and asked if he could leave work so we could drive to the hospital nursery that evening. I needed to meet that baby! We left within the hour.

"I'm so excited I feel like the kid on a trip who asks 'Are we there yet' every five minutes. Lucky we aren't having a blizzard so we have this chance to go there."

"To see our Christmas baby," Larry laughed. "We'll be there soon. I can't remember when you were this excited. You're all over the place!"

I barely heard him, thinking that I'd look in the baby's eyes and feel a connection—instant, undeniable, unbreakable forever.

That's not exactly how the evening unfolded. We had the place to ourselves and a few hours before visiting time ended. Larry and I made ourselves at home in the nursery's waiting room.

Two nurses were busy feeding and checking on the eight infants behind the glass wall. The babies were as cute as newborns are, but I just stared at the one biracial baby—my baby—the only one without a nametag on his bassinette. The little baby with the tan skin was completely engaged in sleeping, at peace, unaware of anything but his dreams.

The full range of emotions engulfed my senses by turns. At any moment, I thought, he could awaken and see his new mom. We would both experience our first bonding moment and I would know we were meant to be a family.

Moments later a nurse came out to ask who Larry and I were and what we were doing there. When she understood the situation, she was glad we had the opportunity to be there, even though it had to be on the other side of the glass.

Thirty minutes passed and the baby without a name slept calmly. An hour passed with no change on his precious face. He had moved around a bit, but sleep was his top priority. I began to think that this decision might be more difficult than I expected.

"I can't believe he's still sleeping. He looks so content," I said to Larry, "and his little face is so cute. I know you said it's my decision..."

"Absolutely. Whatever you want, I'm behind it."

I always wanted a family and figured it would come through a combination of adoption and birth. I had gone through the paperwork seven years earlier, when I was previously married and we couldn't have children. Had the adoption lawyer thought I was nuts? Frankly, I wouldn't have been surprised. First I was on the list with one husband, then as a single woman, not wanting to lose the place on the list. A few years later I called to ask them to add my new husband to the list.

I started mumbling to myself, "How do I know if this is our son if I miss seeing him wake up hungry, or whatever, and I can't even comfort him through the glass or let him feel how I already adore him?"

The hospital loudspeaker blared that visiting hours would be ending soon. The baby slept on.

On the drive home I was thrilled that we'd seen the baby, but I was disappointed that we hadn't actually met.

My husband and I stayed up all night contemplating every angle of this lifetime commitment. It was funny. Only the week before, Larry and I had agreed if adoption didn't happen for us, we were okay with that. We had a good life as it was. We enjoyed traveling together. We enjoyed walking to the park a block away, or flying halfway around the world to hike mountains surrounded by waterfalls. We even thought about buying a vacation home in Florida.

We didn't need the weekend to make our decision. Of course, we were still up all Friday night talking about every side of the issue. That night, during the hours of talking, we kept coming back to thinking of this baby as our own precious boy.

"Just imagine, Larry, being part of this new, little life. We'll be in on everything: playing together, reading to him, sitting in the gazebo in our butterfly garden, kissing his boo-boos, taking him to his first day at school. We'll be the disciplinarians to keep him in line and hold hands to cross the street. We will be there for his first bike ride, then teaching him to drive."

"It'll be a huge change for us. Especially for me, since I'm older. But it's a challenge that will bring a lot of reward. Are you okay with not connecting with him eye to eye?"

"I don't know. Maybe that was unrealistic to hope for, but I think we're ready and I feel really good about this. Committed?" I asked.

"Committed."

Waiting until Monday to talk to Glenna was hard. What if the other couple decided they wanted this baby? For months they had thought of him as theirs. Would Glenna say the baby would be going home with that couple? After all, they had prepared for this particular child for months, but then they said no to him.

I left a message on Saturday so Glenna would know our answer first thing on Monday. Larry and I would love to raise this baby. When her office opened Monday I called again.

Paul Travis came home with us two weeks later and the adoption was finalized in court the usual one year later.

Paul was such an easy baby that I wished he'd been twins. He loved to smile, was easy to amuse, and had a good appetite. He loved to sleep. In fact, he was sleeping through the night at three months— many months before the average baby does.

That's when I realized Paul had been communicating with me from the moment I set eyes on him. The joke was on me. As he was napping soundly that first night in December, he had shown me what I had to look forward to: my content, sleeping little sweetheart. Our family was complete.

Shara Pendragon Smock

SHARA PENDRAGON SMOCK wrote the books *Living with Big Cats* and *Hooking the Reader: Opening Lines that Sell.* She has written for numerous magazines and newspapers. See her work at www.sharasmock.com.

Messages In A Bottle

Another bottle washed up to the shore.

"You'd think somebody'd have the decency to throw out a full one," Mac mumbled as he lifted a white zinfandel wine bottle from the waves.

He pulled the cork from the bottle, and using a stick, fished out the note.

Help! it read, I'm stranded alone on a deserted island!

Mac went to his signal fire, yanked a small stick from the flames, and with the burnt end wrote, Me too! on the back of the note. He put the note back in the bottle, corked it, and threw it into the ocean.

Sitting on a rock beside his signal fire, Mac looked at the dozen-plus bottles he'd collected—all of them having similar notes inside.

"Is this island some kind of post office?" he shouted to the sky. "Or am I going crazy?"

And so we're introduced to the saga of the note-holding wine bottles finding their way to Mac's lonely island somewhere in the vicinity of nowhere. Is it possible so many wine connoisseurs had become stranded on deserted islands? If not, why all these bottles, all these messages? All of them ending up on Mac's beach. Is this some kind of Bermuda Triangle thing, or is Mac crazy and hallucinating?

◇

Destiny scanned the ocean from shore, her long blonde wet hair glistening against her tan skin. For weeks, she'd spent most of her days watching for ships. Food was plentiful on the island, and were it not that she was alone, Destiny believed she could come to love the island's natural beauty and bounty.

Oh, well, she thought, might as well try again.

She went to the several dozen wooden cases of white zinfandel lying strewn on the beach, uncorked a bottle, poured the wine onto the sand, and slid a piece of paper inside the bottle. Having replaced the cork, she tossed the bottle into the sea.

"See you around sometime, person who gets this. Yeah, right."

◇

After weeks alone, Mac decided he'd never be found. He gathered tree limbs, some of which he broke off, and the biggest vines he could tear away from the tropical forest's dense undergrowth. He'd build a raft. He'd rescue himself.

◇

On another beach, Destiny, too, decided she'd never be found, so she made herself a hut from sticks, vines, and palm fronds, not unlike the huts she'd seen on television, although the huts on TV looked better than hers.

While combing the beach for driftwood, Destiny found a bottle washed ashore. She pulled the cork from its mouth and shook out the note inside. It read, Me, too!

"Me, too? What kind of message is that?" Frowning, she turned the note over and read her handwriting, Help! I'm stranded alone on a deserted island!

"This is too weird," Destiny said. "I send a message in a bottle, and it comes back with a reply from somebody else who's stranded. What could be worse than that?"

Sitting in her campsite, she slid the note back into the bottle and pulled a small notebook from her purse.

◇

A few days later, Mac again saw a bottle floating in the cove. But this time, it held two notes—his Me, too! answer and a new one.

Please tell me you're a handsome young man on your way to

rescue this beautiful sea nymph who's stranded alone on a deserted island.""

Chuckling, Mac went to his signal fire and pulled out a small burnt stick with which to write.

~

Destiny walked the beach, her clothes tattered, her skin as deeply tanned as if she were native to this part of the tropics. "I can't believe I married that guy," she mumbled. "If I hadn't gotten married, I wouldn't have been miserable, and I wouldn't have divorced and gone on a cruise that sunk in the middle of the ocean. And I wouldn't be dreaming about being rescued by some guy who sails up to my beach on a homemade raft. How stupid is that?"

The sun glinted off something in the sea. A bottle bobbing in the waves.

"What the heck," Destiny said, stripping on her way to the water. "It's not like anyone's going to see me."

Moments later, she walked back onto the sandy beach, her skin glistening in the sun with the seawater droplets that covered her firm young body.

She read the note. Send a full bottle next time.

"What kind of idiot expects full bottles of wine to float up on his beach?""

She shrugged and went to the wine cases, pulled a bottle from an open case, and tossed it into the sea. "Enjoy, whoever you are."

~

"Well, I'll be," Mac said, laughing as he picked up the bottle. "She sent me a full one. Who would've ever thought it? I wonder what she's like."

Mac awoke the next morning in the sand next to his signal fire. It had burned out in the night.

He shrugged. "Doesn't matter anyway. I'm taking off tomorrow, so I won't need it."

Mac took one of the bottles from the pile he'd collected, removed the note from inside, and wrote on the back of it, I'm setting sail on my raft tomorrow morning. Best I can tell, it takes about three days for our messages to reach one another, so look for me the day after you find this.

He tossed the bottle into the sea.

Early the next morning, Mac dragged his crudely built raft into the cove and, using a pole, pushed his craft past the coral reef that protected his beach and into the open sea. "Goodbye, you wretched island. I hope I never see you again."

A strong swimmer, Mac had made it to shore after his plane went down. He spent several days looking for other survivors but found no one.

∿

"Well," Destiny said after reading the note, "if he makes it, at least I won't be alone. Nothing's worse than spending your life alone." She looked down at herself. "Maybe I should try to look better. Maybe find a rock sharp enough rock to shave my legs with before Mister Mystery Hero gets here."

∿

Without tools, Mac had been unable to cut logs, and his unsubstantial raft took a beating in the waves. To make matters worse, he couldn't get beyond sight of the island. It appeared some freak ocean current was going to have him circling it.

∿

Destiny sat on the sand watching the sea. "Okay, Mister Mystery Hero, where are you? It's been twenty-four hours since I found your note. Are you coming or not? Don't tell me you beached yourself on some other island. Please, not that."

Later that day, Destiny saw skinny logs and pieces of vines washing ashore. She looked hard but saw no raft, no boat, nothing but ocean all the way to the horizon. She sank to the beach and pounded it with her fists.

"No! No, no, no! I don't want to think you didn't make it! I don't want to think about spending the rest of my life alone on this island! Nothing could be worse than life alone."

"Yeah? How about spending the rest of it trapped on a deserted island with your ex-wife?" a voice behind her said.

Destiny turned. "You!"

"Till death do us part, baby."

APRIL STAR

JOMARIE GRINKIEWICZ, who writes under the pseudonym of April Star lives in Sebring, Florida. She's the author of the wanderlust mysteries, *Tropical Warnings* and *The Last Resort* are the first two titles in the series. She has written for numerous magazines and newspapers. See her work at www. authoraprilstar.com.

An Anniversary Remembered

Eileen looked across the dinner table at Harold, her husband of almost sixty years.

"Harry, you're not eating again—what's wrong?"

"I'm not that hungry. That's all."

"But you never seem to be hungry anymore. I keep wasting food with you."

"Aw honey, would you quit worrying?"

"Maybe I should take you to the doctor."

"Stop being such a worrywart, I'm fine."

"In all my years, Harry, I never thought I'd see the day when you wouldn't eat my meatloaf dinner."

"I'm sorry. I just have some stomach bug or something—it'll pass."

"Well, I hope it will pass by tomorrow evening—it's our anniversary, Harry."

"I know that doll, and not just any anniversary, it's our 60th."

"It's times like these that I regret not having kids," Eileen said.

"Oh, none of that, now. You can't think like that, we've had a wonderful life together."

"Of course, I know that, but...never mind. Where should we go for our big dinner?" Eileen asked.

"Where we always go on our anniversary—Eugene's restaurant."

"I thought you might want to go somewhere different this year."

"But it's been our tradition forever. Besides, Eugene will be upset if we don't show," Harold said with a chuckle.

"I suppose you're right. We don't want to disappoint your friend, now do we?"

"We always have a wonderful meal there too—let's not forget that."

"I just have a weird feeling about eating there this year."

"Nonsense, dear. You and your premonitions. We'll have a great time there, as always."

"I know that, dear, I know we will. I'll make reservations tomorrow."

Eileen put on the television for Harold and began cleaning the dishes. When done, she made a pot of coffee and poured two cups. She brought them into the living room where Harold relaxed in his favorite recliner. After placing the coffees on the table between their recliners, she sat down next to him, glancing at her husband from time to time, admiring his good looks.

"What are you watching, Harry?"

"Oh, I don't know. Whatever was on when you twisted its tail."

"That doesn't sound like you—no ballgame tonight?"

"Nah, I'm not interested."

Eileen focused on the program; it was a 60 Minutes special on senility and the ever-increasing percentage of the elderly who suffer from it.

"Why watch this nonsense, our minds are sharper than most youngsters, Harry."

"Oh, I know that. Like I said, just watching what was on, something to occupy my mind."

"You're not touching your coffee, Harry."

"Sorry. Don't think it would do me much good. My stomach's acting up."

Eileen watched him with concern, but soon began to relax and watched TV with Harold until bedtime.

The next morning Eileen woke to a healthier Harold. He beamed at her.

"I love you, honey, more and more every day," he said. "I breathe every waking breath for you. My heart pounds out every heartbeat for our love. You are my life."

Harold gave her a big kiss, as he pulled Eileen back to the bed where they held each other for what could have been hours. Throughout the day, they expressed their love by showing little signs of affection that were often neglected or taken for granted by couples their age. Eileen felt young again.

It was almost time for their big dinner. As Eileen donned her gold earrings, she felt the stirrings of excitement about their anniversary.

Harold stepped into the bedroom wearing his best suit. "Well, doll, I think not eating yesterday has really worked up my appetite."

"I'm glad, Harry. I was worried about that."

"You worry too much about me—I told you I'd be fine."

"And you were right, dear."

"You look beautiful in that dress."

"Ya think? This old thing?"

"Old? I guess it suits you then," he said and they laughed.

"Oh Harry, you old bugger," she said and laughed some more.

"Honest, honey, you are as beautiful now as when I first laid eyes on you."

"Oh Harry." They kissed and held each other. Tears welled up in her eyes as sixty years of marriage flashed by.

They took the F-train into the city and cuddled up on a seat near the exit door. At the East Broadway stop, a large black man almost sat down on Harold.

"Stop, stop it—what are you doing?" Eileen asked with urgency.

"Trying to sit down, lady."

"On my husband?!"

The man looked at the space beside her, then back to Eileen. "What are you talking about?"

"There's only room for me and my husband on this bench—you'll have to find another seat."

The man looked at her oddly and then scrambled up the train looking for another seat before it started moving.

"Crazy man," she said to Harold.

Harold laughed. "You almost had a pancake for a husband."

She laughed too. "What was he thinking?"

"You know, there are quite a few crazies in this city."

From their stop, it was only a short walk to Eugene's. As they entered the restaurant, Eugene and his staff welcomed them warmly. Eugene shook Harold's hand and gave Eileen a hearty hug and a kiss on the cheek. They were led to a table set with flowers and a complementary bottle of champagne chilling in a bucket of ice.

"Congratulations, my friends! Sixty years and still madly in love! How do you do it, old pal?" Eugene asked, patting Harold on the back. "I'll check up on you two lovebirds a little later. Please let me know if you need anything at all. Enjoy your evening."

"This is so nice, Harry, isn't it? You were right about coming here."

"Eugene always does things in style," Harold said.

"He sure does."

The waiter brought the bread board and filled their glasses with champagne. He went over the specials and gave them time to ponder. Harold decided on the fish special and asked Eileen to order while he went to the restroom. The waiter returned right after Harold disappeared into the men's room down the hall. Eileen ordered Harold's special and requested the spaghetti dinner for herself. Then she sat back, relaxed, and soaked up the ambiance.

Eileen was waiting for Harold's return when a commotion erupted near the front of the restaurant. Two men in ski masks stormed into the restaurant yelling for everyone to remain calm. They wanted money from the register and from everyone's wallets, and they'd be on their way. One of the gunmen was standing near the men's bathroom door when it opened.

It was Harold.

Eileen looked on in horror as the masked gunman whirled in fear and pulled the trigger.

"What'd you do, man?!"

"I don't know, I don't know. He surprised me—I didn't mean to."

"Let's go—we gotta get out of here."

As the gunmen fled the restaurant, Eileen hurried to Harold's side. He lay motionless, spread-eagle on the floor. His blood was everywhere. Eileen knelt down, cradled him in her arms, and wailed. "Why, oh why?" she asked over and over again.

Eileen felt a strong pair of hands grab her shoulders and help her up.

"Eileen, Eileen—it's okay. Let me help you back to your seat."

She closed her eyes for a moment, and when she opened them, the floor below was empty—no Harold, no blood. She looked around while stunned patrons looked on. As it all came back to her, she put her hand to her mouth and let Eugene assist her back to her booth.

Once she was seated, she asked, "I did the same thing last year, didn't I?"

Eugene nodded.

"And the year before that?"

He nodded again. "Every year since Harold was taken from us six years ago this night."

"Why do you keep putting up with me?"

"Harold was a great man and a wonderful friend. I can understand why you want to keep him alive, so I do what I can to help . . . I'd be dishonoring him if I didn't." Eugene rubbed her back. "Can I get you anything?"

She looked up and tried to smile. "A cold glass of water would be nice." And then she sat back, numb and grief stricken. She felt terribly alone, like an in-patient after visiting hours.

Tomorrow, she would begin the painstaking process of resurrecting Harold in her mind again, so they could live happily ever after, at least until their next anniversary.

JEFF SWESKY

JEFF SWESKY is currently working on a literary novel titled Such a Dreamer and the Rogues Gallery Writers collaboration Writing is Easy. He is also ghostwriting a holocaust memoir for Rabbi Samuel Cywiak of St. Augustine, FL. Website: www.JeffSwesky.com

Keepsakes

At the funeral home, my aunt told me that you never get over losing your mother. It's the nurturing that you miss. The special bond that can't be replaced, but you learn to get by. During bad days, you envision good memories as you try to push tear-stained cheeks into a smile. For me, it's been the routine things. I can't tell you how many times I've picked up the phone to call her since she's passed.

I'm at Mom's house now, going through the possessions in her bedroom. Dad didn't want to be bothered. Actually, he's hardly talked since her death. He just parked himself in front of the living room television where he watches black and white movies. Truth be told, he seems more to stare at them than to watch.

In the bottom drawer of her nightstand, I find oodles of fabric with partly crocheted designs. One has a teddy bear with one arm and no legs. One says, "Home Sweet Ho."

The top drawer contains hundreds of greeting cards for all occasions. They're dated back years and years. What had she planned to do with all of these? Amongst the cards I find her Bible, a King James Version with a black leather cover that has crease marks down the middle. The binding is coming loose and the pages will soon begin to fall out.

I flip through the Bible and am shocked. Mother was so organized and kept the house immaculate, yet her Bible has scribbles, crumbs from pencil erasing, and little scraps of paper throughout. Near the back of the Bible, in Revelation, I find an old black and white photo, so old it's actually more like brown and yellow. It's a portrait of an older man, posing and smirking at the camera, his pale thinning hair brushed back and teased by the wind. His wire-rimmed glasses seem too small for his face, maybe because his eyes are squinting in the sunlight. Wearing a white long-sleeved dress shirt, he stands in front of a large tree. The dress shirt is pressed to perfection and lies against his thin frame. A diagonally striped tie is knotted at his neck, but the thin bottom part hangs down lower than the wider portion as if he left the house in a hurry and did not notice the uneven tie job. It looks like a nice picture taken after church on Sunday morning.

I look at this mystery man. He means nothing to me, although it vaguely reminds me of a conversation I had with Mom in her hospital room. Her bedside table was cluttered with flowers and get-well cards. She was sitting up so I could massage her back to get the blood moving and to prevent bedsores. A steady hum enveloped the room and occasional blips sounded from a machine on the other side of the partition—the woman over there seemed in much worse condition than my mother. My nose stung from the scent of alcohol-rubbed metal and over-bleached linoleum. While the television suspended from the wall spat out worthless daytime programming, my mother looked over her shoulder at me and smiled.

"I'm worried about you," she said, her voice raspy, but still soothing to my ears.

"Oh please, Mother. I'm not the one that's sick."

"You know what I mean."

I didn't have a response.

"He's making you miserable. You know this. You've told me time and time again. He doesn't respect you. He's verbally and physically abusive. That's no kind of husband to have . . . and what kind of father would he make if you two decide to have children?"

I felt an ache in my womb. I already knew the answer to that question. It was one thing I never quite told my mother the truth about.

"Mother—stop."

"There's a good man out there for you – one who will treat you right. You need to leave Thad—he's no good for you."

"Oh, how would you know?" I snapped. "How do you know that I would be better off without him?"

"Honey—life's too short . . . don't make the same mistake I made. The right man is out there for you. And when he comes along, believe me, you'll know it. Don't live out your life in regret."

"What are you talking about—what mistake did you make? What are you regretting?" I asked.

She turned her head from me and began to weep. It was so unexpected that my hands left her back for a moment as if I was unsure whom I'd been touching. I tried to soothe her, to find out what mistake to which she had referred, but she refused to answer. All of a sudden, I did not want to know. I continued to rub Mom's back while staring at the prone shadow against the partition beside us. The occasional machine-assisted deep breath from that side of the room kept me company.

The recollection makes me sick. The nausea increases because, looking at the picture closer, I recognize myself. The large smooth forehead, the slightly sunken eyes, the prominent nose, and retracted jaw. It's the similarities I had always looked for in my father, but could never find. Even the way this stranger's head is slightly tilted to the right resembles me . . . it's exactly how all of my pictures turn out.

This doesn't make sense. This cannot be what it seems.

Sure my father has been stubborn his entire life and never said so much as a kind word to my mother. "Get me this" and "get me that. Stop lollygagging and get cleaning. Get back inside the kitchen and make my dinner."

Still, would she cheat on him? She was such a pious woman. She attended church every Sunday despite the weather or her health, at least until those last few months. On the other hand, Father never attended church.

I'm an only child and Mother was in her fifties when she gave birth to me. It always seemed strange that they conceived so late in life. Maybe Father wasn't fertile—although he would have blamed her regardless—but Mom, in her later years, meeting the love of her life?

No, I don't want to think about this—it's making me nauseous, my head is reeling. I look at the back of the photo. There's writing, but it's only barely legible. The ink has been worn to a light gray, but I can make out some portions. One part says, "Life's choices are never easy, and I know that yours was the most difficult." The middle is too hard to discern, but I do see words like "love" and "miss". The last sentence reads, "I respect your decision and agree not to interfere."

It's signed, "Your Beloved." There's no name, but the date jolts me. It was written almost 33 years ago. Only a few months before . . . I was born.

Jeff Swesky

JEFF SWESKY is currently working on a literary novel titled Such a Dreamer and the Rogues Gallery Writers collaboration Writing is Easy. He is also ghostwriting a holocaust memoir for Rabbi Samuel Cywiak of St. Augustine, FL. Website: www. JeffSwesky.com

Memory Lake

I froze when the huge snapping turtle clamped on to my line.

The new rod and reel I'd insisted on purchasing with most of our monthly pension check shook in my hand. My wife would kill me if I lost them.

The turtle's dark eye looked like a black hole as it fixed on me, collapsing all my dreams of catching a big bass.

It reminded me of another turtle, its shell etched ebony, its neck smooth leathery folds, and its face, just like this one: all mouth clamped on my line.

Back on that July day, I was all of eleven. The forecast promised temperatures in the 80s, perfect for fishing at the local clay banks. My best friend Joey tapped on my door at six in the morning.

"Hey, Tommy, let's go," he called from the front porch.

I grabbed my bamboo pole, stuffed extra hooks and line in my pants pocket, and yelled goodbye to my mother, who was already working in the basement, sorting laundry.

First, Joey and I stopped at Mrs. Letty's bakery. She gave us a bag of day old jelly donuts and a bunch of fresh dough trimmings that we could use for bait. I don't know how she ever made any money. Things were sure different back then.

We wound our way through waist-high grass buzzing with gnats and passed the Matthews apple farm. Back then it was the last house in town, a whitewashed Cape Cod with paint that was peeling off in long strips.

Finally, we reached the marbleized mounds of the clay banks where shades of yellow, orange, and brown colored the soil. In the middle of all that clay sat a wide pond. For some reason, everyone called the pond Horsey's.

Joey pinched a jellybean-sized lump of dough and squeezed it around his hook. I watched his perfect cast break through the clear water as I prepared my own hook. Aiming just to the left of a jagged gray boulder, I threw in my line. The wine cork, tied about a foot from the hook, bobbed with the wave caused by my cast.

Joey landed a sparkling red carp, and I pulled in three sunnies for Mom to fry up for dinner.

"Hey, look at that turtle," Joey called, nodding his head in the direction the gray rock.

I yanked in my line and checked the hook. "He's scaring all the fish away," I complained. I tossed the line right back to my favorite spot, in spite of the looming turtle. The hook plopped right next to the boulder, bluegill territory. I smiled. Another couple to hang on my stringer wouldn't be a bad thing. The turtle slid off the rock and snapped right on to my line.

"Geesh, Joey, look."

"Don't pull. You'll cut the line."

"What'm I going to do?" I held the pole with both hands, ready to yank that turtle to shore.

Joey jumped down from his spot and started looking around. I saw him bend and scrabble around in the dirt. "What are you doing?" I asked.

"You'll see." He picked up a stone and skimmed it over the surface of the water, just shy of the turtle. His next shot dropped closer. The beady eye blinked. The third shot splashed the turtle in the face. His mouth opened as if surprised and the line fell out. I swirled circles of the plastic filament around one hand as I pulled it in. The hook had probably sunk to the bottom of the pond, joining the old bedspring and rusted out Jeep embedded in the muck there, but I still had my trusty bamboo pole, line, and bobber.

With my expensive equipment at risk, I wished Joey was here now to come to my rescue again. I kicked at the dirt along the lakefront and dug up a few stones. After all these years, my accuracy was in doubt, but still I had to try. The first few throws went as wide as a rooky Little Leaguer. After a bit, I splashed one close, but that turtle wasn't moving for anything. Out came the knife, time to sacrifice my hook and fancy lure. When I was a kid, I didn't need a top-of-the-line pole. I didn't even have a reel. Just a wine cork, hook, and some bait. Why was it I had such good times fishing then? To catch a tiny sunny would make my whole day. When had I lost that sense of joy at just watching the water shimmer in the sunlight? At pulling in a rainbow covered bluegill? At listening to the birds sing to each other and the bees fiddle a tune as they searched for some buttercups?

I slit the line and watched the old turtle smile at his victory. Carefully, I carried my pole back to the car and stowed it. I would return it on the way home. I'd hand my wife the money and kiss her until she forgot about my selfishness. My bamboo pole was waiting for me in the attic. Now I knew why I saved it all these years. I had a call to make to my old friend and memories to share.

As I started the car, I imagined that magnificent snapping turtle, swimming back to his special rock with his prize. I'll bet he was thinking how the boy who bested him at Horsey's had finally been taught a lesson.

ELAINE TOGNERI

ELAINE TOGNERI has twenty-five published short stories in markets ranging from webzines and anthologies (*Blood on Their Hands*) to major magazines (*Woman's World*). Elaine holds an MA in English from Rutgers University and has taught courses in English Composition, Technical Writing, and Short Fiction.

Gone Fishin'

My youngest son eased the SUV backward down the shallow mud slope, putting the wheels of the trailer a few feet into the water. The channel leading to the lake seemed not much wider than the row boat, and I stood a few feet to the side, out of the way and out of trouble. I was in thoroughly unfamiliar territory, both metaphorically and literally—I had absolutely no idea where we were. Not that it mattered, since for the next few hours, I was entirely in his hands. It had to happen some day.

We were there on the edge of his favorite lake, putting an aluminum rowboat into the water, at my suggestion. Begging, in fact. Fishing had taken hold of Robert with a vengeance this summer, coinciding with the triumph of getting his driver's license and being able to haul a boat and a trailer behind his small SUV. I had soon turned a little envious of his water-borne adventures with his high school buddies. Okay, the part about getting up at five in the morning for a good start didn't hold any charm for me. But in overhearing snatches of conversation here and there, I formed the wistful impression of hours spent soaking in the grandeur of nature, sunrises, sunsets, loons, ducks, occasional fish caught and released, moonlit excursions under star-studded skies that involved more relaxing and talking about life and politics than actually fishing but still sounded heavenly.

And so I bugged him to take me fishing on one of the last mornings before school started up again. We set a date and hoped for good weather. At the appointed Mom-friendly hour, I drove up to the house bearing bug spray, sunblock, and McDonald's breakfasts for the both of us. Climbed into the front passenger seat, and settled in for the ride. He'd been busy already, industriously packing fishing rods, tackle boxes, a cooler full of drinks, nets, a carton of juicy night crawlers, and lifejackets.

This was definitely his show. He competently pushed the boat off the trailer, parked the SUV, and held the boat steady for me to climb into. We poled our way off the mud bottom and down the channel until the boat started to float on its own, then paddled through an ocean of shiny green lily pads fringed by rushes and tall grass. The last of the lily pads finally behind us, we floated out into wide open spaces. Only a few feet deep, and tiny in comparison to other recreational lakes in our county, this pond nonetheless had rustic charm to spare. Only a few houses ringed its shoreline—nature reigned supreme. Too shallow for larger boats and "personal watercraft," too difficult for access for more than the true die-hards who didn't mind getting muddy to get there, this was a lake for those few who really treasured peace and quiet and, dare I say it, utter serenity.

Great blue herons, standing four feet tall on long twig-like legs, spread their six-foot silver wings and floated along the perimeter of the lake, slow and measured wing-beats indicating no hurry, no worries. Their necks arched back in graceful S-curves, and narrow heads perched regally above their chests, their long legs trailing behind like a ballerina's arabesque. Unseen but still present, sandhill cranes clacked musically from the sidelines, and Canada geese passed, honking, overhead. A pair of ducks shot airborne across the lake, all speed and business, like turbo-charged Mini Coopers compared to the herons' languid touring cars.

Wind riffled the crystalline water's surface, and we passed over forests of strange vegetation below, some plants with leaves curled upward like submarine calla lilies, others with riots of long, furry arms reaching upward and crossways, chenille yarn for fish and mermaids to fantastically knit. A damselfly perched casually on my knee, and I let him sit, undisturbed. The weather was perfect. Sunny, no clouds above but a small handful scattered at the horizons. Light wind, enough to both keep us cool and move the boat, but not enough to rock it.

My son set me up with a casting rod, starting with the basics: an earthworm on a hook, with a plastic bobber attached to let me know if a fish started to nibble. Later in the morning I graduated to an artificial lure and left the bobber behind in favor of the thrill of the chase. He upgraded to a "buzz" lure, hoping to land a northern. I surprised my son—nice to still be able to do that every so often—by casting respectably from the get-go. All those hours spent horse-training decades ago, lightly cracking a long-handled whip to snap the air just behind my gelding's haunches as he trotted in circles on the lunge line, were good for something.

We sat, and drifted, and casted, and occasionally motored to new spots, and detangled our lines from the weeds they snagged in. We landed four feisty bass, two apiece. I marveled at how beautiful a day we'd lucked out with. And I marveled, too, at how lovely it is when the roles get reversed, and I could sit back and enjoy the ride.

There's inevitably a tipping point—or there should be—when you look at the kid you have raised from day one, through diapers and ear infections and teething and bruises and homework and late-night trips to the E.R., piano recitals and back-to-school shopping and driver's ed, and realize that they can do some stuff on their own.

For my older son, that moment came when he was eighteen and I flew to Germany to visit him for a weekend. He was spending several months there as a foreign exchange student. I not only spoke no German, I barely knew which end of the country he was living in. For four days a few thousand miles from home, I took all my cues from my son. He navigated the trains, gave me a walking tour around the neighborhood and the town center, picked a café where we had coffee and ice cream, warned me to keep my purse closer to me when we sat so it would be out of pickpocket range, navigated all the signs and directions and bathrooms and menus, and translated more than adequately at an impromptu gathering of my German cousins before we left.

For my oldest daughter—the "training baby" we mother's have the hardest time cutting the apron strings on—the moment came watching her as she addressed a crowd of about twenty-five-hundred students from an auditorium stage at a convention she'd helped to plan. For the younger one, it came at the end of a long day at the office, a hundred fifty miles of highway under my belt, and an awards banquet we'd attended that evening where she'd received a scholarship. As I sat on the living room sofa of her new student apartment, she kicked into maternal comfort mode. Let me get you a cup of tea, she suggested. Would I like to watch "Sex and the City?" I put my feet up on the coffee table and accepted my new place in the world. It felt good. And now it was time for my "caboose baby."

Three hours after Robert and I first poled and paddled our way out to the middle of the lake, it was time to make our way home. He expertly located the tiny break in the identical stands of tall grass rimming the lake, and navigated us back up the channel to the spot where we'd left the car. Grunting and struggling mightily, he wrestled the boat—usually a two man job—by inches onto the back end of the trailer. I stayed out of the way as he balanced on the trailer and manhandled the full load, then tentatively worked the winch at his direction when the time came. Gear unloaded and boat buckled down, we slowly made our way home and back to reality and routine. "Thanks, honey," I said, "this was just…beautiful!"

The school year has started, the house is again quiet, and autumn is settling in. A few sugar maples have started to brilliantly catch fire and drop their leaves already, signaling an encroaching end to long days spent outdoors in shorts and sandals. I can already anticipate breaking out my snowshoes after a good blizzard this winter, and we haven't had the first frost yet.

The march toward the dead of winter is inexorable, with fixtures of hot chocolate, snowdrifts, crackling fires and frosty windshields on the horizon. But no matter how cold it gets, and no matter how few hours of daylight we have for months on end, it won't take much to get my mind back in that boat. If you see me with a far-off stare and a smile on my face this winter as the winds howl outside and the snowflakes fall like cotton, chances are…I've "gone fishin.'"

Mary T. Wagner

MARY T. WAGNER is a prosecuting attorney, award winning photographer, and the author of *Running with Stilettos: Living a Balanced Life in Dangerous Shoes*. Her by-line has appeared in the *Washington Post*, *Philadelphia Inquirer*, and *San Francisco Chronicle*. Her essays and photos can be found at www.runningwithstilettos.com.

Previously published at www.runningwithstilettos.com, September 7, 2007, and "Running with Stilettos", the book, May and December, 2008.

The Dance of the Butterflies

I'll always remember that date – October 2nd. It was the day I almost killed someone I loved.

An error was made that almost caused the death of a family member who was also one of my patients. I do know that it is not wise to treat a family member, but this was a very special person.

Doctors aren't supposed to make mistakes. I tried to remind myself that I was actually a human being. After all, doctors practice medicine. In reality it is an imperfect art in a world that demands perfection in each and every situation. We are charged with playing God, even though we are mere mortals.

Was the error caused by failure to follow protocol, careless action, or improper diagnosis? Was it due to poor judgment, inadequate training, or mental impairment because of drugs or alcohol?

No. It was caused by a tiny dot, a speck of ink on a chart that looked like a harmless decimal point on a pharmacy order.

Anna Schnell was my great-grandmother, a terminally ill patient. Nana had lived for 97 years. She told anyone who would listen that she was tired and mentally ready to experience the rewards of heaven.

Every morning she smiled sweetly and greeted me with "Guten Morgan, Sherry. It's a beautiful morning and I'm still alive to greet the day."

I usually sat by her side for a while, holding her small, frail hand, her skin so pale and thin that I could see her spidery blue veins. Her face, so sweet and grandmotherly, was framed by her white curly hair tinged with powder blue highlights.

We began each morning with our loving ritual dance of friendship. "Nana", I would say, "you look like sunshine and smell like fresh flowers today."

After Nana had been in the main hospital for about ten days, our family decided to move her to the Hospice unit. We went though our regular morning routine and I was not willing to miss seeing her for even a single day.

Like all other days, the morning of October 2nd began with our daily visit. Nana was not feeling particularly well, but she tried hard not to show it. "I believe I will be heading north pretty soon," she said looking skyward.

"I certainly hope you are thinking of a trip up to Canada and not somewhere else," I pretend-scolded her.

"Now, Sherry," she began, patting my hand to comfort me, "you of all people know that my time here is almost up. I'm not sad. I just want to be comfortable here while I enjoy my memories. I know I will soon see Lewis and that makes me happy. I just hope he still wants me when I get there. He is perpetually only 78 and might not want an old woman of 97," she said with a shy smile.

Nana leaned back against her sunny yellow pillows and told me that she was experiencing some pain. "Can you order me something that will ease the discomfort but not make me fuzzy? You know how I hate that feeling. It's like I'm trying to swim through cotton wool."

With genuine warmth I smiled down at her. "Of course I'll get something for you. Just what the patient ordered."

I knew I would have to call my mother, but I wanted to write the order and ask the nurse to have the pharmacy deliver it promptly. I stopped at the Hospice nurses station. It was a hive of activity with fancy computers, beeping monitors and blinking lights. It made me feel like I was on some kind of space ship.

I wrote the order for 0.05 mg/kg of morphine, just enough to take the edge off the pain, but not enough to make her drowsy and unable to function.

Nancy, the nurse assigned to Nana, took the order off the chart and faxed it off to the pharmacy before I left the station. "Sherry, Anna's been going down quickly. It's sad because she has become special to all of us. We knew her pain has been increasing, but this is the first time she has asked for something."

"Yes, I know. We'll all take very good care of her. When her time comes, she can go peacefully," I said, while looking through the big picture window into the Butterfly Garden. "Just make sure Nana's window stays open. She loves the garden and all those beautiful butterflies."

The order that went to the pharmacy was for 0.05 mg/kg of morphine. The ampoule that was delivered to the nurse's station later that afternoon, bearing with Anna Schnell's name and hospital number, was 0.50 mg/kg.

If that whole ampoule of medication had been injected into Nana's intravenous line, her death would have been swift and quiet. The lights would have gone out for anyone, especially a tiny elderly lady.

Around dinnertime I was notified that Nana was failing. I hurried to her room, but she had already passed on - quietly. The ward clerk told me that she had notified my mother and that she was on her way in. "I'm so sorry, Dr. Krieger," she said with tears in her eyes. "We all loved her, too."

I asked Nancy if Nana had received her Morphine dose. She looked at the chart and said that Cookie, the second shift nurse, had taken the ampoule, intending to give it to Anna. The chart was in her room and I could go by and check.

I checked the order sheet that came up with the drug and was shocked to see that what was sent up to the floor was an order for 0.50 mg/kg, not 0.05 mg/kg! My heart almost stopped in my chest. I became lightheaded and had to sit down. Had I made an error? Did I kill my very own Nana before her time?

How could this happen? Even though the nurse would also be involved, since she gave the drug, I was the one who ordered it. Did I fail to put the decimal in the right place? How could two medical professionals fail to catch a critical error?

I left the station and quickly walked outside to the Butterfly Garden. I sat on the bench outside of Nana's window. I looked upward, and tried to communicate with her.

With tears in my eyes I said, "I am so, so sorry. You only wanted a little relief from pain. You still had memories to replay in your mind. I killed you. Oh, Nana, I didn't mean it. I don't know what to do. How can I practice medicine anymore if I kill people, especially someone I loved with all my heart"?

The tears poured and my body shook with sobs of fear and grief. I really did not know what to do. The garden had been designed as a place of solace for those who were physically ill. I hoped it would grant me some mental peace.

"Dr. Krieger! I'm so glad I found you." I turned to see Cookie, the second shift nurse hurrying over to my side. She was a pretty black woman whose face was awash with relief.

She sat down next to me. "I guess you saw the medication order that came back from the pharmacy for Anna. You need to know that she did not receive the dose."

I looked at her through hazy eyes and was not sure my brain was clear enough to comprehend what she was saying.

"Sherry, the pharmacy order was wrong. You did not order 0.50 mg. Your order was 0.05mg. I went down to the pharmacy to check the faxed order. There was some debris on the copy they received. It looked like the order could read 0.05 or 0.50. The

pharmacist should have caught it. They have taken the fax machine out of service and the new pharmacist will be counseled on checking questionable orders.

Cookie put her arms around me and we held each other tightly. "I loved her too, you know," she said with a sob. "We all did."

"Thank you," I said with a weak smile. I just want her to find her Poppa Lewis again and to be happy. We'll all miss her."

A beautiful butterfly briefly perched on my shoulder. I watched as it was joined by another. They fluttered and danced together around my head, then flew up and away towards the heavens.

I smiled and looked over at Cookie. A silent look of knowing passed between us. God had given us a sign of comfort and closure. Nana and Poppa were together again and he was taking her home.

SHARON K. WEATHERHEAD

SHARON WEATHERHEAD has authored more than 100 articles found in national, local and internet publications. She covers primarily professional sports teams, medical and health topics and local interest articles. She is currently working on her first novel, *It's Not Over,* a medical thriller.

Double Dragons

A bead of sweat dripped off Scott Bailey's forehead onto his Blackberry screen, blurring part of the calendar display.

September 15. He'd thought of almost nothing but this day since May when his seven-year-old son Matt begged him to promise to ride a roller coaster on their vacation in Orlando. He shouldn't have promised. Scott was coasterphobic. A stupid fear, but his psychologist friend assured him there were lots like him.

The things petrified him. The thought of riding one made him gnaw his fingernails to the quick. Four months of sweaty palms, sleepless nights, and anxiety attacks, anticipating the day that now, God help him, was here.

To assure himself the Double Dragons was safe, he'd spent hours researching every aspect of the ride. Scott learned that the coaster had ten loops, reached speeds of sixty-five miles per hour, dropped a hundred fifteen feet at one point, and took exactly two minutes and six seconds start to finish.

He became obsessed with those one hundred twenty-six seconds. When he walked from his car to his office, he counted backward from one-twenty-six to get an idea what the time felt like. He knew the first thirty of those seconds would be spent in a slow ascent in tandem with a parallel coaster to the top of the track and its first perilous drop, so actually, the ride was only ninety-six seconds of twisting, stomach-lurching hell. He practiced counting down from a hundred twenty-six with his eyes closed, the same way he planned to ride the Double Dragons—eyes closed.

By God, I'm a grown man, he told himself. There's no danger. It's the illusion of danger that makes people ride it. I'll have to suck it up, show my son I'm a man. I can do it. It's only a hundred twenty-six seconds. Ninety-six of them terror.

Matt ran to him dripping water from the ride he just got off. "Are you ready, Dad? Are you ready for the Double Dragons?"

Scott lifted his eyes to the huge coaster's parallel cars twisting into hairpin turns, sometimes within a foot of each other. He suddenly felt cold, and his teeth chattered. Cyndi put her hand on his shoulder.

"You don't have to do this, Scott. Matt and I won't think any worse of you if you don't ride it with us."

"Aw, c'mon, Dad, you have to. You said you would. Please?"

He did have to do it. How could he face his son at dinner if the boy thought him a wuss? A hundred twenty-six seconds. A little over two minutes.

"I'm okay, Cyndi. Really. I'm okay."

The electronic sign flashed FIVE MINUTES, the time remaining before the next ride. Scott quick-counted the people in line ahead of him. Forty-five. Ten seats, four abreast equaled forty. He'd be on the coaster after this one.

He watched a boy board one of the cars and pull the plastic harness down. An attendant snapped the seat belt that joined the harness to the seat in place. A few seconds later, the floor beneath the riders' feet dropped, and the coaster jerked forward, slowly turning the corner out of the building. Scott looked at his watch.

One hundred twenty-six seconds later, the coaster returned.

The line surged forward, and Scott was pushed toward the coaster's empty seats. He sat on the end, Matt next to him, and Cyndi on the other side of their boy. Scott looked to make sure each car was indeed individually attached to the rail. Is the gap between my roller and the rail bigger than the others? The attendant pulled Scott's harness down and checked its lock before attaching the seat belt. Scott closed his eyes and took deep breaths. His teeth chattered.

Someone grabbed his wrist. "Are you all right, Scott?" Cyndi.

His teeth were chattering so violently, he couldn't answer.

The coaster jerked forward. Scott kept his eyes closed and counted. One hundred twenty-six, one hundred twenty-five, one hundred twenty-four. . . .

Scott listened to the loudly clicking chains pull their car alongside the parallel dragon up the thirty-degree incline, where the cars would detach from the chains and plummet in a hundred-and-fifteen-foot freefall. He thought he heard the chain snap, and his eyes popped open. He should yell, tell them to stop the ride! He looked over the side. The chain seemed fine.

He looked up. They neared the top and the one-hundred-fifteen-foot drop. He looked to the side. A walkway. He could reach it. There was still time.

He turned to his wife and yelled, "I can't do can't do this, Cyndi, I can't!"

Cyndi put her hand on his knee and shouted over the noisy chain, "It'll be okay, Scott! The ride will be over before you know it! Don't worry!"

"No! I can't!" He unbuckled the seatbelt. He yelled, "I can't do it, Cyndi!" and pushed up on the harness with all his strength. The harness moved only an inch, but it widened the gap enough to let him slide one of his legs out beneath it. Cyndi slapped at him and screamed for him to sit down. She pointed ahead. They were about to crest the incline.

Scott slipped his other leg out and started to step onto the walkway, but the coaster dropped straight down at sixty-five miles an hour. The centrifugal force pushed him against his harness. He wrapped both arms tightly around it anticipating the ride's first inverted loop He'd lost count and estimated. Eighty-four, eighty-three, eighty-two. . . .

The coaster whipped into the loop, the force flinging his legs out, his feet landing on the shoulder of a stunned passenger in the parallel dragon. His car banked hard to the left in a ninety-degree turn. The enormous torque flopped him into Cyndi's harness, which he grabbed onto and held as tightly as he'd held his own. Cyndi's eyes went wide, and she yelled something, her face only inches from hers, but Scott didn't hear it over the glee-filled screams of the other riders. He estimated. Forty...thirty-nine...thirty-eight. . . .

He prayed to hold on for the rest of the seconds, but he his arms were losing strength. Thirty...twenty-nine...twenty-eight. . . .

Only one loop to go, the one where both coasters barreled head-on toward each other at fifty miles-per-hour, a hair breath from collision before shooting straight up. Mustering everything he had, he tightened his grip on Cyndi's harness just as his legs flung out and slammed into the side of the parallel coaster, both dragons hurtling toward the cloudless Florida sky. He felt his right ankle snap and his foot flop completely around as if attached by nothing but tendons and ligaments.

Fifteen...fourteen...thirteen. . . .

The force of the last ninety-degree turn knocked him off Cyndi's harness, and he catapulted skyward and out. Scott experienced zero gravity when he reached the apex of his unintended flight. He stared at the scene below and watched both coasters slow to a stop at ride's end.

Scott felt like he landed on concrete when his body hit the pond next to the ride. He passed out. When he came to on the grass, he knew by the excruciating pain in his right ankle that he wasn't dead and screamed. His scream was drowned out by the screams of the coaster's riders, as once again the parallel dragons plummeted a hundred-fifteen feet.

"Oh God, Scott! You're alive," Cyndi shouted, grabbing him in a hug.

"Sir," a park employee said, "the ambulance and paramedics are on their way. Are you all right?"

Scott raised his head and looked at his cockeyed foot.

"I think so, but I think my foot's broken."

A kneeling Matt patted his shoulder.

"I'm sorry, son," Scott said. I just couldn't do it. I'm sorry."

"It's okay, Dad. You tried." The boy leaned to his father's ear. "Dad, while they're helping you, can I go on the ride again?"

 ## J. J. WHITE

JOHN J. WHITE has won numerous writing awards for his novels, short stories, and poetry. He has written for several newspapers, magazines, and websites. You can see his work at www.jjwhite.org.

About Florida Writers Association, Inc.

At the FWA, some 900 professional authors and aspiring writers come to learn, grow, network, and find the resources they need to improve their writing, learn to navigate the treacherous shoals of the publishing industry, and cultivate their inner muse.

Florida Writers Association was founded in May 2001 and officially approved as an IRS 501(c)6 trade association in 2002. Our motto is: "Writers Helping Writers." In the beginning, FWA was administered by a board of regional directors and officers, with local "palm" group leaders nominated by RDs and appointed by the president. All members received the quarterly *Florida Palm* magazine and invitations to the annual FWA conferences. Other services included presentations by industry leaders in FWA publications and at meetings and networking by email. Except for some magazine staff, all leaders and workers were, and still are, unpaid volunteers. Volunteers have allowed us to keep dues low for such a quality professional organization.

Over the years, we've added other benefits: local one-day conferences, a better and constantly improving website, more and better local groups, streamlined day-to-day management, electronic technology innovations, and bigger and better annual conferences. Growing at a rate of about 100 members annually, FWA is recognized nationally and has members from around the world; we even have an Asheville, NC, writers group.

November 2007 witnessed the birth of an unaffiliated sister, Florida Writers Foundation, bringing writers' unique love of books and reading to focus on enhanced literacy for adults and families. This new 501(c)3 educational charity collaborates with established organizations to benefit individuals and communities. Florida writers will be proud of their association with FWA and FWF in future years.

Dan Griffith
FWA President

Florida Writers Association [FWA] is proud to be the sponsoring organization for this, the first collection of short stories written by our members.

FWA's Collection #2—Slices of Life

Florida Writers Association is already busy planning our next book in the *Collection* series . . . *FWA's Collection #2—Slices of Life*. Watch our website, www.FloridaWriters.net, for entry guidelines and more details.

Life at its best, or worst—this is where you can write about real or imagined snippets of life as it is—or should be—or could be—or might be. Nonfiction or fiction, share your *Slices of Life* with us.

Just as Suzette Standring is the Person of Renown for *FWA's Collection #1—From Our Family to Yours*, Eliot Kleinberg will serve in that position for our second *Collection*. Eliot Kleinberg is that rarest of Floridians—a native.

Born in South Florida, he spent three decades in both broadcast and print news, including a twenty-plus year stint at the *Palm Beach Post* in West Palm Beach. In addition to covering local news, he writes extensively about Florida and Floridiana.

He's written eleven books, all Florida-related, including *Black Cloud*, a 75th Anniversary Book on the great 1928 Okeechobee Hurricane; two Weird Florida books, and *Palm Beach Past* and *Wicked*

Palm Beach, collections of his weekly local history columns for the Post. His tenth and first fiction outing, *Peace River*, is a recently completed historical novel that takes place at the end of the Civil War.

Eliot was born in Coral Gables in 1956, graduated from Miami-area public schools in 1974, and received two degrees from the University of Florida. His career as a radio and television reporter and editor from 1979 to 1984 included work in Miami and at the Cable News Network. He was a reporter for the *Dallas Morning News* from 1984 until 1987, and returned to Florida to join the *Palm Beach Post*.

Mr. Kleinberg is a member of the Florida, South Florida and Palm Beach County historical societies. He lives at Casa Floridiana in Boca Raton with his wife and two sons.

LaVergne, TN USA
08 October 2009
160180LV00005B/2/P